CHARLES NODIER

THE STORY OF
THE KING OF BOHEMIA
AND HIS SEVEN CASTLES

Translated and with an Introduction by
Brian Stableford

THIS IS A SNUGGLY BOOK

Translations and Introduction
Copyright © 2023 by Brian Stableford.

ISBN: 978-1-64525-123-1

THE STORY OF
THE KING OF BOHEMIA
AND HIS SEVEN CASTLES

CHARLES NODIER (1780-1844) was one of the pioneers of French Romantic prose; his salon at the Bibliothèque de l'Arsenal, begun in 1824 and known as *Le Cénacle*, brought together many of the key figures in the Movement and spun off other *cénacles* in which it was anchored, including Victor Hugo's. His best work consists of short stories and novellas.

BRIAN STABLEFORD's scholarly work includes *New Atlantis: A Narrative History of Scientific Romance* (Wildside Press, 2016), *The Plurality of Imaginary Worlds: The Evolution of French roman scientifique* (Black Coat Press, 2017) and *Tales of Enchantment and Disenchantment: A History of Faerie* (Black Coat Press, 2019). He has translated more than three hundred volumes from the French, mostly in the genres of *roman scientifique*, *contes de fées* and Romantic and Symbolist fiction. His recent fiction includes the visionary science fiction novel *The Revelations of Time and Space* (2020) and its sequel *After the Revelation* (2021); the last in his long series of "Tales of the Genetic Revolution," *The Elusive Shadows* (2020); and the comedy fantasy *Meat on the Bone* (2021), all published by Snuggly Books.

SNUGGLY BOOKS

Contents

Introduction

This collection of fiction by Charles Nodier follows two earlier volumes: *Outlaws and Sorrows*, which assembles works published in the first phase of his fiction writing, from 1802-06, and *Jean Sbogar and Other Stories*, which contains works published in the second phase, in 1818-22. The present volume features the work that began the third and final phase of his fiction writing, the bizarre visionary fantasy *Histoire du roi de Bohême et de ses sept châteaux* (1830; tr. as *The Story of the King of Bohemia and his Seven Castles*), supplementing it with three related works: an essay on dreams and two "biographical fantasies," one of "Polichinelle," which expands on one of the episodes in the novella, and the other of a "Bibliomane" [bibliomaniac] the principal character of which is Théodore, presumably the dreamer featured in *Histoire du roi de Bohême et de ses sept châteaux*. The article, "De quelques phenomènes du sommeil," tr. as "On Some Phenomena of Sleep," first appeared in the *Revue de Paris* in February 1831 and was reprinted as a booklet, as well as in the volume of the author's collected works entitled *Râveries littéraires morales et fantastiques* (1832). "Polichinelle" and "Le Bibliomane" both appeared in separate volumes of a series of anthologies, *Paris, ou Le Livre des cent-et-un*, in 1831; both were reprinted in the posthumous collection *Contes de la Veillée* [Fireside Tales] (1875), along with the article, there retitled "Le Pays des rêves" [The Land of Dreams].

It is not obvious why Nodier published no fiction in the eight years that separated the publication of his previous novella, *Trilby, ou Le Lutin d'Argail* (1822),[1] from the puhblication of *Histoire du roi de Bohême et de ses sept châteaux*, given that he had published one novella a year for the previous five. One important factor distracting him from such work was undoubtedly his appointment in January 1824 as librarian at the Bibliothèque de l'Arsenal, but his occupation of that position did not prevent him producing fiction regularly, on a more prolific scale than ever before after 1830, including the works contained in the remaining volumes of the present set, *The Memoirs of Maxime Odin, Perfectibility and Resurrection* and *The Four Talismans and Other Stories*. The likelihood is that he did continue writing fiction after 1822, at least for a while, but had difficulty publishing it and became temporarily disheartened. In particular, it seems highly likely that he wrote *La Fée aux miettes* (tr. by Ruth Berman as *The Crumb Fairy*) soon after *Trilby*, but was unable to get it into print until he included it in the set of his collected *Oeuvres* in 1832.

Nodier always felt that the marketplace was fundamentally hostile to his work, and he had had specific problems compounding that hostility before. The gap in his fiction publications between 1806 and 1818 was partly caused by the fact that he was exiled from Paris and placed under police surveillance in his home town of Besançon after a brief period of imprisonment after admitting authorship of *La Napoléone* (1803 tr. as "The Napoleonad"), an "ode" criticizing Napoléon, not long before the latter declared himself to be the Emperor of France. Ironically, Napoléon also became involved in his career again, while in exile himself on Saint Helena, where he was reported

---

1 *Jean Sbogar and Other Stories* does not contain *Trilby* or its immediate predecessor *Smarra, or Les Démons de la nuit* (1821) because translations of both works by Ruth Berman are in print in the Black Coat Press collection *Trilby; The Crumb Fairy* (2015), but it does include the three shorter pieces appended to the first edition of *Smarra*.

to have read the anonymous *Jean Sbogar* with great interest, thus prompting the revelation that Nodier was its author. Although Nodier was not under formal surveillance during the Restoration, he was known to have been a Jacobin during the Revolution, and in order to help get himself out of jail he had swiftly written a second ode praising Napoléon to the skies, thus giving grounds for suspecting him of Bonapartism. Although he received an invitation to the coronation of Charles X in 1825, along with Victor Hugo, he was undoubtedly considered by the increasingly repressive Bourbon regime to be a potential trouble-maker, and although it is unlikely that there was any formal censorship of his work, his reputation was probably sufficient to induce a certain wariness on the part of publishers. That is unlikely to have been a decisive factor, however, and if one compares the nightmare fantasy *Smarra*, the delusory fantasy *La Fée au miettes* and *Histoire du roi de Bohême et de ses sept châteaux*, it seems probable that the principal factor determining suspicion of his work on the part of publishers during the 1820s was its bizarrerie.

While the three works in question are not entirely without precursors, and the pattern of their publication made it difficult to see them at the time as a triptych, if they are considered in terms of what they have in common, they do look like aspects of a common enterprise that was unprecedented and unusual in the extreme. At the time, and subsequently, the fact that *Smarra* employs the motif of vampirism allowed it to be separately associated by readers and critics with other fiction employing the same motif, especially the notorious drama *Le Vampire*, which enjoyed a sensational success at the Théâtre de la Porte Saint-Martin in 1820-21, and to which Nodier made a minor contribution. When *La Fée aux miettes* eventually appeared in 1832, its title alone invited linkage with *Trilby* rather than *Smarra*, and at the time when the eccentric *Histoire du roi de Bohême et de ses sept châteaux* ap-

9

peared it did not seem to have any evident connection with anything, and no one knew what to make of it for a long time afterwards. From a modern viewpoint, it can readily be seen as a remote precursor of Alfred Jarry's "pataphysical fiction," Guillaume Apollinaire's "surrealism" and Dadaism, especially the key aspect of surrealism that wanted to draw inspiration from the unconscious mind via dreams, reproducing the apparent incoherence and perversity of "dream logic," but no such accounting-scheme was available to critics and readers in 1830, and the critics of the day were just as puzzled as the fictitious critic whose malevolent hypothetical review is incorporated into the text.

The memoir of her father's work published by Marie Mennessier-Nodier (1811-1893) in 1867 revealed that *Histoire du roi de Bohême et de ses sept châteaux* was actually written in 1828. Understandably, the memoir is very hazy about the years preceding that date, although Marie began participating in Nodier's famous cénacle in her mid-teens, so it has little to say about *Smarra* and *La Fée aux miettes*, but her childhood memories do provide other insights that might well help to explain how it came about that Nodier's productivity was so patchy, and why it had such a peculiar pattern. In particular, she comments on the fact that her father was often ill, sometimes to the extent that his life seemed endangered.

The physicians of the day were, of course, incompetent to diagnose Nodier's illnesses with any degree of certainty, and retrospective diagnosis is a perilous business, but twentieth century biographers have suggested that his symptoms lend themselves to the possibility that he suffered from hereditary hypoadrenalinism, commonly known as Addison's disease, and that certainly seems plausible. Marie, on the other hand, reports that one doctor consulted in desperation during one of the worst flare-ups of his symptoms, opined that Nodier had a tapeworm of the genus *Taenia*. If so, it might have been producing side-effects that would nowadays be classified as neurocysticercosis. The doctor in question allegedly told Nodier that he could poison the tapeworm for him, but that he would have to be stronger than the tapeworm in order to avoid being fatally poisoned himself. Nodier drank the concoction he was given—Marie is vague about its composition, but says that a main ingredient was turpentine—and allegedly made a complete recovery, in time.

Some additional insight into Nodier's health problems is provided, albeit a trifle dubiously, by the letters written by his friends, and friends of his father, in order to secure his release from prison in 1804, particularly one written by his best friend in Besançon, Charles Weiss. More than one of the letters alleged that Nodier was not in his right mind when he wrote *La Napoléone*, because he had overdosed on opium; Weiss added that Nodier had used opium, presumably in the form of laudanum, as an aid to literary creativity, and that his use of it had eventually precipitated a crisis of temporary insanity. Other sources confirm that Nodier suspected himself of being "epileptic," which was then considered a symptom of "mental alienation," or, more bluntly, madness. More cautiously, Nodier only alleged in his own defense that the balance of his mind had been disturbed by the recent deaths of two close friends. The allegation that he used opium as a medicament, and also as a means of imaginative stimulation, is, however, very plausible.

How familiar Nodier was in 1803 with the work of such English Romantic poets as Samuel Taylor Coleridge is unclear—he made no reference to Coleridge in his works—but he could read English and he shared with Coleridge a strong interest in German Romanticism, so it would not have been surprising if he was aware of Coleridge's use of laudanum then; even though he could not have read *Kubla Khan* in 1803, because it was not published until 1816, he might have read

The Rime of the Ancient Mariner, and by the time he wrote the hallucinatory final chapters of *Jean Sbogar* he was probably not only aware of *Kubla Khan* but of the legend attached to its composition following an opium-induced "reverie". In 1928, when he began to write *Histoire du roi de Bohême et de ses sept châteaux*, Nodier would certainly have been familiar with Thomas De Quincey's *Confessions of an English Opium-Eater*, (1821) which was translated into French in that year—very loosely—by one of the younger members of the cénacle, Alfred de Musset, and which subsequently became a significant influence on other members of the cénacle, particularly Théophile Gautier, Alphonse Esquiros, Alphonse Karr and, albeit briefly, Honoré de Balzac.

Not unnaturally, Nodier kept his illnesses and their treatments discreetly hidden. Modern biographers have found evidence that he spent most of his time in prison in the prison hospital being treated for gonorrhea, but it is hardly surprising that there is no mention of such a circumstance in any of the stories he wrote in which one of his fictional alter egos is imprisoned. On the other hand, several of his fictitious alter egos go into elaborate detail describing symptoms of hallucination and "epilepsy" brought on by grief and amorous disappointment, and his work is extraordinarily rich in sickbed scenes, two especially graphic specimens providing the melodramatic climaxes of *Jean Sbogar* and *Thérèse Aubert* (1819). Such scenes never mention opium, but if the circumstances described had actually occurred, it is difficult to believe that the physicians in attendance would not have prescribed opium as a palliative, perhaps in the pastille form that Theodore admits using. Similarly, whatever the root cause of Nodier's recurrent bouts of illness was, it is highly unlikely that he was not advised to employ opium as a palliative by his physicians, even though they would surely have been familiar with George Young's *Treatise on Opium* (1753), which had warned of the drug's dangers and the complications consequent on its usage.

If one considers *Jean Sbogar*, *Smarra*, *La Fée aux miettes* and *Histoire du roi de Bohême et de ses sept châteaux* with the aid of modern hindsight, as a sequence of literary explorations of hallucinatory experience, in connection with Nodier's subsequent attempts to analyze and explain such altered states of consciousness, it is difficult to avoid the conclusion that the last-named and longest of the stories can not only be classified as an account of a drug-induced hallucination, but also as an attempt to explore by literary means the process by which such visions are composed and the peculiar pseudo-logic of their connectivity. In particular, it is radically innovative in splitting the protagonist's "dream-self" into a trinity of distinguishable but inseparable identities, in which the workaday conscious self becomes subservient to more flamboyant alter egos kept under a much tighter rein in waking experience. Sigmund Freud and Carl Jung do not seem to have been aware of *La Fée aux miettes* or *Histoire du roi de Bohême et de ses sept châteaux*, but subsequent psychoanalysts have certainly got their teeth into the former, and the latter surely offers even richer fodder for their interpretations.

Given the relationship between the works in question, it is tempting to suppose that periodic illness probably played a considerable role in occasioning the gap in Nodier's publication record between 1822 and 1830, and that its treatment might well have had a significant role in the inspiration of the works bracketing that gap. In spite of its starling originality, therefore, it could be argued that the most puzzling thing about of *Histoire du roi de Bohême et de ses sept châteaux* is not its composition or its publication—although that must have represented a very brave decision on the part of its publisher—but the fact that it brought an abrupt punctuation mark to that phase of the author's career. Dreams and madness continued to play a very significant role in his subsequent work, but always in a much more distanced, controlled and disciplined

fashion, never again attempting the deliberate stylistic experi-
mentation and reckless fragmentation of the novella featured
in the present volume. As to whether or not that was because
he had expelled an inconvenient worm from his gut and its
errant eggs from his nervous system, we can only speculate,
but the hypothesis might at least make an interesting *conte
fantastique*.

The revivification of Nodier's career after 1830 was certainly not merely a medical matter. In that year the so-called
July Revolution got rid of Charles X, and although it disappointed its republican instigators when the government of the
day found a substitute king in Louis-Philippe, it instituted a
constitutional monarchy to replace the oppressive absolutism
of the former regime. For a brief period, political censorship
was considerably relaxed and publishers believed, at least for a
while, that they had acquired a new and much greater freedom.
Nodier, along with all the other members of the Romantic
Movement, took rapid advantage of that thaw, which enabled
him to issue his twelve-volume set of his *Oeuvres*, recovering
most of the fiction from the earlier phases of his career as well
as numerous recent works.

The presumed license granted to publishers was interpret-
ed by the editors of several periodicals as an opportunity to
publish more controversial work, and several began to pro-
mote the Romantic Movement enthusiastically as a potential
regenerative force in French literature. One of the periodicals that did so most pugnaciously was the *Revue de Paris*,
which became Nodier's principal showcase for several years,
both for philosophical articles flamboyantly setting out his
controversial theses regarding literature and its historical and
psychological contexts, and for fiction in which he practiced
what he preached. Perhaps inevitably, he began revisiting the
ideas that had fuelled his early fiction, in order to recapitulate
and re-examine them from a more mature viewpoint. The

essay appended to the present volume was one of the earliest of those articles; although it is less inclined to scrupulous scholarly caution than many of the others he produced in series with it, it still gives the impression of a certain conscientious reticence, and his fiction also became more studied and more circumspect in its representations of altered states of consciousness, as can be seen in many of the stories in the remaining collections in the present series.

In 1831 Nodier began to publish a series of "Extraits des mémoires de Maxime Odin" in the *Revue de Paris*, but only published two episodes bearing that label there, and interrupted it when he put together a volume of the *Oeuvres* entitled *Souvenirs de jeunesse* [Souvenirs of Youth], for which he borrowed the title of the *Revue de Paris* series as a subtitle, even though the second item in the series was not included on the collection and one of the four items it did include does not feature Maxime Odin. Although they fill an intriguing spectrum from sentimental tragedy to farcical comedy, they all contrast very markedly with *Histoire du roi de Bohême et de ses sept châteaux* in the determined orthodoxy of their narrative form. It was not long before Nodier began to dabble with the surreal again, in two stories that began another incomplete series in the *Revue de Paris* in 1832, collectively entitled "Perfectibilité" (tr. as "Perfectibility" in *Perfectibility and Resurrection*). They are, however, far more carefully controlled than *Histoire du roi de Bohême et de ses sept châteaux*, and Nodier's subsequent work was further restrained in its use of grotesquerie, even when the pedantic Don Pic Fanferluchio—the oddest of all the author's fictitious *alter egos*—was ungagged and allowed to indulge his pedantic authorial idiosyncrasies to the full, as he was, tacitly, in "Le Bibliomane" and in the last story that was published during Nodier's lifetime, the bibliomaniac fantasy "Franciscus Columna" (1843; tr. in *The Four Talismans and Other Stories*).

15

Histoire du roi de Bohême et de ses sept châteaux is a very remarkable literary construct, although it is content to describe itself as a "pastiche" and it gives an elaborate account of its own literary ancestry, taking its immediate inspiration from Laurence Sterne's *Tristram Shandy* and remoter encouragement from Rabelais. The liberation of the imagination and the mining of the unconscious fraction of the mind via the imagery and strange sequentiality of dreams, which are key to the philosophy and methodology of surrealism, are put into practice quite deliberately by Nodier; *Histoire du roi de Bohême et de ses sept châteaux*t is by no means the first long work of fiction to be represented as a dream, but it tries harder than any of its predecessors to reproduce some of the odder phenomena of the dream state, and Nodier's idiosyncratic theory of the nature and substance of dreams, as contained in the appended essay, is intimately connected with it, although it is far from offering a detailed explanation of its content and narrative method.

The novella juxtaposes and intermingles several of Nodier's past and present obsessions, including etymology, entomology, the art of writing fiction and the essential hopelessness of amour, the sum of which had largely constituted his unusual life. If the work can be fully understood—and there are certainly passages within it and elements of its construction that a deliberately designed not to make sense—that cannot be achieved without some knowledge of Nodier's biography and the awkward shape of his career prior to the July Revolution, as outlined in the introductions and illustrated in the contents of the previous collections in the present series. Exactly how the author's biography, his previous literary work and the vision of 1828 are linked and interrelated is, however, a matter for intricate analysis and evaluation.

Les Tristes, ou Mélanges tirés des tablettes d'un suicide (1806; tr. as "Sorrows; or, Miscellaneous Extracts from the Notebooks of a Suicide"), had included "Un Heure, ou Le Vision" (tr. as "One o'Clock; or, The Vision"), a story, in which mental disturbance occasioned by the grief of lost love formulates a consolatory hallucination. That motif established a template for many later stories and exemplifies a theory of madness and hallucination further elaborated, not only in the essay included in the present volume as an appendix but by several of Nodier's crucial contributions to the development of the *fantastique* in French fiction. The story of Gervais and Eulalie contained within *Histoire du roi de Bohême et de ses sept châteaux*, deliberately broken up into four increasingly cursory fragments, is a quasi-allegorical variant of the recurrent theme of frustrated amour, which links the encapsulating dream-fantasy to the whole sequence of Nodier's fictional representations of the existential treachery and hopelessness of the sentiment in question.

What Nodier's wife, Désirée—who was sixteen when she married him in 1808—thought about her husband's addiction to writing stories of allegedly perfect amour that all end in tragic death and despair we can only speculate, but it might be worth noting that his principal fictitious alter ego, Maxime Odin, remains unmarried after losing one of his perfect amours mere minutes after a deathbed wedding. It is unclear whether the dreamer in *Histoire du roi de Bohême et de ses sept châteaux* is married, but if he is, it is probably to one of the two voices that occasionally intrude into his dream-space as "Victorine" and "Fanny," although the reader is perfectly at liberty to infer that they are two of his mistresses. If both have real equivalents in Nodier's mundane life, though, one is likely to be a transfiguration of Désirée and the other of Marie. Although there is room for doubt as to which one is which, if that interpretation is favored, the probability is that Victorine, for whom he sometimes seems to be telling up the story, while promising others, is Marie. The Théodore of "Le

Bibliomane" is definitely married with a young daughter, but their names are not given.

As to why the dreaming narrative voice of *Histoire du roi de Bohême et de ses sept châteaux* is called Théodore, we can only speculate, but there are oblique references in the dream to several of the fellow writers with whom Nodier was in regular communication in the *cénacle* he hosted throughout the late 1820s, some of whom also included oblique references to him in their own works. It might not be simple coincidence that Jules Janin, who knew Nodier as well as anyone in the cénacle, in one of his finest stories, "La Soeur rose et la soeur grise" (reprinted in book form in 1837; tr. as "The Good Sister and the Bad Sister") employs a hallucinating protagonist who is addressed in the story by the Devil as his "beloved secretary, Théodore." Janin links that name directly to one of the forenames of the German writer of classic alcohol-induced hallucinatory fantasies E. T. A. Hoffmann, who was undoubtedly one of the sources of inspiration for Nodier's hallucinatory fantasies.

We do not learn very much about Théodore, in course of *Histoire du roi de Bohême et de ses sept châteaux*, and when he makes an arithmetical division of the three components of his dream-self he rates himself as zero and even Don Pic de Fanfrelucio as one in a thousand, but if one were to attempt an analysis of him on the basis of the fragmentary data, one would probably have to conclude that his dominant characteristic, there and in "Le Bibliomane," is frustration— not surprising, given the point that Nodier's literary career seemed to have reached in the 1820s, especially if it really was stalled continually by repeated bouts of illness. The effects of frustration are very evident in *Histoire du roi de Bohême et de ses sept châteaux* and help to explain its defiantly eccentric format as well as its tone. Although the dreamer's "mission" is continually sidetracked by a number of personal distractions and digressions, their sum is symptomatic of general frustration induced by the sensation that his imagination, whether symbolized as a horse, a carriage or a combination thereof, is being weighed down and held back, unable to get to where it wants to go.

In theory, as Théodore insists more than once in the novella, his imagination can go absolutely anywhere, but in practice it is by no means so easy. He has his own handicaps, including Don Pic Fanferluchio's relentless pretention and academic esotericism, but even when Don Pic is temporarily excluded from the text, the contents of the dream and its attempted directionality are subject to all kinds of deflective pressures and forces. Although *Histoire du roi de Bohême et de ses sept châteaux* was eventually reprinted integrally, an extract of the story of Gervais and Eulalie, stitched together to form a continuous narrative, as "Les Aveugles de Chamouny" [The Blind Couple of Chamouny] has always been much more easily accessible, and the similarly extracted "Histoire du chien de Brisquet" (tr. as "The Story of Brisquet's Dog") was reprinted even more frequently, although the fact that the former narrative is broken up and distributed within its frame is essential to its narrative topography and purpose, and the second is pointless except when seen as Breloque's critical response to the former story, and the theoretical justification that he gives of it, in opposition to the supposed faults of its predecessor (and, tacitly, of the greater part of Nodier's fiction).

Even if one sets aside the elaborate overt discussion within the narrative frame of the nature and substance of the work, *Histoire du roi de Bohême et de ses sept châteaux*, if it is considered as a story, is fundamentally a story about the composition and narration of stories, and the hows and whys of that activity, on the part of a writer all-too-uncomfortably aware of the fact that his own personal obsessions have little in common with those of the audience that he is compelled by circumstance to address. His decision in the present novella to challenge that audience, flamboyantly, rather than attempt to flatter it, is inherently hazardous and deliberately provocative, but necessarily original and, in its own fashion and, at least in parts, brilliantly so. The novella asks the question of what stories can and ought to do, and answers both aspects of that question, and although the entire remainder of the author's subsequent career deliberately avoided those answers, doing different things for different purposes, Nodier never entirely sacrificed the combative and subversive spirit of *Histoire du roi de Bohême et de ses sept châteaux.*

Maxime Odin and various unnamed narrators took over Théodore's role in the author's subsequent work, having perhaps already featured in some of the work done in the 1820s that did not surface until 1832. None of those narrators aspired to be the Devil's secretary, and most were very insistent that they were on the side of the angels, even though divine Providence appeared to have it in for them, and one of Maxime Odin's memoirs explains how he "gave himself to the Devil" by means of the reckless employment of an old grimoire. All of them, however, disdained the strategy of simply improvising analogues of the story of Brisquet's dog, in the interests of currying favor with the bulk of their audience, and if they sometimes succeeded in gagging Don Pic Farferluchio, or blindfolding him with a symbolic ribbon, they always remained aware of his unacknowledged presence, and never completely escaped the presumed effects of his censure.

It is not really surprising, in spite of the relative liberation of the literary marketplace after 1830 and his continued interest in the nature and content of dreams, that Nodier never tried to publish anything else akin to *Histoire du roi de Bohême et de ses sept châteaux.* The wonder is that he contrived to do it once, seventy years before the brief fashionability acquired by Alfred Jarry and Guillaume Apollinaire, in a much more hospitable literary climate, and a hundred years before the publication of James Joyce's *Finnegans Wake* (1939), with which it has a kinship at least as significant as its advertised kinship with *Tristram Shandy*. It is not what would nowadays be called a "reader-friendly" work, and it poses a considerable challenge even to those professional academics who are paid, as it were, "to like that sort of thing." It is not, however, a book without its rewards even for the most casual of readers, and its humor, although odd, is genuinely funny as well as anarchically exuberant, while its tragedy, in the enclosed narrative of Gervais, is genuinely moving.

As literary experiments go, even if it is not to be reckoned a complete success, *Histoire du roi de Bohême et de ses sept châteaux* is very far from being a complete failure, and it can be enjoyed as well as judged intriguing. It is deliberately incoherent, and in places deliberately incomprehensible, but its incoherence is never without an underlying purpose and an underlying schema, partly because it takes for granted the thesis that the apparent incoherence, inconsequentiality and incomprehensibility of real dreams must have an underlying purpose, however arcane, and an underlying schema, however bizarre—and that expeditions in literary surrealism are valuable processes of exploration, capable of offering valuable and unique rewards. It is, in its own peculiar fashion, a masterpiece of intelligence, wit and literary artistry.

The translations of *Histoire du roi de Bohême et de ses sept châteaux*, "Polichinelle" and "Le Bibliomane" were made from versions of the texts preserved on the Blibilothèque Nationale's invaluable *gallica* website. The accompanying essay was translated from the version of *Rêveries* reproduced by Google Books.

—Brian Stableford

THE STORY OF
THE KING OF BOHEMIA
AND HIS SEVEN CASTLES

There was once a King of Bohemia who had seven castles.
Trimm.[1]

1 Corporal Trim is the character in Laurence Sterne's *Tristram Shandy* who relates a truncated version of an anecdote about the king in question. The misrendering of the name here might be deliberate.

Introduction

Yes! If I had for a mount the sophistic and pedantic donkey that argued against Balaam . . .

If I were reduced to bestriding the ticklish nag that made another Absalom of Brother Jean des Entommeures,[1] or the restive mule whose infernal stubbornness compromised one day the salvation of the abbess of the Andouillettes and the gentle Marguerite . . .

If it were prescribed to me by a law of the State or a canon of the Church never to run to a relay except on the fantastic hack of Lenore[2] or the pale horse of the Apocalypse that bore a rider named *Death* . . . that one, alas, is whinnying outside my door . . .

But who the devil can tell me what a pale horse is?

If I had to borrow, in order to go there, the adventurous flight of the hippogriff, to suspend myself like Montgolfier from a bladder of gummed cloth, or to perch like Sinbad the Sailor on the shoulders of an accursed afrit . . .

I would go!

"Deadly ambition, where do you intend to take me? Is it to Corinth?"

"No, Théodore, it's to Bohemia."

I shall pen the diptychs, I shall spell out the diplomas, I

---

1 A character in Rabelais.
2 In Gottfried Bürger's eponymous ballad.

shall collate the charts; I shall know in what time that King of Bohemia lived, and I shall mark the location of his seven castles with a precision worthy of Pausanias, Antonin or Rutilius, in such a manner as to cause the exact, punctual and conscientious Dodwell to die of chagrin, if he had not already died in 1711, the worthy Henry Dodwell, a few days after flowery Easter.[1]

Although, in Dodwell's time, hardly anyone was occupied with the King of Bohemia and his seven castles!

And that is why societies progress slowly. Every century has its needs.

The most pressing need of our epoch, for a rational man who appreciates the world and life at their true value, is to discover the end of the story of the King of Bohemia and his seven castles.

Personally, I only need a horse; either by necessity or by caprice, I will not go to Bohemia without a horse. An enterprise like this one is well worth the expense of a horse, and yet I have seen twenty subscriptions go by without there being any question of a horse to go to Bohemia.

A horse, a horse! My kingdom for a horse![2]

---

1 Henry Dodwell (1641-1711) was elected as a professor of history at Oxford in 1691, but was deprived of his post for refusing to swear allegiance to William and Mary, who had come to the throne following the "Glorious Revolution" of 1688; Dodwell thus became a heroic exemplar of religious dissent, although the quality of his scholarship was highly controversial.
2 This quotation from Shakespeare's *Richard III* is rendered in English in the original.

Retraction

What would I do with a horse, anyway? I wouldn't give a univalve mollusk for one—I don't care whether it's a cone or a spindle, an olive or a trochus, a spiral or a buccina; I believe that it's a cowry—no, I wouldn't give a fragment of that primitive money that the sea casts up on your beaches, poor and fortunate islander, for Alexander's horse, which had the head of an ox, or Caesar's which had the feet of a ram.

Can I not travel without a horse in all the spaces that God has opened to human imagination? Do I not have at my service the comfortable and obedient carriage of which he has made me a present as part of my celestial heritage, and which I have sometimes preferred to a pharaonic chariot?

I cannot tell you precisely what your vehicle is called. It is not the disobliging solitary of Monsieur Dessein; it is not the presumptuous tilbury of the fop; it is neither the rapid sediole of the Italian, which flees on two burning wheels, nor the fuming sleigh of the Laplander that glides over the snow, whistling, and disappears in the middle of a cloud of icy dust.

It is a carriage of my own, where I can sleep peacefully in the four corners, sometimes alone, sometimes accompanied, and which I steer at my ease toward all the points of the universe.

It is sufficient for me to flick my thumb against my middle finger or click my tongue against my palate three times to take it from Delhi to Tobolsk, or to send it from the Orkneys to Chandernagor—and if I have chewed a few leaves of the great convolvulus that produces betel;[1] if the juice of the poppy, transformed into solid and perfumed pastilles, reawakens in my mind the laughing family of dreams; if I inhale in a long glass the spirituous and spiritual gas that emanates from casks of Epernay; or if I take several pinches from my pretty Lumloch snuff-box of that intoxicating and poetic power with which a minor diplomat of the sixteenth century endowed France . . . oh, how far I would leave you behind me, timid Vesta, grave and modest Pallas! How many times I would cross, Jupiter, the orbit in which your satellites roll! How many times I would break your pallid ring, somber and silent Saturn! I remember having touched a barrier on which one read in letters of a form and color unknown on Earth: *Tollbooth of Uranus*. God, how cold it was!

What is convenient about my carriage is that it is always ready. Would you care to climb in, Madame? There is no axle to grease, no cotter-pin to tighten. It does not lack a bolt. Have no fear of road accidents. If the equipage of Cervantes or Rabelais, if that of the beneficiary of Sutton or the dean of Saint Patrick,[2] has passed this way, I have followed the rut very carefully, or have deviated from it with great skill! The ditches are, in truth, as deep as space. They would give an eagle vertigo. But the path is as broad as the channel of the Manche, multiplied by all the drops of water in the Atlantic. I tip up sometimes, but only when I want to—or when you want to—and it is on to sand so soft, on to grass so supple, so flexible and so fresh, that you will never regret, I swear,

---

1 Betel is not a hallucinogen, but it does have psychotropic effects, which combine a feeling of euphoria with a sensation of increased alertness and concentration. Honoré de Balzac notoriously overdosed on coffee beans, employing caffeine to obtain a similar effect, and it would not be surprising if he and Nodier had experimented with betel for the same purpose,
2 i.e. Laurence Sterne and Jonathan Swift.

either the soft eiderdown of your bed or the silken stuffing that inflates your sofas.

Yesterday, Fanny, my eyes fixed on that little yellow beauty-spot over your dark eyebrow, for there is too much danger for me in looking at lower down . . . no later than this morning, Victorine, fingers entangled in the golden curls of your floating hair . . . tell me, traitress, who undid your hair?

O Victorine, O Fanny, how far you have traveled with me without knowing it!

But it is a matter today of more serious things. For the first time in my life, I have taken it into my head to have a fixed will, a determined goal. I am leaving. I have left.

"Where are you going, then, Théodore?"

"To Bohemia, I tell you! Whip, coachman!"

Convention

Only I won't go without them. I have good reasons for that.

One is Don Pic de Fanferulchio.

The other is my faithful Breloque.[1]

The former entertains me in secret with those studies of little value in which one forgets pleasantly to live. He is the most assiduous of the friends of my youth. At twenty-five I had never sought any other conversation but his, and what conversation! The tallest of men, the thinnest, the narrowest, the most geometrically abstract in all his dimensions; with a smattering of Greek and Latin, onomatopoeias, theses, diatheses, hypotheses, metatheses, tropes, syncopes and acopopes; the head that contains the most arguments against an idea, sophisms against a reasoning, paradoxes against an opinion, names, forenames and surnames, forgotten titles and useless dates, biological stupidities, bibliological nonsense, philological absurdities, the living table of the subject-matter of Adelung's *Mithridates* and Saxius' *Onomasticon!*[2]

1 A breloque is a seal or charm appended to a watch-chain; the name thus symbolizes the humblest of the links in the narrative voice's identity-chain, contrasted with the pretentious scholar Don Pic, whose surname is a corruption of *fanfreluche*, another term for decorative trimmings.

2 *Mithridates, oder allgemeine Sprachennkunde* (1806) is an incomplete work by the German philologist Johann Christoph Adelung, who set out therein to track down all the roots of the various dialects of the Germanic language. *Onomasticum Literarium* (1788) by "Christophorus Saxius" [Christoph Sach] is a series of biographical and critical annotations of

The latter is a bizarre and capricious creature, a singular jest of Providence amusing itself after molding a genius in the form of Achilles or Apollo in building with the splinters escaped from its chisel a deformed and grotesque monster: a fortuitous mixture of elements that one would have thought incompatible, a temporary but unique accident in the innumerable modes of being, a ridiculous unfinished sketch of a human being; a being without a name, without a purpose, without a destiny, who was always seen laughing, always singing, always mocking, always gamboling, ever disposed to do nothing or to make nothing . . .

Alas, my dear Victor,[1] I do not have your golden pen and tour ink of a thousand colors; I do not have, my dear Tony,[2] the palette richer than the rainbow with which you charge your brushes—and I would be trying to paint a dwarf!

When I had won the lottery of the German principality that I lost this morning when I woke up—a plague on the shaker—I gave Don Pic de Fanferluchio the seals of the chancellery and the keys of the library.

Breloque had the treasury and the petty apartments.

O you whom fortune has exposed in an elevated rank to the jealous gazes of the multitude and who has nor read fruitlessly the life of Alcibiades, you can address yourself to Breloque in all security. He will cut off the tails of your dogs.

No, no one has ever been proven to the same degree as me . . .

Not Cleobis and Biton,[3] who died of fatigue pulling their mother's triumphant chariot . . .

---

eminent writers in all languages, in chronological order.

1 Victor Hugo.

2 Tony Johannot, another key member of the cénacle, the illustrator of the original edition of the present volume.

3 Cleobis and Biton are featured in a story told by Herodotus, named by Solon, somewhat ironically, as two of the happiest people in the world

Not Sire Gontran de Léry who expired depositing his fiancée on the summit of the Côte des Deux Amants[1] . . .

Not Euthyme de Locres,[2] to whom nothing less happened for having transported an enormous rock destined to close the walls of his city . . .

What am I saying? Not even the giant that sustains the world: Antheus, Epimetheus, Prometheus or Atlas . . . I'm very sorry if I've mistaken his name, but I don't even have an almanac here . . .

No, no one had felt the weight of that compact and immense virtue, that ideality of absolute perfections, that prototype of all innate and acquired faculties, that exemplar of human soul and intelligence almost divinized, the overwhelming superiority of which exercises an involuntary but hostile and perpetual censure upon society entire . . .

"Help me, Breloque," I cried, "save me from my innocence! Remove, if necessary, from my chaste forehead, the crown of timid purity that women once awarded me. Deliver me from that infallibility of mores, from the inflexible austerity that will end up attracting the hatred of the whole human race to me. Dance, Breloque, dance on . . . Give me faults that are not vices, tastes that are not excesses, manias that are not passions. Dance, Breloque, dance forever . . . and if your little bells are ever audible in the formidable concert of the trumpets of judgment, do not fear that they will inform me of a remorse!"

Breloque made the perilous leap.

Poor Breloque; without you, what would I become?

---

1 The Breton confluence known as the Côte des Deux Amants features in one of the lays of Marie de France; the legend on which it is based, which features the named knight, is also developed in Breton ballads.

2 "Euthyme de Locres" [i.e, Euthymos], was mentioned in the *Annales de l'Instiute de correspondence archeologique* (1830) as well as several eighteenth-century treatises as a pugilist honored in the Olympic games who was said to have battled a demon as well as his great rival Theagenes.

What would I have been without them, I ask? The formless statue of the Titan, the doll of the ideologue, the anthropomorphic monster of Godwin?[1]

When the archangel that melts the figure of a man in the furnaces of nature had perceived the mistake that had made him confound such diverse elements—Don Pic, Breloque and Théodore—his first impulse was to break the image and throw the fragments into space . . .

O povero mi! How many centuries would it have required to bring my constitutive molecules back into harmony, to re-attach my atoms, to idiosyncratize my monads, to reestablish the intimate and perfect adherence of so many antipathetic surfaces between the myrmidon Breloque and the filiform Patagon Don Pic de Fanferluchio?

Fortunately, the angelic practitioner looked at it twice, three times, returned to it again, and became accustomed to tolerating, and then to loving his model. He went as far as confiding to him an emanation of the bountiful breath with which the angels are so miserly, and imprinting his thumb forcefully on the end of his still-inanimate manikin's nose, in order to be able to recognize him one day by that original flattening.

"Go," he said to him, "and be Théodore." And my father wept with joy over a cradle.

---

1 Presumably the "monster" in *Frankenstein* (1818), Godwin being Mary Shelley's maiden name; the novel in question was adapted for a dramatic production, *Le Monstre et le magicien*, at the Théâtre de la Porter Saint-Martin in 1826, in an attempt to repeat the success of *Le Vampire*, and Nodier might have lent a hand to the script.

Demonstration

If, however, by chance, this fiction does not suit you . . . for I see no difficulty in declaring that it is fiction . . .

If you are among the number of positive minds who are only content with absolute verities, and who will not receive an idea struck in the coin of Montaigne and Plato without submitting it to the proof of an assay-balance . . .

If you give more credit to a good addition than a similitude, or even a comparison . . .

Well, my God, you only have to say so!

It is only necessary to agree on a point of departure—which is to say, on the calculation of Diocles of Smyrna,[1] which represents the human mind as the number one thousand.

Thus, sum received on account: 1000.

Let us pass on to the analysis

Item, Théodore, or my imagination: 0.

Item, Don Pic de Fanferluchio, or my memory: 1

Item, Breloque, or my judgment: 999.

I have no need to make the synthesis before you, but you can easily verify it with your professor of mathematics, your steward, or even your laundress.

I posit boldly the total: 1000.

---

1 The reference is to the Greek mathematician Diocles (c240 B.C.-c170 B.C.), but Nodier's insistence on referring to him as "Diocles of Smyrna," here and elsewhere, is idiosyncratic.

Which signifies, identically: the author of *The Story of the King of Bohemia and his Seven Castles*; for the mind is the whole man, and it is its three faculties, imagination, memory and judgment, which compose—unless something has changed therein—the mysterious trinity of our intelligence, in rather irregular proportions, as you see, and which can suffer modifications so multiple that the encounter of two intellectual twins would probably be the most unexpected event in the world, and the one that would add the most piquant charm to our future Palingenesis.

What an incredible variety of physiognomies! What an inexhaustible source of harmonies and contrasts! How many souls that will be astonished not to have flown to one another! How many affections that will revolt against the yoke to which a deceptive sympathy has subjected them! How many modesties reassured too late! How many great men I have seen, and—it costs me to admit it—who will arrive there, negatively stamped with three zeroes, like the beard of Diocles![1]

Breloque has not reserved any other pleasure for himself for the first thirty myriads of the centuries of eternity.

---

1 Nodier was undoubtedly aware of an anecdote relating that in 176 A.D. the Roman Emperor Marcus Aurelius created four chairs of philosophy in Athens; when one fell vacant the committee appointed to choose his successor preferred the aged Diocles to Bogoas on the grounds that the latter did not have a beard; Bogoas argued that if philosophers were to be judged on the merit of their beards, they ought to appoint a billy-goat, and the confused committee-members referred the question to the Emperor for a Solomonic judgment.

Objection

"Well, Monsieur, I see what this is! Another bad pastiche of the innumerable pastiches of Sterne and Rabelais . . ."

Bad, it pleases you to say? And then, what the devil do you want if you don't want pastiches?

Dare I demand of you what book is not a pastiche, what idea can pride itself today on hatching out primal and typical?

(Dalgarno[1] reduced all primitive ideas to six, and Don Pic de Fanferluchio claims that that is a luxury.)

Dare I demand of you, I was saying, what author has proceeded by himself, like God, except for the unknown author who started the day after the invention of letters?

Perhaps that was Enoch, but his book has not been found[2] . . .

Perhaps it was Abraham, but the *Jezirah* is apocryphal and the Holy Spirit swept it, like the false gospels, from the table of the Council of Nicea . . .

Perhaps it was Mercury, alias Hermes Trismegistus; but there is no more question of that particularity in Apollodorus than Père Gautruche.[3]

Who took it into his head to trace for the first time, on the sand . . .

---

1 The linguistic philosopher George Dalgarno (1616-1687).
2 In fact, a copy of the *Book of Enoch*, discovered in Ethiopia, had been presented to Louis XV by the explorer James Bruce in the 1770s.
3 The Jesuit scholar Pierre Gautruche (1602-1681).

Or on a rock . . .

Or on a brick . . .

Or on an ivory tabella coated with virgin wax . . .

Or on some other natural or plastic, but penetrable and tenacious, substance . . . or on a leaf of papyrus . . .

Or on the membrane of the placenta of a quadruped . . .

Or on the broth of hemp or linen, cotton or silk, straw or nettles, stretched, flattened and dried . . .

With a sharpened reed . . .

Or a pointed graver . . .

Or a friable metal pencil . . .

Or a fragment of colored stone . . .

Or a goose-quill . . .

To trace (as I was saying) a few vertical or horizontal lines . . . from bottom to top or top to bottom . . . from right to left or left to right . . . or even from left to right and from right to left alternately, as is practiced in the *Boustrophedon* . . .

And to cry out in a language that died before the deluge: *Exegi monumentum!*[1]

That man (original writer, I salute you!) only wrote, however, according to all appearance, what had been said before him; and, a marvelous thing, the first book written was itself only a pastiche of tradition, a plagiarism of speech.

A new idea—great God! Not one remained in circulation in the time of Solomon, and Solomon only said it after Job.

And you want me, a plagiarist of the plagiaries of Sterne . . .

Who was the plagiarist of Swift . . .

Who was the plagiarist of Wilkins[2] . . .

Who was the plagiarist of Cyrano . . .

Who was the plagiarist of Reboul[3] . . .

---

1 The full quotation from Horace is *Exegi monumentum aere perennis* [I have erected a monument more durable than bronze].
2 Bishop John Wilkins (1614-1672), an associate of Dalgarno.
3 The violent satirist Guillaume de Reboul (1564-1611).

Who was the plagiarist of Guillaume des Autels[1] . . .

Who was the plagiarist of Rabelais . . .

Who was the plagiarist of More . . .

Who was the plagiarist of Erasmus . . .

Who was the plagiarist of Lucian . . . or of Lucius of Patras, or of Apuleius, for no one knows which of the three was stolen by the other two, and I never cared to know . . .

You would like me, I repeat, to invent the form and the foundation of a book! Heaven help me! Condillac says somewhere that it would be easier to create a world than to create an idea.

And that is also the opinion of Polydore Vergil and Bruscambille.[2]

---

1 Guillaume Desautels (1529-c1599).

2 The Humanist Polydore Vergil (c1470-155) was chiefly noted for a collection of Latin proverbs; "Bruscambille" was the pseudonym of the famous farceur Jean Gracieux (1575-1634).

Declaration

Furthermore, you will agree that I have not announced the slightest insensate retention to be new in the most tediously exhausted métier that one can exercise in the world: that, as Rabelais would say, of sophisticator of thought and siever of words.

You could search fruitlessly for a hundred years for a title that would reveal a plagiarist more naively than these ingenuous lines: *The Story of the King of Bohemia and his Seven Castles.* Scarcely have they struck your eyes than three or four ideas suddenly spring from your memory, full armed, like Minerva from the head of Jupiter, charged with insignia, blazons, fields and devices, circled by ramparts, moats and counterscarps, bristling with barbed openings and bastions . . .

"Aha!" you say. "I've seen that somewhere, in Olaus Magnus, Rudbeck or perhaps Sterne . . ."

One last box opens, that of reflection, and a more intelligent, clearer and more lucid idea emerges, which says to you in a sardonic tone, shrugging its shoulders slightly . . . (O divine Entelechy, the shoulders of an idea!)

"But that's it, that's absolutely it! It's in Sterne! It's only a pastiche!"

And then, reentering disdainfully: "Thank you, Madame!"

I would have been so easy for me to dissimulate that borrowing of an exhausted imagination, by saying, perhaps:

The Story
of the King of Hungary
and
his Eight Fortresses

or, even better:

The Chronicle
of the Emperors of Trebizond
and a Description
of their Fourteen Palaces.

But my natural candor finds such artifices repugnant.

A pastiche, a true pastiche, all that there is of pastiche . . .

And that suits me all the better because I do not know what it is.

It only depends on you to make me take that sincere abnegation of all personal merit to its ultimate expression . . .

(I am talking to the peevish expression that emerges obstinately from its niche at the end of all my pages like the importunate automata of the clocks of Nuremberg).

Gentle and prudish Modesty, inspire me with a concession so humble, so resigned that it will finally disarm the wrath of my enemies!

Eureka! I've found it!

And I ought to reassure my pretty female readers that I am not writing this "in simple apparel"—in the negative costume of Archimedes. I have a blue linen jacket that I have only worn three times. In any case, it isn't me that it's a matter of looking at. It's the following page, where you will find the definitive title of this volume . . .

Definitive, inasmuch as it is permissible for a man to attach that reckless adjective to one of his conceptions . . .

Definitive, if God and my aneurism permit . . .

Poor Théodore!

𝕿𝖍𝖊 𝕾𝖙𝖔𝖗𝖞
𝕺𝖋
𝕿𝖍𝖊 𝕶𝖎𝖓𝖌 𝕺𝖋 𝕭𝖔𝖍𝖊𝖒𝖎𝖆
𝕬𝖓𝖉
𝕳𝖎𝖘 𝕾𝖊𝖛𝖊𝖓 𝕮𝖆𝖘𝖙𝖑𝖊𝖘

A PASTICHE

O imitators, servum pecus!
Horace *Epistle* I, xix, 19[1]

PARIS
At the Bookshops
That do not sell novelties.

---

1 The quotation translates as "O imitators, servile crowd!"

Continuation

As for imitators without conscience . . .

As for the juggling ape who counterfeits without taste, who sees without intelligence, a living automaton whose physiognomy is a caricature and whose laughter is a grimace . . .

As for the surly parrot who sings the song of Psaphon[1] because Psaphon has sung it, who thinks he is inventing what he is repeating . . .

As for the brazen crow who ornaments himself insolently with the spoils of some unknown peacock, and who displays in your museums and academies a diamond crest and golden plumes with azure eyes that he has not borne . . .

I would sooner count Toralva's goats, a calculation that frightened the infallible judgment of Don Quixote, and whom the most perspicacious infinitesimal mathematicians, from the Marquis de l'Hôpital[2] to the editor of the latest *Almanac of the Muses*, have sagely left out.

Who would dare to complain today that there was one goat—a single goat—too many in Toralva's flock, which was capering there in the manner of the others?

---

1 According to Maximus of Tyre, in a story cited in 1828 by the Chevalier de Méry in his history of proverbs, Psaphon was a young Libyan who taught a multitude of birds to pronounce his name in order to make it famous.
2 Guillaume de l'Hôpital (1661-1704), author of the first systematic account of differential calculus.

The sheep of Dindenaut[1] have never been found to be too numerous; however, they drowned, whereas Toralva's goats only asked to jump. And provided that my goat passes in the number; that she is neither old, nor deformed, nor peevish; that she is near, elegant and speckled; that she has the natural sentiment and dignity and decency of her sex . . .

Provided, I say, that she files past, nose in the air, her nostrils open to scent at a distance the flowers and the dew, her head slightly inclined over the left clavicle, because she is putting on airs . . .

Or, standing up on her hind legs, her forelegs modestly curved back on themselves, her neck extended, her eyes bulging, her mouth elongated and quivering, she can break from time to time, from the summit of a bush that does not belong to anyone, one of those long bouquets of leaves or parasitic fruits that exhaust the bush without embellishing it . . .

Fructu careolus volvitur gestiens croceo . . .[2]

(That was probably the corymb of an immature sorb-tree.)

O pitiless critic, one will ask no more of you . . .

With your permission, Messieurs, make way for Theocritus' goat![3]

---

1 A character in Rabelais.
2 "A saffron-colored fruit agitated by the wind . . ."
3 Theocritus' first Idyll, which a rutting billy-goat plays a symbolic role, is generally considered to be an allegory of the origins and essence of bucolic poetry.

Protestation

Plagiarist! Me, a plagiarist! When I wanted to find a means of preserving myself from that reproach by disposing letters in an order so

N   O   V   E   L
    or subjecting lines to rules
       of disposition so bizarre
          —or, to put it better, so
            Madly unusual!!!

When, with such violent inversions, I would like to torture words!

Or marry ideas and hostile words incompatibly, which would roar on encountering one another!

When I only aspire to bear you away on the wings of the Oriental Condor to the summit of some inaccessible mountain that has braved the invasion of the Deluge . . .

Or precipitate you with me on a charger compared to which Mazeppa's would have cut no better figure than Sancho's old donkey, into the depths hollowed out five hundred million leagues beneath the subterranean worlds of Klimius . . .[1]

---

1 The hero of the satirical *Nicolai Klimii Iter Subterraneum* [Nils Klim's Journey in the Underworld] (1741) by Ludvig Holberg. Written in Latin and published in Germany in order to dodge an inevitable reaction in the Danish author's homeland, it was rapidly translated into several other languages, including French.

You would accuse me of imprisoning you by means of a cowardly impotence in this petty corner of our little land that is known as Bohemia!

Alas, perhaps I shall never go as far as Bohemia, although it is, I swear on my honor, the only project that occupies me today—and if I go, I shall arrive so late that no one of this generation and the twenty-two generations that will follow it will be able to read the news on the posters of Prague. I have so many things to do on the way!

First of all, I am firmly decided, I shall only enter Bohemia via Austria . . .

And Austria via Styria . . .

And Styria via Carinthia, where I owe a tear to the empty tomb of Édouard[1] . . .

And Carinthia via Carniola, my second and dear homeland . . .

And Carniola via Istria, where, lying on the cheerful beaches of the Blue Gulf, we shall scan with our delighted eyes at our pleasure the walls of Trieste and the tower of Aquileia . . .

And Istria via the land of Venice . . .

Behold Venice, and its port, and its gondolas, and its old Christian mosque, and its black palace, and the marble steps where the traces are visible of the blood of Faliero,[2] rejuvenated by the verses of Byron and the brushes of Delacroix . . .

And Venice via Mantua, which recalls Virgil . . .

---

1 Carinthia was incorporated into Illyria in Napoléon's Empire; it was where Napoléon's *grand armée* fought the battle of Dürrenstein in 1805, at which the French sustained very heavy losses, although Édouard Mortier, Duc de Trevise managed to secure the vital Danube crossings; the latter was still alive when the present story as written.
2 Martino Faliero (1274-1355), Doge of Venice, executed after a failed *coup-d'état*, the central character of a novella by E.T.A. Hoffmann, "Doge und Dogaresse" (in *Der Serapionsbrüder*, 1819) which Nodier had undoubtedly read.

Or via Brescia, which recalls the continence of Bayard[1] (since Heaven finds him more to its liking than me) . . .

Or via Bergamo, which recalls another hero, more modest and more popular, whose compatriots you recognize by the rabbit's tail that floats elegantly over their white felt hats . . .[2]

And if you believe me, we'll leave Bayard and Virgil there in favor of Harlequin . . .

Into Italy, finally, via Mont Saint Bernard and the valley of Chamouny, which I came to penetrate walking backwards with a marvelous skill along frightful paths, although my mind is doubly distracted by vertigo and by a confused memory of the adventures of Gervais and Cecilia . . .

But are you as disposed to hear them as I am to recount them? I've only come for that.

---

1 Pierre Terrail, seigneur de Bayard (c1473-1524), who distinguished himself at the siege of Brescia in 1512 and defended the daughters of a nearby house from attempted rape after being carried there when wounded.
2 A hat trimmed with a rabbit's tail was a distinguishing feature of Arlequino [Harlequin] a key character is the *commedia dell'arte*.

Dubitation

"I shall not raise any opposition to that," said Don Pic, "As long as your Cecilia isn't blind . . ."[1]

(She is.)

"I have a horror of these unnatural fictions in which the name of the principal character indicates to you in advance the subject and the purpose of the story, without regard to the illusion that is all the charm of it.

"What interest do you want me to accord to the death of Hippolytus, the misfortunes of Oedipus and the combats of Diomedes when I am so well-informed that the first will perish a victim of his furious horses, that the swollen feet of the second will have been traversed in childhood by a bloody strap, and that the third is nominally predestined to triumph over the gods themselves?

"Have I any need of a story to know that Philip loved horses passionately and that Alexander conquered nations? Is it not a bad joke to call Augustulus the last of the emperors?

"I have no objection to make against Nicias, since it appears that by reason of that name he was give command in the war against Sicily; and there is probably no one who imagines that the name of Scaevola and that of Cocles had been given to them before the former burned his wrist in Porsena's bra-

---

1 Saint Caecilia is the patron saint of music, whose name comes from the Latin *caecus* [blind].

zier and the second had bravely put out an eye in the dense of a bridge, which was nevertheless not the Pons Emilius or Palatinus, as some ludicrous antiquarians have proposed.

"But you will find people who have made adequate studies and who believe sincerely that the man whose eloquence was for a long time the strength of his people was named Demosthenes in the cradle, and that nature had inscribed the titles of model of sages in the baptismal certificate, or, if you wish, the birth certificate of Aristides.

"When the monks of the Middle Ages took it into their heads to pass ancient names under the leisure of their obscene and disorderly muse, how did they designate the author of a collection of gracious songs, as light and tender as the modulations of the shepherd's flute to which young girls danced? They called him Tibullus. When it was a question of a supple, dainty and mordant poet who played with a sparrow, the name of Catullus presented itself of its own accord. The volume that gave birth to the idea of an arsenal in which were displayed, in a thousand hostile forms, the cruelest weapons that had ever offended all the estates and mores of society since Archilochus, was attributed to Martial.

"What judicious critic would be credulous enough to adopt the individuality of a concise, almost enigmatic writer whose art is hiding many ideas under a few words, whose name was Tacitus? Or an elegant, pompous, sonorous orator who grouped choice words in bouquets and phrases in enameled compartments, whose name was Florus?"

"What, you think . . . ?"

"Inventions of studious idlers who relaxed sagely from the ennui of the offices by composing Latin classics for the usage of ignorant posterity![1] What afflicts me profoundly is that

1 This passage echoes the theory of the Jesuit Classical scholar Jean Hardouin (1646-1729), who alleged that many of the classic works of antiquity—he excepted Homer, Herodotus and Virgil, among others—had been forged by Medieval monks.

our Holy Church, the infallibility of which is so averred, was able to render itself accomplice to these maladroit frauds, in adopting the garish fable of a second edition Hippolytus, a Herculean Christophorus or Christ-Bearer, and a pretended Veronica or Veritable Image, whom one cannot name without revealing the impudent gaucherie of a forger . . .

"Oh, if your Cecilia were blind . . ."

(You know that she is.)

"I would like it a hundred times more if she were called Sappho or Lucrezia, Phyllis or Dorimene, Radegonde or Deborah, although I hold all those names in execration."

"What if she were called Eulalie?"[1]

"You would believe yourself obliged to make her speak with the redundant and mannered abundance that is all too familiar to you . . ."

"I give you my most sacred word of honor, as the euphuists of the court of Barras[2] said, "that I do not know a word of what she will say . . ."

"Good."

---

1 The object of the hopeless adoration of the Wertherian hero of Nodier's quasi-autobiographical novella *Le Peintre de Salzburg* (1803) is called Eulalie, but is not subject to Don Pic's criticism.
2 Presumably the protagonist of the scurrilously anti-Napoleonic *Amours et aventures du vicomte de Barras, ex-membre du durectoire exécutif* (1817).

Narration

I had travelled through the gracious forest of fir-trees that envelops the village of Bois with a new pleasure. I arrived at the small esplanade, invaded by glaciers from day to day, that dominates in such a majestic fashion the most beautiful peaks in the Alps, and which ends via an almost insensible slope at the picturesque source of the Arveyron. I wanted to contemplate again its portico of azure crystal, which changes aspect every year, and demands some emotion from those great scenes of nature. My fatigued heart had need of it.

I had not taken thirty steps when I perceived, not without astonishment, that Puck was not with me. (Alas, you would not have decided to draw away from your master at the price of the tastiest macaroon or the most delicate ring-biscuit.) He was even a little slow in responding to my appeal, and I was beginning to worry, when he came back, my pretty Puck, with a countenance embarrassed by dread, and yet with the caressant confidence of amity, his body rounded in a semi-circle, his gaze moist and suppliant, his head so low that his ears were trailing on the ground like those of the dog in *Zadig*.[1] Puck was also a spaniel.

If you had seen Puck in that posture, you would not have had the strength to be annoyed.

---

1 The reference is to Voltaire's 1747 novella, in which the distinctive trail left by a dog with floppy ears occasions a feat of deduction that gets the eponymous hero into trouble.

I was not annoyed; but he set off again, and then he came back again, and as that game was repeated, I approached in his wake the point of attraction that was summoning him, until, equally attracted by perfectly isogenic sympathies—or, if, like me you prefer it, by two entirely similar powers—he remained motionless, like a magnetized clapper between two iron bells placed at an equal distance.

On the bench of rock from which Puck separated me with a precision so exact that Laplace's compass would not have found a means on either side to insert a single geometric point, a young man was sitting, with the most amiable face, the most touching physiognomy, clad in a sky-blue blouse in the manner of a tunic, his hand armed with a log laburnum staff curved back at the top: a singular accessory that gave him some resemblance to Poussin's antique shepherds. Blond curly hair was rounded out in large ringlets around his bare neck and floating over his shoulders. His features were grave without austerity, sad without dejection; his mouth expressed more displeasure than bitterness. His eyes alone had a character of which I could not take account; they were large and limpid, but fixed, extinct and mute. No soul moved behind them.

The noise of the breeze had covered that of my approach. Nothing indicated that I had been perceived. I thought that he was blind.

Puck was studying all my impressions, and at the first sentiment of benevolence that he saw spring from my gaze he ran to that new friend. Who can explain the fervor of the most generous being in nature toward the most unfortunate being, of the dog toward the blind man? O Providence! I am, then, the only one of your children that you have abandoned!

The young man passed his fingers through Puck's long hair, smiling at him with candor. "How do you know me," he said to him, "you who are not from this valley? I had a dog as frolicsome, and perhaps as pretty, as you, but he was a barbet with woolly fur. He quit me like the others, my last friend, my poor Puck!"

"A strange hazard! Your dog had the same name as mine."

"Oh, Monsieur," the young man said to me, standing up, leaning on his laburnum staff, "forgive my infirmity . . ."

"Sit down, my friend. You're blind?"

"Blind since infancy."

"You've never been able to see?"

"I've seen, but so little. I have, however, some memory of the sun, and when I raise my eyes toward the place t must occupy in the sky, I think I can see a globe rolling, which reminds me of its color. I also have a memory of the whiteness of snow and the aspect of our mountains."

"It was an accident, then, that deprived you of the light?"

"An accident that was, alas, the least of my misfortunes. I was scarcely two years old when an avalanche descending from the heights of La Flégère crushed our little house. My father, who was a mountain guide, had sent the evening at the Priory. Imagine his despair when he found his family engulfed by the horrible scourge. Helped by his comrades, he succeeded in digging a hole in the snow and penetrating into our cabin, the roof of which was still sustained by its frail supports. The first object that was presented to his sight was my cradle; he extracted it from a peril that was augmenting incessantly, for the work of the diggers had itself favored the collapse of a few new masses and augmented the instability of our fragile dwelling. He went back in order to save my unconscious mother, only saw her for a moment by the light of the torches that were burning outside, and picked her up in his arms—but then everything collapsed. I was an orphan, and it was perceived the next day that an icicle had struck my eyes. I was blind."

"Poor child! So you remained alone, absolutely alone!"

"An unfortunate is never absolutely alone in our valley. All our good Chamouniers united to ease my misery. Balmat gave me shelter, Simon Coutet nourishment, Gabriel Payot clothing. A good widow who had lost her children took charge of caring for me and guiding me. It's her who still serves me as a mother, and who brings me to this place every day in summer."

"And those are all your friends!"

"I had several others," replied the young man, placing a finger over his lips with a mysterious expression, "but they've departed."

"Never to return?"

"According to all appearance. I've thought for a few days, however, that Puck might come back, and that he had only gone astray . . . but one doesn't go astray with impunity on our glacier. I won't feel him bounding at my side again. I won't hear him yapping at the approach of foreigner . . ."

The blind man wiped away a tear.

"What is your name?"

"Gervais."

"Listen, Gervais. These friends you've lost . . . explain to me . . ."

At the same moment I made a movement to sit down next to him, but he launched himself swiftly into the empty place.

"Not here, Monsieur, not here! This is Eulalie's place, and no one has occupied it since her departure."

"Eulalie?" I said, sitting down in the place he had just quit. "Tell me about this Eulalie and you. Your story interests me."

"I declare," said Victorine, "that it is beginning to interest me too . . ."

And how could I refuse? Decidedly, Breloque, we're not yet in Bohemia today.

Gervais, therefore, spoke thus.

Insertion

Or rather, he did not speak, because I interrupted him, launching myself with all the force of my thought into the editorial office of the best newspaper of the epoch, the *Infallible*, the *Impartial* or the *Disinterested*, distracted by an obsession that my literary modesty forces me to lock away under the key of parenthesis:

(The extremely urgent necessity of assuring myself of the sale of this story or work of fiction, this joke or poem, which the bookshops don't want.)

However, I confess that I am not quitting Gervais' story without regret. And I take Heaven as my witness that I remember the story as if I had just heard it and that I shall write it before having arrived in the drawing room . . .

In the antechamber . . .

On the porch . . .

On the landing . . .

On the main staircase . . .

In the vestibule . . .

On the parvis . . .

In the courtyard . . .

At the door . . .

In the avenue . . .

At the turning-point of the first of the seven castles of the King of Bohemia . . .

But it is so good and so sure to render an account oneself of oneself to oneself!

That privilege is so common, so comical, so convenient and so commercial, and I have made such scant use of it! Call me a liar if you dare, avid and mercenary demon who presides over the tariff of reputations!

"What prevents us," said Breloque, "reading tomorrow, in all the archives of renowned contemporaries, these equitable lines written to our glory:

"The illustrious Anonymous . . .

(Illustrious because of our magnificent sovereignty of Nihil-no-not-night.)

"The illustrious Anonymous will not remove himself from public admiration . . . 3 f. 50 c.

"One has recognized in his style the cachet of a tender, eloquent, energetic, harmonious, sublime writer . . . 7 f. 25 c.

"Who has left far behind him Cyrano de Bergerac, Homer, Byron, Chateaubriand, the Seigneur des Accords,[1] Montesquieu and Turlupin . . . 9 f. 00 c.

"*The Story of the King of Bohemia and his Seven Castles* will produce an immense revolution in literature . . ."

"What nonsense are you spouting, Breloque?"

"I'm writing a newspaper article."

"Dispense with that trouble. Here's one ready-made. Go, my friend, buy glory, since you prefer that stupid smoke to the suave vapor of my Havana cigars. Buy glory, Breloque. Pay cash and pay without counting; otherwise it's dearer!"

"Empedocles acquitted himself at such a high price that nothing remained of him but his pantoufles."[2]

---

1 The poet Étienne Tabourot (1549-1590), also known as Seigneur des Accords, best-known for *Les Bigarrures* (1572), a collection of word games, including acrostics, which he followed with collections of epigrams and folktales.

2 The word *pantoufle*—which I am not translating as "slipper" because of the manner of its usage elsewhere in the novella, including a whole chapter

"His pantoufles, Breloque, nothing but his pantoufles, that's what I wanted to say to you. Pantoufles! That word makes one of those dolorous strings vibrate in my heart that resonate for a long time, the emanation of which sympathizes with all the melancholies of the soul . . .

"If I had, by chance, a Stradivarius or an Amati violin and I could submit to the savant method of Baillot or animate it with the pathetic fingering of Viotti . . .

"Or if I only possessed what is necessary of the turpentine of Kolophon—there is mention of it in Meursius[1]—in order to make the raucous bow of a village Amphion screech less disgracefully . . .

"With what impetuous sensibility I could make the heart-rending expression of my memories pass into your soul!

"But I am stimulating the languishing wick in vain; the oil that remains in my lamp will take us, at the most, to the end of this feuilleton."

---

devoted to its hypothetical etymology—had more than one usage in the argot of the era in which the story was written. It was sometimes used as a supplement to "etc." to signify the triviality of the items that a speaker could not be bothered to add to a list. By extension, it could be applied disdainfully to a person, implying insignificance or impotence. Théodore, however, eventually favors a euphemistic interpretation, which is not in any dictionary but can safely be left to the reader's imagination, and which adds a belated gloss to the remark with which he follows Breloque's innocuous reference to the item of footwear allegedly left by Empedocles on the rim of Etna, which led the philosopher's followers to hypothesize that he had committed suicide by leaping into the crater.

1 The Classical scholar Johannes Meursius (Jehan van Meurs, 1579-1639).

Transcription

LITERARY ANNOUNCEMENTS

THE STORY OF THE KING OF BOHEMIA AND HIS SEVEN CASTLES[1]

I cannot say to the author of this work what Tacitus said of Otho, Galba and Vitellius: *nec beneficio, nec injuria cognitus*. I would say, on the contrary, if my impartiality did not prevail over any other consideration, like Corneille of Richelieu:

He has done me too much good to speak evil of him;
he has done me too much harm to say anything good.

He was one of those beings accidentally identical to our existence, whose indivisible intimacy we are obliged to tolerate throughout life, without conceiving in their regard either a permanent affection or a permanent hatred, and from whom we nevertheless receive in turn two impressions, in accordance

---

1 The author inserts a note here which pretends to be a footnote attached to the review in the newspaper: "One volume in octavo, bound in the English manner and ornamented by fifty engravings in wood by Porret, after drawings by Tony Johannot. Price: Cavalier vellum paper, satined . . . 15 fr.; Holland paper, limited to 12 copies . . . 50 fr. Colored paper, limited to 6 copies . . . 60 fr.; China paper. Limited to 6 copies . . . 1120 fr. Paris, chez Delangle frères, publishers-booksellers. Rue Batoir-Saint-André-des-Arcs, no. 19."

with our mental dispositions, especially following those of our affairs, balanced from one hour to the next between the need to free ourselves violently from an inconvenient tyrant and that of welcoming all his fantasies, caressing all his caprices and lavishing time, gold and baubles upon him. Fortunately, he hollowed out an immense interval between us by entering the perilous and ridiculous career of letters and selling his intelligence to monopolizers and publishers:

since Albe has named him, I no longer know him.[1]

Or rather, I know him well enough to be sure that he only expects from me a rigorous impartiality, of which this article will probably be the sole example in all newspapers past, present and future.

Until now the reputation of the author of whom we speak has been entirely due to the temporary vogue of a morsel of eloquence that had for its title: *Eulogy to a Mistress Pantoufle*, and which remained unpublished after having made the delight of three consecutive sessions of the Société des Bonnes-Lettres. It is true that at the last reading, the exhausted anagnost fell asleep so profoundly that before he was able to perceive it, the manuscript entered into immediate communication with the flame of the candle, and was consumed all the way to the almost imperceptible corner of its inferior part, which remained grasped mechanically between the thumb and index finger of the patient, with the result that all that exists of it today are imperfect vestiges, from which the indefatigable Angelo Mai[2]

---

1 The quotation is modified from Pierre Corneille's *Horace* (1640), dedicated to Cardinal Richelieu, which dramatizes the famous quarrel between the Horatii and the Curiatii, as recounted by Livy. The actual line is "Albe vous a nommé, je ne vous connais plus."
2 Cardinal Angelo Mai (1782-1854) caused something of a sensation after being appointed as custodian of the Ambrosian Library in Milan by deciphering the original text of a number of palimpsests wiped clean for reuse.

and Doctor Furia have had a great deal of difficulty recovering twenty-two words and an exclamation mark, of which it would be absolutely impossible to make logical sense, or even romantic nonsense, as absurd as one can imagine.

We have therefore to judge him on those of his works that have been submitted to the proof of publicity—if one can call publicity the existence of a printed book that is not read—which is to say, on a small volume of poetry composed at college, or at least at the age when one ought to be at college, and on a slender romance whose success, unknown to everyone occupied with literature and criticism, has been keenly contested for a month among clothes-merchants. One can judge the merit of the verses by the complete forgetfulness into which they had fallen after two days, five hours and a few minutes, although recommended by a coquettish poster with a filigree frame and ornamented with a delightful vignette by Deveria.[1]

As we propose to be just above all, we would like to recognize that the prose of the pseudonymous Théodore is not quite as bad as his verses; that it is not even devoid of the fluid luxury of syllables, the pompous arrangement of words, the loquacious verbosity, as Montaigne said, *ampullas ac sesquipedalia verba*,[2] as Horace said, which seduces up to a certain point unexercised ears and injudicious minds; but that buzzing of sonorous phrases, so laboriously and so painfully studied in all the keys of human speech, so fruitlessly submissive to a diapason of which the vibration is only sensible for the very small number of dilettanti of prosody, and the displaced melody is cast over conceptions so negligible, so denuded of taste and reason, so falsely grasped and so gauchely ordered, that we have never heard it resounding through the immense wave of

---

1 The painter and lithographer Achille Deveria (1800-1857) painted portraits of many of the writers of the Romantic Movement, and a notable portrait of Nodier's daughter Marie during her brief career as an actress.
2 Approximately, "He spouts his high-flown language and his long words."

the author's ideas without crying, like Fontenelle at the sonata: "Prose, what do you want of me?" and without regretting from the depths of our hearts the inimitable naivety of *Petit Chaperon rouge* or the Gothic energy of *Robert-le-Diable*.

It is necessary to admit, however, that of all the extravagances committed by the most obscure—alas—and the most indefatigable of arrangers of periods (he is the one who has found for them the fortunate comparison of a stringed instrument that only resonates because it is empty), none is as pitiful as *The Story of the King of Bohemia and his Seven Castles*. We doubt, in fact, whether there exists in any language a term appropriate to characterize the intrepidity of the reckless scribe who has not feared to counterfeit clumsily what even talent cannot imitate: the originality of a writer unique in his species and forever unique in all ages; for if Sterne had been reserved by the providence of genius to that rational, serious and potent era in which all useful verities could be shown without a mask, he would have thrown far away the crutch of Trim and the little bells of Tristram. There was, however, at the fundament of his ingenious satire an interest, a family, an action and a romance. In the insignificant sketch of the copyist I see nothing but the tedious idleness of a professional *phrasier*, who covers the paper with words drawn at hazard from the inexhaustible lottery of dictionaries and launched noisily through a book like dice in a game of tric-trac.

That unexampled monomania cannot even be explained by a physical accident, such as the excessively vertical action of the solar rays to which the author has imprudently exposed in his distant voyages the bony container that the physiologists make the mysterious *scrinium* of our rational faculties, which have been desiccated to such an extent through the frail envelope of his triply trepanned sinciput—the long nervous rag rolled up into a wad that is vulgarly called the brain—that our author's has been reduced, in the opinion of all anatomists, to proportions incomparably inferior in dimension, consistency and capacity to those of the occult organ that takes the place of the common sensorium in the tiniest of the microscopic animalcules vulgarly known in science under the name of infusoria.

He will owe the kindness we have employed toward him to that consideration, and in order to bear it, with all the benevolence of which we are capable, to its superlative expression, we agree that it is not given to everyone to display, in the flow of the pen, so much pedantic cynicism and so much grotesque erudition. This ostentation of ill-placed science only announces, however, studies incompetently made by a man who cares little for learning and hardly remembers having learned; but we have excellent reasons for thinking that his knowledge is reduced to some skill in memory. What we would prefer to find in *The Story of the King of Bohemia and his Seven Castles*, and what readers will seek there in vain, are delicate perceptions, criticism of the time, satire of circumstances and, above all, gaiety.

The idea of writing such a book when one has never been remarked by the spirit of wit, when one has become sad and one is almost old, is one of those misconceived extravagances that are only signaled in all times by ugly minds. Is it not a singular ambition for a profoundly morose writer, who seems to be ulcerated by incurable dolors, to play with a fool's bauble? Is not a foolish deception that of a man serious in studies and mores, who tries to cheer up the curious with the sound of a grave tambourine and a sentimental flute? On what pretention does one dare to found such an enterprise? Perhaps that of passing, in a future of a few weeks, for the most jovial of melancholy scribblers or the saddest of buffoonish balladeers!

There is, I admit, in this extraordinary combination of the ironic folly of an embittered intelligence and the somber disillusionment of a deceived heart, something that merits more pity than derision, but that is one of the misfortunes of position of which members of the public take no account in authors who bore them; and we would be very surprised if there exists in Europe an idler sufficiently denuded of sense, or a prodigal sufficiently disgusted by money, to drop on the counter of a bookshop the smallest fraction of the tiniest coin of the vilest metal that has ever been illustrated by an imperial, royal or consular effigy, in exchange for these inept pages, blackened with printer's ink to the shame of civilization.

This text leads us naturally to solicit from the elevated wisdom of the chambers a law of repression against the ignorant mud-slingers who make the benefit of the press a subject of opprobrium for the human race, by debasing the divine art of the masters of thought and style. That will be the subject of another article.

(*To be continued in the next issue.*)

Conversation

DON PIC DE FANFERLUCHIO

What, Monseigneur, without regard for our high social position!

Without respect for our principled literature?

Oh, rare and generous pride of the man of letters worthy of that name!

Oh, how I have always admired the noble independence of the journalist who has taken for a motto the *viram impendere vero* of the Genevan philosopher![1]

THÉODORE,
with concentrated chagrin

Say rather the *nil mirari* of Bolingbroke.[2]

BRELOQUE,
with an assurance that does not testify in favor of his modesty

Fortunately, we can cover ourselves like a butler with Marot's motto: *La mort d'y mord.*[3]

---

1 Jean-Jacques Rousseau adopted this motto from Juvenal, meaning "a life devoted to truth" in 1759.
2 This motto, meaning, "be surprised by nothing" originates from Horace.
3 The motto of the poet Clément Mariot (1496-1544), meaning "Death

DON PIC DE FANFERLUCHIO,
a trifle ironically

Combining it with that of Montaigne: *What do I know?*
Or that of La Mothe Le Vayer: *De las cosas mas seguras, la mas segura es dudar.*[1]

THÉODORE,
a trifle disdainfully

They have taken both of them from Rabelais, who said: *Perhaps.*

DON PIC DE FANFERLUCHIO,
with a fine air

In any case we have for a resource the motto of Master Abraham Wolfganck[2]: *Quaerendo.*

THÉODORE,
in a bitter tone

Or that of the Mercure Galant: *Vires acquirit eundo.*[3]

DON PIC DE FANFERLUCHIO,
launching himself linearly in all his perpedicularity

Or that of President Espagnet[4]: *I hope.*

---

does not bite."
1 François de La Mothe Le Vayer (1588-1672), a close friend of Molière. The proverb means "Of all safe courses, the safest is doubt."
2 Presumably the printer Abraham Wolfgang Küfner (1760-1817).
3 "We gather strength as we go."
4 Jeabn d'Epagnet (1564-1637) President of the Parlement of Bordeaux

BRELOQUE,
fidgeting concentrically in all his convexity

Or that of Faret, Boissat, Giry, Alary, Abbé Cottin[1] and forty others of the same strength: *To Immortality!*

THÉODORE,
with the marked intention of drawing the conversation away from its original object

If I adopted a motto, I'd take Tabourot's: *To all accords.*

DON PIC DE FANFERLUCHIO,
with the pronounced design of transporting the question on to scientific terrain

I prefer mine, which appears to me to contain in abridgment all the Encyclopedias, which I would gladly call the *Epitome*, the *Elenchus*, the *Pinax* or the *Compendium* of human wisdom: *Yes or no.*

BRELOQUE

I prefer *Neither yes nor no.* And I'd have that one engraved on my lambrequins, if I didn't have another.

THÉODORE

What, Breloque, you have a motto?

---

and associate of the witch-hunter Pierre de Lancre.
1 Nicolas Faret (1596-1646); Pierre de Boissat (1603-1662); François Giry (1635-1688); Pierre-Joseph Alary (1689-1770); the Abbé Cottin cited is probably the minor associate of the Encyclopedists rather than the sixteenth-century poet.

BRELOQUE

Eh! Who doubts it, Monseigneit! You haven't seen my emblematic portrait, then, in your gallery of paintings. I have my right foot on the nacelle of an aerostat, and the left on the prow of a submarine.[1] I'm holding in one hand a large cluster of rosebuds, and in the other a dried poppy. A dazzling butterfly is caressing my ears and hair with its multicolored wings. An enormous bat is beating them with its black membranes, ready to fold up around its hairy body. To my right is my shield of arms, divided in azure and sable, with a golden phoenix and a drowned dog. And above all of that is my motto in ultra-capital letters:

WHAT DOES IT MATTER TO ME?

---

1 The author of the 1820 dramatic adaptation of John Polidori's novelette *The Vampyre* for production at the Porte Saint-Martin theater, to which Nodier contributed additional dialogue, was Achille de Jouffroy (1785-1859), more notable as a mechanician and the constructor of an experimental submarine.

Combustion

It is too true . . . *infandum jubes renovare dolorem* . . .[1]

It is too true that the *Eulogy to a Mistress Pantoufle*, which was to have been sealed one day in the pedestal of my literary statue—I have not renounced others—disappeared in a partial and limited fire, the result of which causes frissons . . .

It is since that time that there has been no more talk of the pitiful conflagration of Baruch's library, which, in truth, was only composed of the prophecies of Jeremiah, which made a certain Johoaikim, king of Juda, burn . . .

Of the library of Cnidus, which was devoted to the flames by Hippocrates, as a punishment for the credulous confidence of the people in an ignorant quack, audacious enough to cure, incongruously and without license, the maladies of the great man . . .

Of the library of the Ptolemies, with which Omar made for Islam a bonfire of four hundred thousand volumes, and whose cooled ashes still cost my venerable friend Monsieur Boulard[2] tears after twelve centuries . . .

---

1 Aeneas' response to Dido, which translates literally as "you are commanding me to renew human suffering"—a way of saying that he doesn't want to talk about it.

2 The translator and bibliophile Antoine-Marie-Henri Boulard (1754-1825), whose library was said to contain half a million books. The Library of Alexandria had been burned long before the time of Caliph Omar in the seventh century A.D., and accounts of his destruction of its residue are probably apocryphal.

Of the library of Julian, whom we call the Apostate, which the pious Jovian burned in the temple of Trajan on the conclusions of his commission of censure . . .

Of the library of Byzantium, which perished under the reign of Basilicus or Basiliscus in a popular movement. (It was there that the famous dragon intestine was found on which all the poems of Homer were written in golden letters, and of which we will probably never see a facsimile, because of the great rarity of dragons) . . .

Of a second Byzantine library formed by Theodosius, which Léon Isaure, who I more gladly pardon for being a heretic and a magician than for being a barbarian, had burned pitilessly by virtue of virile hatred against the cult of holy images, to the great detriment of the librarians who burned with it . . .

Of the Hebraic library of Cremona, which contained twelve thousand volumes of beautiful commentaries on commentaries of the Talmud, which is the commentary on commentaries on the Pentateuch, which went up in flames in 1553. What a loss for the synagogue . . . !

Of the library of London, which disappeared in 1666 in the catastrophe of that beautiful capital, but unknown to the pope and his adherents, whatever the insolent and calumnious column of Christopher Wren might say . . .

Of the library of the savant astronomer Hevelius of Danzig[1] and that of the prodigious antiquary Olaus Rudbeck of Uppsala,[2] a few rare volumes of which escaped the destructive scourge, still exhaling an odor of burning highly esteemed by bibliomaniacs . . .

Of the library of the excellent Thomas Bartholin,[3] whom I beg you to absolve in my favor of a few learned and naïve pranks, and who sagely wrote at the news of his misfortune:

---

1 Joannes Helvelius (1611-1687).
2 Olaus Rudbeck (1630-1702).
3 The physician Thomas Bartholin (1616-1680).

Liberi me salvi sunt, libri valeant; a sentiment full of grace and philosophy, which can excuse the wordplay . . .

Of the library of the sage and modest Valincour,[1] a true philosopher, who had learned by reading books to do without books and who merited a friend more sensitive than Boileau . . .

Of the shop of Master Pierre Le Petit,[2] our modest Elzevir, and that of poor Monsieur Trattner of Vienna, the joists of which I saw burning, exhaling in smoke the learned lucubration of Scopoli . . .

Great gods, on what depend the long solicitudes of patience and genius, of which Buffon made the same thing! On what hang the expectant enjoyments of the posterity that is not represented there by anyone; that orphan posterity, *longe orba*, of which a prudent but facile attention might have preserved the future joys, either by waking the fatigued reader with an auxiliary coughing fit or by turning away from the hearth of light with an adroit gesture the pages that I destine for immortality!

O Guttemberg . . . or Geinsfleisch,[3] for it's all the same to me . . . what was the good of your inventing the typography, I don't know where and I don't know when, which you brought to light in Mayence? Or that you did the same thing, industrious Mentel, in the illustrious city of Strasbourg? Or you, laborious Coster, creative and prodigious genius who was not put to sleep by the noxious vapors of the marshes of Harlem, which gave me such an obstinate coryza last year! Or anyone else who might have had the same idea, even in China!

---

1 Admiral Jean-Baptiste-Henri de Valincour (1653-1730), to whom Boileau dedicated his satuire "On true and false honor."
2 The printer Pirrre Le Petit (1616-1686).
3 Johannes Gensfleisch zur Laden zurn Gutenberg (c1440-1468) was allegedly the full name of the man credited with the invention of the printing press employing movable type; as the text suggests, he was not the only claimant, Johannes Mentelin (c1410-1478) and Laurens Coster (c1370-c1440) being other contenders.

What does it matter that Nicolas Jenson[1] designed those admirable characters that our arch-typographers will never surpass? That Laurent François de Alopa opposed to him the marvelous capitals that served for the beautiful editions of Lascaris? And that old Aldus Manutius rivaled them in grace and imagination in the slim and gracious figure of his brilliant italics?

Why did Geoffroy Tory[2] rack his brains to measure the proportion of Attic, Antique and Roman letters?

Duret, to rediscover the protography of Adam;[3]

the Cabalists, the hagiography of Solomon;

the Egyptian priests the hierography of Horus;

the bonzes and the literates, the ideography of Fo-Hi;

voyagers and missionaries, the anthography of Mexico and Peru;

ingenious antiquaries, to spell out under parsimoniously superimposed manuscripts the piquant enigmas of palimpsestography;

Jarry, to perfect calligraphy;[4]

Kircher, to discover or renew polygraphy;[5]

Legangneur, technography, and rizography as well;[6]

---

1 The Venetian printer Nicolas Jenson (c1420-1480), who later became master of the French Royal Mint, created the first of the "Roman" typefaces that are still in widespread use. Laurent-Franscisci de Alopa, also known as Laurent de Venice, was an early printer in Florence, while the scholar Venetian Aldus Pius Manutius (c1450-1515), founder of the Aldine Press produced scrupulous editions of Greeek and Latin writers that remained important models for centuries.

2 The French humanist and engraver Geoffroy Tory (c1480-553) was the printer who added the accents to French letters that are still in use today.

3 The intended reference is probably to Albrecht Dürer (1471-1528).

4 The calligrapher Nicolas Jarry (1620-1674).

5 Athanasius Kircher (1602-1680).

6 Guillaume Legangneur (1553-1624), secretary to Henri II and Henri IV, published his *Technographie* and *Rizographie*, the former on French and the latter on Italian handwriting, in 1599.

Vigenère and Colletet, pseudography;[1]
Du Carlet, cryptograohy;[2]
Du Vignau, mimography;[3]
Ramsay, tacheography;[4]
Coulon-Thévenot, tachygraphy;[5]
Taylor and Bertin, stenography;
Schott, Hiller and Addy, steganography;[6]
Uken, steganometrography;

Leibnitz, preceded by Wilkins, who was preceded by Dalgarno, who had been preceded by the Almanach of Nuremberg, pangraphy;[7]

---

1 Blaize de Vegenère popularized the substitution cipher named after him, which requires a keyword in order to be deciphered, after revealing it at the court of Henri III in 1586, although he had not invented it. The juxtaposition of his name with that of the poet Guillaume Colletet (1598-1659) is a joke, referring to errors in his history of French poetry.

2 Jean Robert du Carlet's handbook *Le Cryptographie* was published in 1644.

3 Nicolas de Vignau attempted to learn the Algonquin language in 1611 while he was an associate of the colonist of New France Samuel de Champlain; the latter denounced him as a liar when he claimed to have discovered the Northwest Passage.

4 Charles Aloysius Ramsay published *Tacheographie, ou l'art d'escrire aussi vite qu'on parle* [Tacheography, or the art of writing as rapidly as one can talk] (1681), an early account of a system of shorthand.

5 Jean Coulon de Thévenot (1754-1813) published his account of tachygraphy, a system of stenography, while working for Louis XVI, but joined the Jacobins and became a significant orator during the Revolution before fleeing the Terror and eventually ending his life in Bohemia. The competing system of Samuel Taylor (1748-1811), developed in the 1770s, remained much more popular in Britain, and was adapted for use in French by Théodore-Pierre Bertin (1751-1819); it was reportedly one of the latter's disciples who denounced Thévenot to the Convention.

6 The Jesuit scientist Gaspar Schott (1608-1666) developed a method of concealing messages in musical scores, which is, therefore, a text of steganography. The other texts cited, Luigi Enrico Hiller's *Mysterium artis stenographiae* in 1683 and William Addy's *Stenography* (1664), are not. Melchias Uken's *Steganometrographia* (1751), however, which describes a method of hiding messages in poems is.

7 *Programme de la Pangraphie* by the professor of mathematics in

Chappe, after Polybius, telegraphy;[1]
the poor and modest Fyot, archeography;[2]
Benedictine scholars, paleography;
Firmas, palingraphia;[3]
Bricaille, panlexigraphy;[4]
Susse, mnemography;[5]
Dublar, multilinegraphy;[6]

Mannheim, Heinrich Bürmann, published in French, was a proposal for a universal system of phonetic representation intended to replace all the various alphabets currently in use. It occasioned some debate, but did not catch on.

1 Claude Chappe (1763-1805) and his brother Ignace (1760-1829) devised a mechanical semaphore system that was established throughout France during the 1790s, with the enthusiastic support of the Revolutionaries

2 Abbé Claude Fyot (1630-1721) wrote a history of the church of Saint-Estienne de Dijon, which probably influenced the chapter in Victor Hugo's *Notre-Dame de Paris* (1831, but begun in 1829, while Nodier and Hugo were still in close communication) which represents the church, metaphorically, as a kind of book.

3 Palingraphia is mirror-writing; "Firmas" is enigmatic, the practice being most famously associated with Leonardo da Vinci.

4 A patent was filed in Paris for a *Panlexicographie, ou syllabaire mobile*, an instrument designed for teaching reading, by "M. Bricaille, avocat" in 1829.

5 This reference is enigmatic, but might conceivably relate to the Susse brothers, who manufactured the first daguerreotype camera a decade after this story was published; Nodier's friend Théophile Gautier was known to have taken an interest in the development of photography by Nicéphore Niépce in the 1820s and Nodier knew Daguerre because of his invention of the diorama in 1822 and its use in the theater. On the other hand, *susse* is the first person imperfect subjunctive of savoir [to know].

6 L. J. Dublar was advertised as the inventor of the "Multinégraphe" (an instrument for teaching writing) in notices for his book *Les Cinq orders de lécriture* in *L'Égide, journal de la société d'encouragement pour l'execution des nouvelles découverttes* in 1832; the second and last issue contains a poem by him and his is credited as the editor of the newspaper. The signature also appears on various song lyrics and poems in the 1830s and 1830s. He published details of a system of shorthand that he called *Zigzagraphie* (1833), which Nodier would surely have included in his list had he known about it.

the Atheneum of Marseille, panteugraphy;[1]

Boinvilliers, after Joubert, cacography;[2]

Vidal, notography;[3]

Sennefelder, lithography;[4]

Some anonymous person or other, autography, from which preceded in a straight line the stupid and disgraceful isography;

Baïf, Taillemont, Meigret, Pelletier, la Ramée, Rambaud, Richesource, Cordemoy, Adanson, Rétif de la Bretonne,[5] and other powerful grammarians of that caliber, phonography;

---

1 A prospectus for *Panteugraphie, ou nouvelle méthode pour enseigner l'orthographie* (1829) was signed Philippe Mathieu, with a certification by the Administrative Committee of the Civil and Military Hospitals of Marseilles that it had worked on four children confided to his care.

2 *Cacographie* (1826) is a collection of phrases in which the spelling of words is deliberately mangled, by the prolific grammarian Jean-Étienne-Judith Forestier Boinvilliers (1764-1830), who also published poetry in the *Almanach des Muses*. The association with the moralist Joseph Joubert (1754-1824), Napoléon's inspector of universities, is sarcastic.

3 *La Notographie, alphabet universelle des sons* (1819) by Étienne Vidal, was yet another system of shorthand.

4 The German dramatist Alois Senefelder (1771-1834) invented lithography in the 1790s.

5 Jean-Antoine de Baïf (1532-1589) founded the Académie de musique et poésie, with the aim of establishing a closer union between the two arts and also elaborated a system of "measured verse"; Claude de Pailemont (1504-c1558) and Louis Meigret (c1510-1558) were both from Lyon; the latter pubished the first significant French grammar in 1550; Jean Le Pelletier (1633-1711) was an eclectic scholar; Pierre de La Ramée (1515-1572) was a humanist murdered during the Saint Bartholomew's Day massacre; Rambaud is also a common surname, but the reference might be to the seventeenth-century writer Camille Rambaud de Champrenard; Jean de Richesource (1616-1694) wrote books on rhetoric and oratory; the philosopher Géraud de Cordemoy (1626-1684) wrote a significant discourse on language; Michel Adanson (1727-1806) was a botanist who devised a system for the nomenclature of plant species. Nicolas Edmé Rétif (1734-1806), who preferred to style himself Restif de la Bretonne was a prolific writer who worked as a typesetter and set all his own work in type, including his monumental pseudo-autobiography *Monsieur Nicolas* (1794-1797), which set out to "lay the human heart bare."

and Toho-Bohu, neography?

I ask you!

Futile efforts, unfruitful labors, since, of the only essential book of our time, of the only simply human writing that a man of righteous sense and healthy intelligence would have some interest today in conserving, there only remain to me exactly twenty-two small fragments burned at the edges, which you could seize all too easily with the index finger and the thumb, and between which there only exists, as you said a moment ago, a feeble point of moral contact, a slight philosophical analogy, a vague possibility of oratorical or grammatical relationship from which the most subtle commentator might be able to extract the most fugitive induction for the eventual wellbeing of modern societies.

Nevertheless, I know not what fear of leaving that debris of my written thought abandoned to the malevolent interpretations of hatred and hypocrisy; I know not what irresistible consciousness of a vague clarity, of an unperceived reason that still animates them; I know not what need to bequeath to you, my friends, on these quasi-or mock-sibylline pages the sparse and scattered imprint of my last sentiments; the need, above all, to satisfy my printer by offering you herewith the specimen of a font that would make the shades of Sanlecque or Garamond shiver;[1] have all decided me to cast before your eyes, in the order in which they come to hand, the few words escaped from the flames and criticism, *combusti membra poetae* . . . !

---

1 The references are to the type designers Jacques Sanlecque (1572-1648) and Claude Garamond (c1510-1561).

Exhibition

Science – Philosophy – Verity
Independence – Justice – Amour – Amity
Glory – Honor – Consolation
Compensation – Reparation – Remuneration
Mystification
Sphinx – Endriague – Dragon
Tarasque – Wyvern – Harpy – Coquecigrue
Pantoufle!

Explanation

Pantoufle! What does that word signify?

What is it usual meaning?

Where is its logical definition to be found?

From what ancient or modern language is its etymology drawn?

Is it indigenous or exotic?

Is it autochthonous or of secondary formation?

Is it radical or derivative?

Does it represent a material fact or does it hide an emblem?

Is the author employing it in its literal meaning or metaphorically?

And if the prudish and pious censor to whom this book will necessarily be submitted, before it is introduced into seminaries and lycées, were to suppose . . .

Never! That odious interpretation is that of an epoch foreign to our mores. It could not present the slightest appearance of verity to the grave and modest appearance that only smiles while blushing at the cynical buffooneries of Rabelais, and has long forgotten in the mud, the brazen effrontery of Diderot, Duclos and Crébillon.

The pantoufle of which there is question here is quite simply that of my gracious master Popocambou the Broken-toothed, the 42,665th autocrat of Timbuktu, under whose reign the famous pyramid was erected that Philo of Byzantium did not count among the wonders of the world because people rarely went to Timbuktu in his time. It was eighteen times as high as the tower of Babylon, which surpassed by as much the pyramid of Cheops, and it was built on its point.

Whether by virtue of the prejudice of education, the inveterate bias of habitude, political obstinacy, religious fanaticism, instinct or experience—which is worth a great deal—Popocambou, since he had come to power, had seen nothing that appeared to him to be preferable to that pantoufle. He thought about it all day and he thought about it at night; he thought about it in the evening and the morning. He turned on his left side; he turned on his right side; he slept on his belly; he slept on his back, but he only saw that pantoufle.

It is true that the pantoufle was not to be disdained; one could have gone a long way without encountering a similar pantoufle.

It was a furry pantoufle;

it was a padded pantoufle;

it was a satiny pantoufle;

it was a refined pantoufle;

it was a perfected pantoufle;

it was a winter pantoufle and a summer pantoufle;

it was an elegant, svelte, good-looking pantoufle, a distinguished pantoufle;

it was a well-conditioned pantoufle, neither too large nor too tight, a solid pantoufle, elastic, soft and comfortable, an essential pantoufle;

it was a pantoufle that did not make the slightest crease;

it was a naïve, natural pantoufle, devoid of affected mannerisms and pretentions, a pantoufle that did not put on the flighty airs of a brodequin, not the advantageous airs of a cothurne, which you would have recognized at fifty paces as an honest pantoufle.

It was not a backward pantoufle, a greedy pantoufle, a pantoufle with fourteen quarters, a Loyalist pantoufle, an ultramontane pantoufle or an absolutist pantoufle;

it was not an argumentative pantoufle, a liberal pantoufle, an industrial pantoufle, a legal pantoufle, a electoral pantoufle or an opposition pantoufle;

it was not an antique pantoufle, a systematic pantoufle, an Aristotelian pantoufle, an economic, encyclopedic, academic or classical pantoufle;

it was not a Gothic pantoufle, a mystical pantoufle, an eclectic pantoufle, a romantic, Germanic or frenetic pantoufle.

It was an excellent little pantoufle. It was one of those pantoufles from which one would never want to remove the foot.

It was the queen of pantoufles!

Annotation

Its etymology, you say?

I shall not dissimulate that it would have been notably useful, in a work destined to become classic, to consecrate at least a supplementary chapter to the important matter that Baudouin has brushed so superficially in his treatise *De pantoufflis veterum*, but that task would have required research so prodigious that the volume would have risked not appearing before the full edition of the Académie's Dictionary, and supplying it with piquant novelties that could not be avoided.

And then, you would be frightened by the poverty of ancient and modern notions of the etymological value of the word *pantoufle*.

Pan is a Greek monosyllable, of which everyone knows the meaning, says Schrevelius[1]; or of which everyone is free to seek the meaning on page 723 of my dictionary, says Monsieur Planche.[2] Under the sixteenth letter of the alphabet, says Scapula. Henri Étienne,[3] who has so much complaint to make of Scapula, does not say the contrary.

As for *toufle*, I would give half a foot of my nose to know where it came from, said Turnèbe, who actually had a nose

---

1 Theodorus Schrevelius (1572-1649).

2 Presumably the playwright James Planché (1796-1880).

3 Henri Étienne was the name of two sixteenth-century printers, father and son, of whom the son (1538-1598) was the more famous; Scapula was a contemporary and rival.

long enough to permit that sally.[1]

"It might come," replied Don Pic, smiling, from the Syriac *tophel* or the German *stiffel*, which is the same as the Italian *stivale*[2] . . . but it is probable that the name of the pantoufle is produced from the Greek signifying something hollow employed for walking—which is, in parenthesis, an excellent definition of a pantoufle, unless your prefer to derive it from variant terms signifying footwear appropriate for treading on friable and light soil; and I would not advise you to employ them on the angular paving stones of Vire, the pedicidal shingle of Fécamp or the rolling gravel of the Lido of Venice.

I would perhaps stop at that explanation if I had not suddenly experienced the profound conviction that the completing element of the research in which we have gone astray for too long is the Greek name for cork, of which the soles of pantoufles are ordinarily made, *quod est probandum.*

"Eh! What can doubt it?" I exclaimed, pushing away with my foot an old stool of staved-in wicker, which had no need of that final hitch. "What do the origin and meaning of the word *pantoufle* matter to me," I added, tearing myself away abruptly from the chaise longue that I acquired at the Matanasius[3] auction and launching myself toward the door in order to get away from the demon who was crucifying me pitilessly with his stupid etymology.

"I would truly be quite mad," I said, slamming the door behind me, "to fret about knowing what the elements are in the construction of the name of a pantoufle." *And if I wanted to be bored this evening,* I thought as I traversed the landing,

---

1 Extant portraits of Adrien Turnèbe (1512-1565) do not seem to support this allegation.

2 The Italian *stivale* means "boot" but *stiffel* is not a German equivalent, and it might seem odd that a linguist in search of a possible German equivalent of *toufle* would overlook *teufel* [devil].

3 "Chrisostome Matanasius" was a pseudonym of the satirist Thémiseul de Saint-Hyacinthe (1684-1746).

is it not the day of the Bouffes and the session at the Atheneum?
"And besides," I went on as I

    went

        down

           the

               seven

                  flights

                of

                    stairs,

"Popocambou's sole wasn't cork, it was cabron."[1]

"What did Monsieur say?" said the porter, opening his smoke-obscured glass vasistas, or *was ist bas*, and passing through his grotesque head, illuminated by October ruby.

"I said that it was cabron."

---

1 Borrowed from Spanish, the literal meaning of this term is "goat"— or goat-skin in this context—but it is usually used metaphorically as an insult; hence the porter's reaction.

Observation

... On which note I ought to observe once and for all—these chapters require an explanation that should have preceded it (but that observation is unnecessary for readers who begin to read the book at the end)—that the word pantoufle is taken in the example in the singular number because the said number represents its intrinsic and virtual value, and not by reason of the device known as metonymy, by means of which one takes the part for the whole, or the one named synecdoche, which has exactly the same property; which leads me to believe that there is at least one of those terms that is superfluous.

And it would be the same with Popocambou's pantoufles if that great prince had more than one pantoufle. Not that it is necessary to conclude from that, with Orus Apollo,[1] that Popocambou was one-legged, like Hermes' trousers; or, with the members of the Celtic Academy, that one of his feet was bare, flat, membranous and palmate, like that of the Reine Pédauque;[2] or, which would be more plausible, that he had a wooden leg like Agesilas[3] or a club-foot like Don Sébastien.

1 *Orus Apollo* is the abbreviated title of a sixteenth-century manuscript by Nostradamus, based on a 1551 translation by Jean Mercier of *Hieroglyphia* by Horapollon of Manuthis, a work referenced by Rabelais and other French scholars.
2 La Reine Pédauque [the goose-footed queen] is a legendary Occitan monarch said to have ruled the region around Toulouse prior to its incorporation into the Visigothic kingdom in the fifth century.
3 The Spartan king Agesilas, the protagonist of a 1666 play by Corneille,

The fact is that the constitutive laws of Timbuktu constrained the sovereign of that land to stand on one foot every time, and throughout the time, that he was exercising one of his royal functions—which would not imply in strict consequence that a king of Timbuktu ought to spend his entire life with one foot shod and the other bare . . .

But the reign of Popocambou was so fertile in colossal enterprises,

the construction of the great pyramid diverted so many arms from the exploitation of common mechanical estates,

that the raw materials necessary for the confection of a well-established pantoufle became so rare,

economic theories so parsimonious,

politics so arithmetical, and arithmetic so popular,

the majorities so umbrageous and so argumentative, principally in the matter of pantoufles, that there was no example of the budget committee passing more than one pantoufle for the King of Timbuktu.

"Fortunately," said the king, "it's a very fine pantoufle."

---

did not have a wooden leg, but the play was generally thought to be lame. Nor did Don Sebastian de Mora, the jester featured in a famous portrait by Velasquez, have a club-foot.

Preterition

If you would prefer, however—and what author can divine tomorrow's tastes?—

a Greek scolia;

a Roman stellane;

a Gallic farce;

a Scandinavian parade;

a Celtic or Gothic buffoonery;

a Germanic bardit;

an Italian masquerade;

an Iberian satirel;

an Illyrian pismé;

a Rabbinical chronicle;

a Talmudic fable;

a Beresithiac history or an apocalyptic romance . . .

you have only to say so, Mesdemoiselles! Breloque's bag is richer in that genre than that of Sammonokhodom.[1] Berloque gives the finger with his bag to the *Edda* as to the *Koran*, to the *Voluspa* as to the *Vedas*, to the *Lamaastambam* as to the *Landnamabok*,[2] to Volney's *Catechism* as to Matthieu

---

1 Nodier almost certainly found Sammonokhodom, reportedly a figure in Siamese mythology, in Jean-François de La Harpe's mammoth *Histoire des Voyages* (1780), an abridgement of which was published in 1830.

2 *Lamaastambam* is a name attributed to one of the religious writings of India by the Jesuit Augustine Calmet, cited by Chateaubriand in the *Génie du Chistianisme*; *Landnamabok* [Book of Settlements] is a twelfth-

Laensberg's *Almanach*.

Perhaps you will ask me where Breloque found his bag? He inherited it from Jean des Vignes.[1]

---

century Icelandic document describing the colonization of the island by Norsemen.

1 Saint-Jean-des-Vignes was an Augustinian abbey in Soissons, which gave its name to a famous Burgundy wine.

Damnation

In my last voyage to Africa, if the memory I have conserved of it is anything but a dream, a strange adventure happened to me of which I shall try to fix the memory. Vanquished by the heat of the day, I was abandoning myself to the slow walk of my horse alongside of a river that I shall not name, because it has never had a name, when suddenly, through the curtain of golden clusters of aloes, baobabs with huge leaves and giant reeds that veiled its banks, a little skiff appeared, manned by a single man, who was negligently following the watercourse without paying any heed to the oar or the tiller; and at the same instant I saw an enormous crocodile, which seized the poop with its scaly hands and beast the waves with its tail, like a flail.

I uttered a scream, but everything had disappeared: the boat, the monster and the traveler. I stopped, struck by fear, and had difficulty containing my horse, whose horror was no less than mine. Imagine my astonishment when I saw the water redden with blood and the stranger, indifferent to his wounds, come toward me placidly, walking on the surface of the water, as if it had been overtaken momentarily by winter ice. I had scarcely had time to look at him but his features were ineffaceably engraved in my memory, for those who have seen him can never forget him.

His stature was tall and straight, his movements supple but sudden, his stride abrupt and precipitate, not like that of fear but like that of impatience. The details of his face lacked neither regularity nor grace, and yet their ensemble was sad and menacing. His long mouth; his narrow lips, which allowed his white and tightly-packed teeth to be seen, quivering; his thick black beard; his warm and bronzed complexion; his hollow cheeks, less tanned than livid; his profoundly sunken eyes from which sprang a fiery gaze, like lightning from a dark background; the inexplicable contrast between the most powerful forms of vigor with the infallible vestiges of age and time, all made that physiognomy an enigma that human reason could not resolve.

The first sentiment that the man inspired, after that of terror, was the idea of the perpetuity that artists lent to their gods. As his physical aspect belonged to all the epochs of life, the strange costume that he had adopted belonged to all countries. The red headband that covered his brow seemed to be the sign of initiation into some monastic order. He wore an Oriental turban, an Albanian dolman, Basque trousers, Scottish plaid and Spanish escadrilles. His leather belt held a Slavonian cangiar, a Moorish assegai and a Venetian stiletto, but it was easy to see by the brilliance with which they shone that those parade arms were a caprice of luxury and not the precaution of a needless prudence.

As his eyes were turned toward me and he was looking at me with a gaze that congealed the blood, I was extracted from that species of fascination by the whinnying of a horse that was not mine. I made a movement and I saw the man's horse bounding at my side. It was one of those small Siberian horses whose coat resembled curly wool, and which initially offered something fantastic, like the imaginary animals that astonish us in dreams. It was prancing with an incredible lightness, but which announced fear rather than joy. Its ardent eyes, filled with a sort of human intelligence, testified that it had been brought to that place by the power of a strange will, and that all its supernatural agility could not shield it from the summons of its cavalier. There was something about it as mysterious as the incomprehensible stranger. Its bit appeared to be pure gold and terminated in ruby studs. The cord that subjugated its head had the flexibility of silk and the brilliance of metal. Its mane, braided with silver thread, fell in long waves, and balanced knots of crystal and precious stones, linked by rubies the color of fire; its harness was entirely fashioned with the polished and perfumed leather that the Levantines tan with incense, and its foot struck the sand with an iron shoe with diamond nails. The voyager leapt on to the crimson horse-blanket, and was about to draw away forever when he seemed to be retained by one of my thoughts, for I doubt that I had the strength to express it in an intelligible voice.

He remained motionless before me, therefore, on his motionless horse, and everything remained motionless around us, including the inflamed vapor that took the place of an atmosphere, and the cloud of red sand overhead that veiled the sun at its zenith, and the solar disk itself had stopped in space, as in the time of Joshua, agape over that lake of fire like a bloody mouth. One might have thought that nature entire had been surprised by death, if the long plaint of a jackal, the cry of which is like a woman having her throat cut, had not been audible in the distance, in muted mewls and lamentable gasps.

"You want to know me," he said, penetrating the depths of my soul with a sharp gaze, "and I consent to satisfy your curiosity, for I can tell, on seeing you, that we are following the same route . . ."

While he pronounced those words he had seized the bridle of my horse, and he bore me away in the course of his own with a rapidity of which none of the memories of our terrestrial life can give any idea, but which had the strange quality that I did not even experience the movement, and wondered for a moment whether it was not the desert, the river and the sky that were fleeing.

"You want me to tell you a story," he continued, "whose like has never been told . . . a story that I will not tell either for the present, which I detest, nor for the future, which I abhor, nor for the glory of the name that only falls from my mouth with disgust, nor for the fortune that I could steal so easily from the pretended fortunate of the earth, if the sentence of my condemnation had not heaped me with treasures as well as dolors . . . nor for amour, the only one of those stupid illusions that leaves a regret after centuries. I will not tell it to you in order to free myself from the great crime that has weighed upon the heads of humankind, for that crime has remained all my pride and all my joy. I will tell you in order to obey, unfortunate as I am, the will of the eternal tyrant of the human heart that is called Hell in the other world and conscience in this one.

"You want it," he continued, "but will the mere revelation of my name leave you the strength or the will to hear me? Mortal man—and how I envy you that privilege!—indiscreet and curious man, hang on with a firm hand to the mane of my horse. I am the vagabond, the eternal reject of the world, who must, more unfortunate than ever, become its master. I am the Wandering Jew. I shall be the Antichrist!"

At that horrible revelation I sensed a cold sweat streaming in my hair, and, my eyes fixed on the accursed one, I waited for each of his words with the terror that seizes the patient beneath the cold and heavy iron of the executioner; but I gradually became accustomed to it, like a fever-sufferer at the return of a fit, an exhausted victim of periodic torture.

It is not those illusions of the soul that I can try to enable the rest of humankind feel, for nothing would be capable of rendering them in the uncertain expression of our ideas that a breath draws through the air, that the march of a little insect effaces on the sand, or that the stroke of a pen destroys on the paper. Only a dream could communicate them to solitary thought in all their grandeur, and it requires nothing less to translate them than a faculty with which Providence is miserly.

"What's that?" said Victorine.

"The legendry genius of Saint Gengulphus,[1] or the historian of Fortunatus[2] . . ."

"In that case," she said, "I'd prefer another."

---

1 Saint Gengulphus of Burgundy, who lived in the eighth century, renounced his wealth to become a hermit and was then murdered by his wife's lover.

2 *Fortunatus* is a sixteenth-century German chapbook whose protagonist is gifted with a magical purse by the goddess Fortuna, and who also acquires a hat capable of transporting him anywhere in the world—gifts squandered by his quarrelsome children. Nodier's novella *Les Quatre talismans* (1838; tr. as "The Four Talismans") is a similar moral fable.

Commemoration

"I've told you, Monsieur, that my life has not lacked some mildness, for Heaven has placed a kind compensation for misfortune in the pity of good souls."

"I recognize that voice," she said, letting her head fall graciously on to my shoulder. "It must be that of Gervais."

"Another time, my sweet friend, I shall write for you alone; but only a solidly scientific work, nourished by a sound and useful instruction, like *The Story of the King of Bohemia and his Seven Castles* can conduct me to the Societé d'Émulation de Castelnaudary. What soul, however, was ever more inaccessible than mine to the vain illusions of ambition and glory?"

"I was enjoying that happy ignorance of evil," Gervais continued, "when the presence of a new guest in the village of Bois came to occupy all conversations in the valley. He was only known by the name of Monsieur Robert, but he was, in the general opinion, a great foreign lord whom irreparable losses and profound dolors had decided to hide his final years in a solitude unknown to all men. He had lost a wife far away he said, who had been almost all his happiness, since nothing remained from their union but a subject of eternal chagrin, a daughter born blind. People praised, however, the intelligence, the goodness and the graces of Eulalie, equal to her father's virtues; but what perfection could have added anything to the charm of her memory? I can still see her in my mind, more charming than my mother."

"She's dead?" I exclaimed.

"Dead?" he replied, in a tone in which the expression of terror and that of I know not what inconceivable joy were confounded. "Dead? Who told you that?"

"Pardon me, Gervais, I don't know that. I was seeking to explain the reason for your separation."

"She's alive," he said, smiling bitterly; and he remained silent momentarily. "I don't know whether I told you," he added, in a low voice, "that her name was Eulalie. It was Eulalie, and this is her place . . ."

He interrupted himself again. "Eulalie," he repeated, deploying his hand over the rock, as if to search for her beside him.

Puck licked his fingers, and, taking a step back, looked at him with a tender expression. I would not have traded Puck for a million.

"Pull yourself together, Gervais. Pardon me once again for having stirred in your heart a fiber so vibrant and so dolorous. I can almost divine the rest of your story. The strange conformity of Eulalie's misfortune and yours struck the young woman's father. The interest you inspire, poor Gervais, cannot help but be felt in a soul exercised in that kind of impression. You became another child for him?"

"Another child," replied Gervais, "and our Eulalie was a sister for me. My good adoptive mother and I went to lodge in the new house that was known as the château. Eulalie's masters were mine. We learned together the divine arts of harmony that steal the soul toward a celestial life. We read with our fingers, on pages printed in relief, the sublime thoughts of philosophers and the charming inventions of poets. I tried to imitate them and to paint like them what I could not see; for the nature of the poet is a second creation, the elements of which are put to work by his genius, and with my feeble reminiscences I sometimes succeeded in remaking a world.

"Eulalie loved my verses, and what more did I need? When she sang, one might have thought that an angel had descended from the summit of the mountains in order to charm the valley. Every day in the beautiful season, we were brought to this stone, which was known as the rock of the blind, and where the best of fathers followed us with all the cares of amity. There were clumps of rhododendron around us then, carpets of violets and daisies, and when our hand had recognized one of the latter flowers with a short stem, a velvety disk and its silky perimeter, repeating a hundred times over the game that served to interpret the first confessions of amour. If the lying flowers refused the expression of my unique thought, I knew how to conceal it from Eulalie by means of innocent trickery. Perhaps she did the same for her part. Today, however, nothing remains of all that."

As he spoke thus, Gervais had become increasingly somber. His pure forehead was darkened by an angry cloud; he maintained a bleak silence, stamped his foot at random and broke an Alpine rose that had long since dried out on its stem. I picked it without him perceiving it, and placed it over my heart.

Some time went by without me daring to address a word to Gervais, without him appearing to intend to continue his story. Suddenly, he passed his hand over his eyes, as if to chase away a disagreeable vision, and, turning in my direction with a laugh full of grace, he went on: "Ah, have pity Monsieur, on the weakness of a child who has not been able to command thus far the involuntary disturbances of his heart. A day will perhaps come when sagacity will descend in my mind, but I'm still so young . . ."

"I fear, my friend," I said to him, pressing his hand, "that this conversation might fatigue you. Don't ask your memory for recollections that torment you; I shall never forgive myself for having troubled one of your hours with a regret that you feel so profoundly."

"It isn't you who reminds me of it," replied Gervais. "It hasn't quit me for a minute, and I'd rather that my soul were annihilated than forget it. All my being, Monsieur, is my dolor. My dolor is my last amity. There is nothing left but it and me. It's necessary to accustom ourselves to living together, and I find it easier to support when a little benevolence lightens, by listening to me, the weight that is so sadly solitary. Ha ha!" he added, laughing again. "The blind are talkative, and there is so rarely anyone to listen to me."

I had not let go of Gervais' hand. He understood that I was listening.

"In any case," he said, "all is not bitterness in my memories. Sometimes they render the past to me entirely; I imagine that my present misfortune is only a dream and that nothing is true in my life except the happiness that I have lost. I dream that she is sitting in this place, a little more distant from me than usual, and that she is silent because she is plunged in a meditation to which our amour is no stranger. Oh, if the eternity that God reserves for benevolent souls is nothing but the infinite prolongation of the sweetest sentiment that has moved them, what joy to be surprised by death in that thought and to go to sleep thus!

"One day, we were sitting on this rock, as we did every day, and we were enjoying, in such a mild ecstasy, the serenity of the air, the perfume of our violets, the song of our birds, especially that of our Alpine warblers—for all the birds of the woods were known to us, and they often flew toward our voices—and we were listening with so much charm to the ice detached by the warmth, which glided along the peaks, whistling, and to the ripples of the waters of the Arveyron, which were coming to die almost at our feet, when I know not what confused presentiment of the rapidity and uncertainty of happiness filled us with anxiety and alarm at the same time. We huddled together urgently, interlacing our arms as if someone were trying to separate us, and we cried out in unison: 'Always! Always!'

"I sensed that Eulalie was scarcely breathing, and that she needed to be reassured by all the strength that my character and my manly courage gave me: 'Always, Eulalie, always! Can the world, which thinks us so unfortunate, judge the felicity that I have savored in your tenderness, and you have found in mine? What importance has the ridiculous movement of that turbulent society to us, in which so many interests that are foreign to us collide, when nature has made a thousand times more for us than the longest apprenticeships in reason provide?

"'For them we are imperfect beings and that is quite simple; they have not yet succeeded in learning that the perfection of life consists of loving and being loved. They dare to pity us, because they don't know that we pity them. The dangerous fascination that the passions exert through sight will never act upon us. Even time has lost its empire over two blind people who love one another. We will never change for one another, since no alteration can disgust us and no comparison can distract us.

"'The sentiment that unites us is immutable, like the waters of our Arveyron, like the song of our favorite birds, like the eternal enclosure of these rocks exposed to the south, to the foot of which we are sometimes guided in the uncertain days of May. It is not the temporary beauty of a woman that seduces me in you, not something that cannot be expressed when it is felt nor forgotten when one has felt it. It is a beauty that belongs to you alone, and which I hear in your voice, which I touch in your hands, your arms and your hair, which I respire in your breath, which I adore in your soul! I have studied their amours in the books that have been read to us, or over which my fingers have been able to seek thoughts, and I protest to you that their advantages over us consist of things of little value. If the sun that I once saw were in your eyes, I would not brush any more voluptuously with my lips the long lashes that shade them, and on which my lips have collected two or three tears when you were little and someone refused, contrary to custom, to satisfy one of your caprices. I do not know whether your neck is as white as the snow of the great mountain, but it would not please me more if it were—and yet it is everything.

"'Oh, if I enjoyed sight, I would beg the Lord to extinguish my eyes in their orbits, in order not to see other women, in order only to have the memory of you, and only to give passage to my heart to the features I would have seen emerging from yours. To see a world, to travel it, to embrace it, to conquer it, to posses it with a glance: a strange marvel! But why? To stun my soul with futile impressions, to stray away from you into frivolous admirations, through what they call the miracles of nature and art! But what would I have to seek there, if not an impression that would render me something of you? It is better and more complete here.

"'Inconceivable poverty of human vanities! Of the arts about which they make so much noise, those prodigies of genius that dazzle them, we know those that the greater number appreciate the most: music and poetry. It is agreed that we have organs to savor them, a soul to feel them, but do you believe that the divine songs of Lamartine have ever resonated as delightfully in my ear as the cry of appeal that you launch to me from afar when you are the last to be brought here? If Rossini or Weber grip me with a more powerful spell, it is because it's you who are singing them. It's you who embellish the arts, and thus you embellish creation, of which they are only the ornate expression; but I can do without those superfluous riches, because I possess the treasure from which they extract the greatest wealth; for after all, your heart is mine, or you're not happy!"

"'I'm happy,' Eulalie replied, 'the most fortunate of young women!'

"'Oh, my children,' said Monsieur Robert, uniting our trembling hands, 'I hope that you will always be happy, for my determination will never separate you.'

"Accustomed to accompany us everywhere with the cares of that attentive tenderness that nothing can reassure sufficiently, he had approached us without being heard and had understood us without listening to us. I did not believe that I was culpable, but I was consternated. Eulalie was trembling.

"Monsieur Robert placed himself *here*, between us, for we were sitting slightly apart. 'Why not?' he said, enveloping us with his arms and hugging both of us with even more tenderness than usual. 'Why not, in truth? Am I not rich enough to buy you servants, and friends? You will have children, who will replace your old father, for your infirmity is not hereditary. Embrace me, Gervais; kiss me, Eulalie; thank God and dream about tomorrow, for the day that will dawn tomorrow will be beautiful even for the blind!'

"Eulalie passed from her father's arms into mine. For the first time, my lips found hers. That happiness was too complete to be happiness. I thought that my heart was about to burst. I wanted to die. I didn't die, alas.

"I don't know, Monsieur, what the happiness of others is like. Mine lacked calm, and even hope. I couldn't sleep—or rather, I didn't try to, for it seemed to me that I wouldn't have enough of eternity to savor the felicities that were promised to me, and the more I sought to enjoy them, the more they escaped all my thoughts under a host of confused appearances. I almost regretted that past devoid of intoxications, but devoid of dread, in which I hadn't feared anything because I hadn't counted on anything. I would have liked to grasp again the pure sensualities of the soul that pass for the future in the heart of a child, in which the future, at least, goes no further than the next day.

"Finally, I heard the ordinary noise of the house; I got up, I got dressed without waiting for my mother, I prayed to God, and I went to the window that overlooked the Arve in order to refresh my burning head with the vapors of the morning mist. My door opened. I recognized a man's footsteps. It was not Monsieur Robert. A hand seized mine. 'Monsieur Maunoir!' I cried. It had been several years since he had come, but the sound of his tread, the contact of his hand, I know not what frankness, ease and tenderness, the individuality of which was not judged by any sense, but which was experienced by them all, had remained of him in my memory.

"'It's really him.' He said, speaking to someone in a slightly altered tone of voice. 'It's my poor Gervais. You know what I said to you at the time!'

"After that he imposed his fingers on my eyelids and kept them raised for some time. 'Ah!' he said, 'The will of God be done! Are you happy, at least?'

"'Very happy,' I replied. 'Monsieur Robert says that I have profited from his generosity. I can read as if I were sighted, and I'm loved by Eulalie.'

"'She'll love you more if she can see you some day,' said Monsieur Maunoir.

"'If she sees me, you say?'

"I thought about the eternal abode in which the eyes of the blind open to a light that no longer has any night. I didn't understand.

"My mother brought me here, as usual, but Eulalie was very late. I tried to understand why. My poor Puck went to meet her, and then he came back, and then he went back again; and when he was far, far away he barked impatiently, and when he was close to me, he wept. Finally, he started yapping in bursts so noisy, and leaping on the bench with so much petulance, that I realized that she must be close to us, although I still couldn't hear her. I leaned in the direction in which I expected her, and my extended arms found hers. Monsieur Robert had not accompanied his domestics this time, and I guessed the reason immediately, which also had to be the reason for Eulalie's unaccustomed lateness; I had forgotten that there were strangers at the château.

"What is strange, Monsieur, is that her arrival, so keenly desired, filled me with I know not what anxiety that was unfamiliar to me. I was no longer at ease with Eulalie, as I had been the day before. Since we were to be everything to one another, I no longer dared ask anything. It seemed to me that her father, in giving me a new right, had imposed a thousand privations on me. I feared to exercise the power of a word, the seductions of a caress. I sensed more fully that she was mine, and I feared touching her even more. I was afraid of profaning her, in listening to her breath, in touching her dress, in seizing a wisp of her hair in my mouth. Perhaps she experienced the same sentiment, because our conversation, for some time, was that of two people who hardly knew one another.

"That could not last long. The illusions of the previous day had not yet grown old. Puck took care to remind us of them, bounding from one to the other, as if he were suffering from seeing us so distant and so cold. I drew nearer to Eulalie, and my lips sought her eyes, the only part of her face that they had touched until the day before. They touched a bandage there.

"'You're injured, Eulalie!'

"'A little,' she said, 'but very slightly, since I'm spending the day with you, as usual, and there's nothing more between your mouth and my eyes but a green ribbon.'

"'Green! Green! My God, what is a green ribbon?'

"'I've seen,' she told me. 'I can see.'

"And her hand trembled in mine, as if she had confessed a fault or recounted a misfortune."

Erudition

"There is more sense than you think in Gervais' question and the modest reticence of your Eulalie," cried Don Pic. "These poor young people, to whom I'm beginning to be attached, and who have probably received some good principles of verbal philology—a particularity that you have inappropriately omitted in your story—understood at the same moment that, because *ribbon* comes originally from the word *rubens*, meaning red, reddish or reddening, *green ribbon* is one of those frightful cacologies, one of those temeritous tropes that put grammar to the torture and frighten logic, so that Gervais' exclamation is equivalent to: 'Oh, dear Eulalie, how can you permit yourself that barbaric catachresis?' and Eulalie's reply signifies implicitly: 'I agree with you, my friend, that I have permitted myself a barbaric catachresis, but I am so far from wanting to justify it that I am ready to talk about something else.'"

"Me too," said Breloque.

"Besides which, if Breloque cares to follow me for a moment," said Don Pic, "which is to say, the time necessary to sketch my monograph on the green ribbon . . ."

"I'd rather have a drink," said Breloque . . .

"I shall consider three things in the green ribbon: *scilicet: materia; color; opus vel fictitio.*

"Primium, materia.

" Id est de animalibus, et oletusb de insectis setigenis in genre; item de bombycivus et bombylis; item de rucis, spectris, larvis, aureliis, chrysalisidibus, papilionibus, imaginibus . . ."

"Et de millionibus diabolibus which will take you in infernibus," said Breloque.

"Secundum, color.

"I shall have the optic, the dioptric and the catoptric;

"the aposcopy, catascopy, metopscopy, helioscopy, physioscopy, microscopy, megascopy, polyscopy, periscopy and kaleidoscopy;

"the panorama, the diorama, the neorama, the georama, the cosmorama and the pantostereorama; the prism, the magic lantern and the opera glasses.

"We shall trip up Newton in passing, thumb our nose at Père Mersenne[1] and deliver a violent kick in the crotch to Algarotti[2] . . ."

"I'll gladly return them to you," said Breloque.

"Tertium,"

(Breloque put on his nightcap.)

---

1 Marin Mersenne (1588-1648) is primarily remembered as a mathematician and pioneer of acoustics, but he also suggested several innovations to the design and construction of telescopes, although he never attempted to build one.
2 Francesco Agarotti (1712-1764) helped to popularize Newtonian theory in France and England, in six dialogues on light and color published in 1739.

"If we consider the green ribbon in its relationship with the history of the arts, industry, commerce and civilization, from the origin of the plastic ideas on which all the typical forms of thought, in its indefatigable and persistent creation, have been molded . . ."

"We shall probably arrive at the Deluge," said Breloque.

"I'm arriving there. The first green ribbon of which there was ever question, if Astruc[1] is not mistaken in his curious *Conjectures on the Materials that Moses employed for the composition of Genesis* . . . listen, Breloque, the first of all the green ribbons . . ."

"I wish that it had served to wring your neck," said Breloque.

". . . Is evidently the one that the dove of the Ark brought back in its beak; but the profound Samuel Bochart[2] thinks that that so-called dove was a seagull, and it is really not probable that Noah, who did not lack sense when he was not drunk, had confided such a mission to a terrestrial bird, having such a fine aviary of amphibious birds on board. Also, independently of the dove and the crow of the Vulgate, Jean Le Pelletier[3] thought he saw a bittern there . . ."

"Three bitterns,[4] neither more nor less: Jean Le Pelletier, Bochart and you," said Breloque . . .

". . . The ribbon that that anonymous, pseudonymous or, rather, polynomic bird offered to the new leader of the human race, the color of which has since become that of hope, doubtless presented to the eyes the cheerful aspect of the verdure

---

1 Jean Astruc's *Conjectures sur les memoires originaux dont il paroit que Moyse s'est servi pour composer le Livre de Genèse* was first published anonymously in 1753.

2 The Protestant Biblical scholar Samuel Bochart (1599-1667).

3 The previously-cited Jean Le Pelletier produced, among many other works, an essay on Noah's Ark.

4 The French *butor* [bittern] is also used metaphorically to refer to a boorish individual; the illustration inserted into the original text at this point depicts three wading birds with human heads.

that was about to ornament the reconquered earth. It was a green ribbon, Breloque—which is to say, a green fabric that we improperly call a ribbon by virtue of a deplorable abuse of catachresis—and not a branch, as certain damned Talmudists claim who are infatuated with the stupidities of the Masoretic text, the reveries of Mishnism, the routine of traditionalists and the six Sephiroths of the Cabala . . ."

"They're the ones who caused my last melodrama to fail," said Breloque.

". . . It's true that Leusden[1] has read 'branch' against the authority of Gabriel Sionite,[2] who has read 'ribbon,' but as they are both dead, Jews, apostates, Marranos, reproved and, what is more, leprous and insolvent, *sub judice lis est*, or even *res agitur in lite* . . ."

"Let's go to bed," said Breloque.

". . . We have, fortunately, in regard to this question, the omnipotential authority—do you hear, Breloque—of our friend Herbinius,[3] who testifies that the immense trees and branches that the waters of the Deluge had charged before their retreat, could easily have furnished the voyaging bird with that equivocal guarantee . . ."

"Oh, if only those immense trees and branches could potentially have furnished fine gallows-form masts and fine forked gibbets from which to suspend you by the throat," said Breloque.

". . . And since those branches and that foliage, which were abundant everywhere, and which the winged ambassador had so much facility in collecting, do not give any miraculous character to its mission, it is less possible, and hence more

---

1 The Calvinist theologian Johann Leusden (1624-1699).
2 Gabriel Sionite or Sionita (1577-1648) was a Maronite scholar who came to Paris from Lebanon, completing the inaccuracy of Don Pic's subsequent judgment.
3 The Lutheran naturalist Johannes Herbinius (1627-1676).

meritorious, to believe that it brought back a ribbon in a time when ribbons were not fabricated, and when the usage of silk was unknown. That reasoning is perhaps what remains most authentic in the systematic, problematic, emblematic, hypothetical and sophistical of ascetic, mystical, parenetic, ethical, enclitic, eclectic, Gnostic, dogmatical and scholastic criticism and hypercriticism, *per omnia saecula saeculorum*."

"AMEN," said Breloque.

Aberration

"Where the devil were we in the monograph on the green ribbon when I fell asleep?" said Breloque.

"It's my opinion," said Don Pic, "that I left us in the home of the Marquise de Chiappapomposa, at the moment when, seizing the green ribbon of her little bell with an entirely Roman dignity—she descended from the chaste Lucretia by the male line—said . . ."

"In truth, Théodore, I don't recognize you, but get on with it, finish, in the name of Heaven, or I'll ring for Spinette."

And Monseigneur, who knew no more about it, reverence retained, imagined that the Marquise de Chiappapomposa would ring. But if the Marquise de Chiappapomposa had rung, it would have been necessary to see whether Spinette had decided to come!

You could have ravaged all the outposts for eighteen leagues around . . .

burned the tent and the flags, the faggots and the wicker baskets, the drawbridges and the palisades, the city and the suburbs . . .

marched, torch in hand through the grain-lofts, the arsenals and the powder magazines . . .

the fire would have commenced to run from the mine to the countermine, from the fuse to the blunderbuss, from the battery to the thunder . . .

And the Marquise de Chiappapomposa would have rung all the church bells and hand-bells;

the songs, the tocsins and the sonnettes,

the grelots and the crotali,

the sistra and the tabales,

the triangles and the atabales,

the tympani and the tympanons,

the tympanioles and the tymbals,

the cymbs, the cymbalons and the cymbals,

the burbelins, the curbelins and the crembalins,

the cri-cris and the crin-crins,

the bombards and the tarabats,

the castanets and the Basque tambourines,

the tom-toms and the rattles,

the belfries and the carillons,

the *clarum oletusbulum* of Catullus and the *clocqua titubans* of Merlin Coccaie,[1]

the campana of Vililli that announces of its own accord, according to the worthy Quinonez,[2] the election of a Pope, and that of Santa Maria of Carabaca, which trembles lightly and cantilenas joyously the vigils of the Assumption . . .

the chimes of Saint-Roch and Saint-Eustache, Bourdon, Georges d'Amboise and the Samaritaine . . .

in sum, all bells of all dimensions that were found clochiatorially arranged in accordance with their chromatic order at the last council of bells, at which the canonization of Janotus de Bragmardo was altisounded carillonically . . . but Spinette would not have come!

No, damn it, she would not have come!

---

1 Merlin Coccaie was the pseudonym of the "macaronic" poet Teofilo Folengo (1491-1544), whose works mingled Latin with Italian dialects.
2 Cardinal Francisco de Quinones (c1482-1540)

Transition

"Away with pedantry and pedants," Breloque continued. "This accursed barbacole has matagrabolized my brain so much with his scientific nomenclatures that I've almost forgotten how to talk Christian."

"It no longer requires as much to arrive at everything," responded Don Pic. "Would you like me to open both battens of the door of the universities to you? When the magnificent rector has awarded you successively the *baccam lauri* and the *togum doctoris*, how will you respond to him?"

"Monseigneur et messieurs, I was never more bored than today, since the last session of the Asiatic Society."

"That's it, and it's not. Listen, Breloque: 'Messieurs, I cannot defend myself, in listening to you, against a somnolent disposition, accompanied by spasms, hiatus and rictus, which progresses, at each of your speeches, to the ultimate degree of prostration, torpor and cephalgia . . .'"

"Cephalgia! I'm dead!"

"No, Breloque, you're bored."

"Me too," said Victorine.

Mystification

"Is that all," said Breloque, "and is it sufficient to sit *in curia et in praesidio*, to comment pedagogically on the thesis of that great simpleton the Prince of Mirandola, *de omnibus rebus scibilibus*, or other bibuses, and to augment *in baroco* in the jargon of the Limousin schoolboy? Here I am. *Favete linguis.*

"Paracelsus had conducted us into the tavern of his quotidian hostelry, where Dioscorides, Archimedes, Abélard, Boetius and Abbé de Latteignant met up from time to time.

"Farinacius[1] was the first to observe that the ambient air contained infinitely little caloric, and the absence of that vehicle had so exulcerated his dermis that you would not have been able to tell whether it was necessary to see therein ambustion or pernionculoid erythema—which is a frightful thought.

"But Flavius Josephus[2] was already equipped with four ligneous prisms three full Italian palms long, crudely carved in the *patula fagus* of the first verse of the *Bucolics*, and he hastened to deposit them on a rather ingenious scaffolding that terminated in the direction of the spectators in cynocephalic masks.

"Budé[3] then took possession of a little iron parallelogram with sharp edges and struck it abruptly with precipitate blows

---

1 The Italian judge Prospero Farinacci (1554-1618), whose name became the subject of a famous play on words by Pope Clement VIII.
2 The first-century historian Titus Flavius Josephus.
3 Guillaume Budé (1467-1540).

of a semi-diaphanous fragment of flint, until that percussion had detached from the metal a few molecules in a state of flagrance, or scintillatory flagration, which set fire repentantly to a dried *agaricus* held by Sulpicius Severus.

"Covarrubias[1] having placed that *agaricus* (I have always thought that it was a *oletus*, as Triptolemus advances peremptorily in his scholia on the juvenilia of Saint Babolin) under the aforementioned prisms, brought into play adpropecireumextraforaneivagoflabralimodulatotrily, by means of a species of hircine leather bladder alternately compressed and dilated between two ebony trapezia armed with spatuliform handles and tubularily terminated by a hollow cylinder, such a large quantity of nitrogen and oxygen in the requisite proportion of 79 to 21 that two phenomena resulted.

"The first, which was explained by Apuleius, is that the mixture lost a part of its oxygen, which was absorbed by the carbon to the profit of the combustion; the second, which was demonstrated by Nicolas Bourbon the elder[2] (he was from Vendeuvre) is that the caloric disengaged progressively stimulated a voluptuous dilation of the cellular tissue of Farinacius; but Farinacius scarcely worried about that; he had blown on his fingers.

"As for the solid part of the feast, which was composed primarily of appropriately unhasty and methodically unseated meats, Ocellus Lucanus admitted to me in secret that there would be a great deal of difficulty in cooking them to a perfectly isochronic degree without an invention that does too much honor to the human mind for me to pass over it in silence. It is a machine whose combinations have a frightful complication, with big wheels and small wheels, tenons, mortices, bolts, pegs, keys, nails, screws, catches, hooks, chains,

1 The Spanish lexicographer Sebastián de Covarrubias (1539-1613).
2 The poet Nicolas Bourbon (c1505-1550), a friend of Rabelais and briefly a protégé of Anne Boleyn, was the great uncle of a similarly-named member of the Académie Française.

of various dimensions, cords, weights, levers, pulleys, springs, pendulums, casings, panels, feet, props, and brackets, which cause a pointed iron axle to turn with great precision.

"What is surprising is that there is no mention of that machine in Diophantus. There is no mention of it in the commentaries of Bachet de Mézirac. There is no mention of it in the description of Grollier de Servière's cabinet.[1] There is no mention of it in the *Mathematici veteres* that have been printed so magnificently at the Louvre. There is no more mention of it in the *Petit Manuels* than in the *Almanach de Liège*, the most savant and most complete of all the collections printed this year. There is no more mention of it in Papin and Parmentier than in Pliny and Apicius. It has escaped the industrial investigations of Monsieur Charles Dupin,[2] and the truly economical lucubrations of the illustrious Monsieur Rumford,[3] who enabled us to eat such bad soups at the Temple. One can only conjecture that it was the chagrin of not having invented it that caused Empedocles to throw himself head first into the crater of Etna, on the edge of which Lord Hamilton found his pantoufles."

---

1 The work of the third-century Hellenic mathematician Diophantus of Alexandria was translated into French in the seventeenth century by Claude Gaspard Bachet de Mezirac; the latter's contemporary Nicolas Grollier de Servières (1596-1689) created a whole series of fantastic machines which he exhibited in a cabinet open to the public.
2 The mathematician and engineer Charles Dupin (1784-1873).
3 Benjamin Thompson, Count Rumford, settled in Paris after marrying Antoine Lavoisier's widow in 1804.

Verification

"How stupid I am," observed my publisher, judiciously, throwing his pantoufle at an old bust of Popocambou. "It's a turnspit."

"The author is sticking out his tongue on the page," said the printer, maliciously, dropping a pinch of eggshell from a nimble hand on to the mobile heel of his compositor. "It's a turnspit."

"Good joke," said the presser, inverting his paper miter on his occiput and drawing back his frame proudly without having marked out the sheet, "it's a turnspit."

"I can't make A or B of it," said the overseer, his carpal and metacarpal broadly imposed on the boxes of the capital As and Bs, "if it isn't a turnspit."

"There are ideas nowadays that truly make one lose one's head," said the book-stitcher, transposing with incredible intrepidity the two most ontologically-connected pages that I have ever written, "but you know, Elodie, doesn't it strike you, as it does me, as a turnspit?"

"Save for a few reserved allusions," said the censor, laying down his pen with a red-soaked nib, "it's difficult for the king's prosecutor to see it as anything but a turnspit."

"The idea isn't fine and the expression isn't fortunate," said the journalist, his two hands in the pockets of his trousers and pacing with his other two feet on the compartments of his parquet, "but I see no inconvenience in the present state of things in supposing it to be a species of turnspit."

"I consent never again to manipulate either the brush or the glue-pot," said the bill-poster, boldly displaying his placard upside-down, "if it isn't a turnspit."

"To the devil with the ignorant ignoramus who has mistaken his thesis!" cried the consternated Don Pic, letting his encyclopedic head fall back with all its weight on to the frayed back of my old black armchair. "He's forgotten, *la leccarda, mio Teodoro, id est, vas adipis exceptorum, vulgo dictum* a drippan . . .

But the university council did not hear that without malice, and although there was no longer, in fact, any question, after reading the *fanfreluches antidotées* of our master Alcofribas,[1] of a Pindaric homily to Saint Thomas Aquinas or a lesson in theology at the Sorbonne, there was no doctor so petty as to give a scholarly opinion affirmatively . . .

And Breloque passed joyfully *inter eximios*.[2]

*

---

1 Alcofribas Nasier was a pseudonym employed by Rabelais.
2 Approximately, "with flying colors."

Numeration

Breloque no longer lacked anything in order to be invested with the rights, privileges, immunities and exemptions of science that are attached to the doctorate except the *Approbatur* of the famous Doctor Abopacataxo, the great logarithmist of the impenetrable consistory of Brouillamini.

The great logarithmist was sitting before a slate parallelogram, on the tablet of which was visible, on one side, a long fragment of a white, mat, friable, brittle, calcareous substance shaped into a sharp cone; and on the other, a kind of soft, irregular, voluminous, light, porous, compressible, elastic madrepore, the name of which is not found in Varro because it was obscene in Latin.[1] He was holding open a scroll of printed paper charged with astral figures, genethliac calculations, sidereal emblems and constellated signs, which Breloque mistook at first for a grimoire, but in the end, after having looked at it more attentively, he assured himself that it was only the *Messager boiteux.*[2]

At the sight of Breloque's thesis the great logarithmist armed himself with this compass and proceeded to measure it magisterially in all its dimensions. Afterwards, following I know not what muted invocation he started tracing and ef-

---

1 The assertion that the word *spongia* was obscene in Latin was popularized in France by Montaigne, who asserts in his *Essais* (1580) that it was because the Romans used sponges to wipe the anus after defecation.
2 i.e., an almanac.

facing horizontal lines of Arabic characters alternately on the magic table, which he named one after another, like so many evocatory formulae, posing or retaining in a loud voice those diabolical hieroglyphs appropriate to his execrable operation.

The sorcerer was sweating with effort, and Breloque trembled in all his limbs.

After that Doctor Abopacataxo drew a large Latin cross, between the crosspiece of which (O profanation!) he hastened to run his hand obliquely, bearing his sacrilegious symbols with a demonic fury to the four cardinal points of the horizon, as if to marshal the entire army of Satan around poor Breloque's thesis.

Breloque's teeth were chattering and gnashing stridently, like those of the accursed of the gospel.

That was not all. Breloque saw him distinctly collect some of the cabalistic rebuses in the last line of the table of talismans, separate them magically by means of formidable and portentous Tironian mimeographisms, in the manner of Abraxas or some other amulatory argot, such as

minorative hyphens (-),
equilitative double dashes (=),
copulative superimposed dots (:),
comparative double colons (::)
and multiplicatory Saint Andrew's crosses (x),

all terminating with the letter X, which is sacred, profane and abominable, lethal and Stygian, in the eyes of God and men, as it is written.

"And when the devil takes me away," cried Doctor Abopacataxo, "I shall unleash that damned unknown!"

At that horrible and blasphematory imprecation, Breloque thought he saw Proserpine herself appear, and his hair stood on end.

(Can you imagine that I had never been able to make him to comprehend the mechanism of the simplest addition, excepting that of Diocles of Smyrna?)

"Sage Breloque," said the great logarithmist of the impenetrable consistory of Brouillamini, eventually, "you can take it for granted that your thesis, composing very nearly, it appears, six pages of impression on the character, format and justification of *The Story of the King of Bohemia and his Seven Castles*, and these pages being formed, more or less, of twenty-four widely paced lines *ad exiguitatem voluminin vitandam*, each of which contains thirty-eight letters, in which scarcely any are lacking, it must contain, approximately, save for error, abstraction being made of commas, full stops, blanks, abbreviations, spaces, reticences and parentheses, quadrats and quadratins, a sum total of printing types that can be estimated at five thousand, four hundred and seventy-two, if Barême has not failed. And as the proportion of consonants to vowels in the vulgar language of which you have made use is commonly fifty-five per cent, according to the average of Court de Gébelin and President de Brosses,[1] which results as you know, from the superabundant paragogy of the fictitious letters of our nominal and verbal plurals, you owe the university five vowels per hundred in exchange for as many valid consonants in good condition, livered without parsimony and without damage, the consonants and the vowels being presently at par in elevated studies—which has not been seen, and perhaps will not be seen again in fifty scholastic generations."

"Oho! That's good!" cried Breloque, reassured. "But my thesis?"

---

1 Antoine Court (1725-1784), who preferred to style himself Court de Gébelin, was an etymologist whose theories regarding the origins of language, extended in the multi-volume *Le Monde primitif, analysé et compare avec le monde moderne* (1773-1781) led him to suggest in one section that Tarot cards were a symbolic repository of ancient arcane wisdom; taken out of context, the notion proved extremely popular, and gave birth to modern cartomancy. Charles de Brosses (1709-1777) had produced a rival, materialistic theory of the origin of languages in 1776, associated with his materialistic theory of the origin of religion.

"You would have experienced another genre of inconvenience in Italian, where the proportion of vowels to consonants is, on the contrary, sixty-two hundredths, or, if you prefer, sixty-two per cent . . ."

"It's all the same to me," said Breloqe, scratching his right ear *velocissime*, which in him is a sign of immoderate impatience, "but my thesis, my thesis . . . !"

"Well, whatever side you might have taken," continued the doctor, without perceiving that he had been interrupted, "what would you have said, Sage Breloque, if you had been dealing with the Icelandic language or the Cherokee language, in which the relative mass of consonants is exactly that of a regiment to the corps of officers and sub-officers? There is only one vowel per squadron."

"Brrrrrrrrrrrrrrrrr," said Breloque, with as much intrepidity as if he had had a regiment of consonants behind him—but the poet laureate had ambushed them all . . .

"Brrrrrrrrrrrrrrrrr," said Breloque, "but talk to me about my thesis."

"You can be assured, sage Breloque, that your thesis composes very nearly, it appears . . ."

"Eh! I know the rest," murmured Breloque, pale with anger. "But my thesis, my thesis!" he continued, in a meteoric voice. "Have I made a doctoral thesis for numerical solution? Can't you see in my quintessential thesis any other combination than that of consonant and vocaliform articulations, and any other consequence than numbers?"

"None," replied the great logarithmist, "Science, Morality, Philosophy, Religion, Literature and Politics, are like a solitary zero about which I don't care. Number is everywhere, everything is numbered. That was the sentiment of Pythagoras, the great logarithmist of the Crotoniates. My affair is numeration, and nothing more, and numerating, I number numerically, baremically philosophizing and philosophically baremizing, logarthimizing Pindarically and Pindarizing logarithmically, drinking as much, and the whole joyfully."

"By the virtue of God, if I broke the thirty-two teeth that garnish your two mandibles with a blow of this hand," said Breloque, showing him a closed fist, "would you tell me how many fingers there are inside it?"

"Five," replied the great logarithmist, without being disconcerted, "which are composed of fourteen phalanges."

"You're lying," said Breloque, lifting the index finger and plunging it into his eye. "I lost the last phalanx of this one in the siege of Koenigsgratz, which is, in order that you know it, the strongest of the King of Bohemia's seven castles. Alas, we had a great deal of difficulty getting there in that campaign."

Interlocution

"'You've seen, I cried . . . ! You can see! Unfortunate that I am . . .'"

But it isn't Doctor Abopacataxo who said that. Doctor Abopacataxo has returned to his figures, and poor Gervais to his story. It is him who is speaking by my side, as he was at the moment when Don Pic de Fanferluchio interrupted him so stupidly . . .

"'The mirror, which was nothing for you but a cold and polished surface, will show you your living image. Its conversation, mute but animated, will repeat to you every day that you're beautiful, and when you come back to the unfortunate blind man, he will only inspire one sentiment in you. You'll pity him for being blind, because you'll imagine that it's the greatest of misfortunes not to be able to see. What am I saying? You won't come back! Why would you come back? What beautiful young woman could love a poor blind man? Oh, woe betide me, I'm blind!'

"As I said that I fell to the ground, but she followed me, pressing me in her hands, linking her fingers in my hair, brushing my neck with her lips and moaning like a child: 'No, never, I'll never love anyone but Gervais. You congratulated yourself yesterday for being blind, because our love would never deteriorate. I'll be blind, if necessary, in order not to leave a care in your heart. Do you want me to tear away this apparatus? Do you want me to put out my eyes?'

"Horrible memory! I had thought of that! 'Stop,' I said to her, seizing the rock violently in order to use up upon it the excess of force that was tormenting me. 'We're talking an insensate language because we're ill, you with your happiness and me with my despair. Listen . . .'

"I took my place again, and she hers. My heart was near to breaking. 'Listen,' I repeated. 'It's very good that you can see, because now you're perfect. It doesn't matter that I can't see and am going to die, abandoned, because that's the destiny that God has made for me—but swear to me never to see me, never to try to see me! If you see me, you'll be forced in spite of yourself to compare me to others, to those who have their intelligence and their soul in their eyes, to those who speak with their gaze and make women dream with one of the darts that spring from their eyes or one of the movements that raise their eyebrows. I don't want you to be able to compare me. I want to remain for you in the vagueness of the thought of a little blind girl, like a dream, like a mystery. I want you to swear to me never to come back here except with the green blindfold—to return every week . . . or at least every month . . . once a year . . . to come back once more! Oh, swear to me to come back once more, and not to see me!'

"'I swear to love you forever,' said Eulalie, weeping.

"All my senses had weakened. I fell at her feet. Monsieur Robert picked me up, gave me a few caresses, and returned me to my mother's hands. Eulalie was no longer there.

"She came back the next day, and the day after, for several days in succession, and my lips had not ceased to find the green blindfold that maintained my illusion. I imagined that I was the same for her as long as she had not seen me. I believed that I could appreciate in my reminiscences the impressions of a sense that I had scarcely enjoyed, and which, it seemed, were not sufficient to distract her from the delectable illusion in which we had sent our childhood. I told myself, with an insensate satisfaction, that she had remained blind for me, that my Eulalie would not see me, that she would love me forever. And I covered her green bandage with kisses, for I no longer loved her eyes.

"A day came, after many days—and if it were to recommence, I would count them—when it happened, I don't know how to tell you, that her hand was united with mine in a tighter grip, that our interlocked fingers were moistened by a warmer sweat, that her heart palpitated here, enough to stir my smock, and my mouth, by dint of wandering, rediscovered the long silky lashes under her green bandage.

"'Great God!' I cried. 'Is it an error of my memory? No, no! I remember that, when I was very young, I saw lights floating over my eyelashes, that they bore radiance, round fires, wandering patches, colors, and it was by that means that the daylight slid with a thousand sharp sparks to wake me in my cradle. Alas! If you were about to see me . . . !'

"'I have seen you,' she told me, laughing. 'What good would it do me to see if I had not seen you? Proud man, who prescribes limits to a woman whose eyes have just ended to the daylight!'

"'That isn't possible, Eulalie! You swore to me . . . !'

"'I swore nothing, my friend, and when you demanded that oath from me, I had already seen you, from further away than the esplanade permitted Julie to discover you. "Do you see him?" I said to her. "Yes, Mademoiselle, he looks very sad." I understood that; I was so late in coming. Well, the ribbon was no longer there. I had been told that that risked losing my sight forever, but after having seen you, I had no need of sight. I only put my green bandage on again when I sat down beside you.'

"'You had seen me and you continued to come. That's good. What had you seen first?'

"'Monsieur Maunoir, my father, Julie—and then this immense world, the trees, the mountains, the sky, the sun, the creation of which I was the center, and which all seemed ready to fall upon me from the depths of I know not what abyss into which I thought myself plunged.'

"'And after you had seen me?'

"'Gabriel Payot, old Balmat, the good Terraz, the giant Cachat, Marguerite . . .'

"'And no one else?'

"'No one.'

"'How fresh the air is this evening! Take off your bandage. You might go blind again.'

"'What does it matter? I repeat to you, I have only gained in seeing by seeing you, in seeing you and loving you by means of one sense more. You were in my soul as you are in my eyes. I only have a new motive for only existing for you. The faculty that they have given me is a new bond that attaches me to your heart, and it's for that reason that it is dear to me. Oh, I'd like to have as many senses as there are beautiful starry nights, in order to occupy them all with our love. I think that it's for that reason that the angels are the happiest of all creatures.'

"They were her own words, for I can't forget them. The conquest of light had further stimulated that vivid imagination, and her heart was animated by all the fires that her eyes had just drawn from the sunlight.

"My days had recovered some charm. One gets accustomed to hope so easily! Humans are so weak in resisting the seduction of a flattering error. Our existence had, however, taken on a new character, I know not what mobile and agitated variety, which Eulalie forced me to prefer to the profound calm in which we had lived until then. The bench of rock on which you are sitting was no longer anything for us but a rendezvous and a station, to which we came to relax in mild conversation from the pleasant exercise of walking. The rest of the time was spent wandering the valley, where Eulalie alone served me as a guide, delighting my ear with the impressions that she collected at the aspect of all the marvelous scenes that sight revealed to her thought It sometimes seemed to me that her imagination, like a powerful fay, was beginning to disengage my soul from the darkness of the body and to enrapture it, illuminated by a thousand gleams, in the spaces of the sky, by lavishing upon it images as gracious as perfumes, and colors as vivid and penetrating as the sounds of an instrument.

"Soon, however, my organs refused that deceptive perception, and I fell back sadly into the bleak contemplation of eternal night. That baleful return to myself rarely escaped the solicitude of her tenderness, and then she spared no effort to distract me. Sometimes, it was songs that brought me back in thought to the time when we were both blind and when she charmed our solitude in that way. More often it was reading, which had become for her a new and singular acquisition, although we had possessed the secret in other forms and by other methods—for the library of the blind is very limited. My attention, drawn into flight by her speech, lost its interior action, and I thought I was living in a new life that I had not divined or understood before, a life of imagination and sentiment where invented individuals less strange to me than myself came to surprise and charm all the faculties of my heart.

"What a vast region of magnificent thoughts and touching meditations opens up to the favored being who has received from Heaven organs for reading and an intelligence for understanding! Sometimes it was a passage from the Bible, like the Lord's discourse to Job, which confounded me with admiration and respect, or the story of Joseph and his brothers, which plunged my heart into a tender emotion of pity; sometimes it was the miracles of epic poetry, with the near-divine naivety of Homer or the religious solemnity of Milton. We also read novels among which a vague, confused instinct caused me to be fond of *Werther*, Eulalie preferred immediately those whose subject was appropriate to our situation. A vividly expressed passion, a dolorously felt separation, the pure joys of a chaste union, the simplicity of a rustic household, sheltered from the interested curiosity and the false affection of humans—that was what troubled her voice and moistened her eyelids; and although there was less mention thereafter of our marriage, when the order of evening reading brought something similar, she kissed me again before her father.

"After some time, I thought I detected that there had been a slight change in the tastes of her reading. She took more pleasure in the depiction of scenes of society; she insisted, without perceiving it, on the vain description of a fête; she loved to linger over the details of a woman's costume or the apparel of a play. I did not suppose at first that she had entirely forgotten that I was blind, and those distractions crumpled my heart without breaking it. I attributed that slight caprice to the extraordinary movement that was making itself felt in the château since Monsieur Maunoir had renewed its aspect by one of the miracles of his art. Monsieur Robert, doubtless happier and more disposed to enjoy the favors of fortune and the graces of life from the moment when his daughter had been given back to him with all the perfection of her organization and all the splendor of her beauty, liked to gather the numerous travelers that the short summer season brought to our mountains every year. The château, I can tell you, had become, in fact, one of those hospitable manors of another age, whose master never thought he had done enough to embellish the sojourn of his guests.

"Eulalie shone in that ever-renewed circle, always composed of rich strangers, illustrious scholars, elegant and witty voyagers; she shone among all the women, by virtue of the attraction of speech that is, for unfortunates like me, the physiognomy of the soul, and a thousand other attractions that I did not know in her. What an incredible mixture of pride and dolor lifted my breast to bursting point when the fire of her gaze was praised in my presence, or when a young man, stupidly cruel, complimented us on the color of her hair.

The people who had come to see the valley gladly prolonged their sojourn in order to see Eulalie. I understood that. I did not have to regret her affection, which never seemed able to alter, and yet I experienced that she was living increasingly apart from me, from us, from the intimacy of misfortune that one does not dare request, but which costs happiness when it is lost. I longed for winter more impatiently than I had ever yearned for the warm breath and the little waves of spring.

"The desired winter arrived, and Monsieur Robert told me—not without a few precautions and not without assuring me that they were separating from me for a few days, at the most, that they were only asking me for the time necessary to make a comfortable establishment in Geneva—that he was leaving with her, that they were going to send the winter in Geneva: the winter so quickly passed . . . the winter passed so close by . . .

"You heard correctly—so quickly! An Alpine winter! So close by! In Geneva, at the extremity of the accursed mountains—a route that chamois would not dare to attempt in winter . . . and I was blind.

"I remained mute with stupor. Eulalie's arms were wrapped around my neck. I found them almost cold, almost heavy. She addressed a few tender and emotional words to me, if my memory doest deceive me, but the sound passed me by like a dream. I only returned completely to myself after several hours. My mother said to me: 'They've gone, Gervais, but we can stay at the château.'

"'Damnation!' I cried. 'Has our cabin disappeared under another avalanche then?'

"'No, Gervais, the cabin is there, and Monsieur Robert's benefits have permitted me to embellish it.'

"'Oh well,' I replied, throwing myself into her arms, weeping, 'enjoy Monsieur Robert's benefits. I don't have the right to refuse them to you . . . but in the name of Heaven, let's go.'

"I had had time to reflect on our position. I knew that she wouldn't marry a blind man, and I would have refused to marry her myself, since she had ceased being blind without ceasing to be rich. It was misfortune that had rendered us equal, and from the moment that sympathy was broken, I lost all the rights that misfortune had given me. What could fill the immense interval that God had thrown between the marvel of creation, an angel or a woman, and the last of its rejects, a blind orphan? But, may Heaven pardon me for the judgment if it is reckless, I believed that she would not abandon me entirely, that she would reserve for me, near to her, the joy of hearing, in a place that she would pass through sometimes, wither the rustle of her ball gown, or the creak of her shoes, or the words, softer from her mouth that an eternal adieu: *Bonsoir, Gervais*.

"Since then, I have nothing more to tell, or almost nothing.

"In the month of October she sent me a ribbon with characters printed on it in relief, which read: *This is the green ribbon that I had over my eyes. I haven't quit it. Here it is.*

"In November the weather was still quite fair. One of the household staff brought me a few presents from her father. I obtained no news of her.

"In December the snows recommenced. God, how long that winter was! January, February, March, April—centuries of disasters and tempests, and in the month of May, avalanches that fell everywhere, except on me.

"When two or three rays of sunlight had softened the air and cheered up the country, I had myself taken along the road to Bossoua to meet the muleteers, but they hadn't come yet, I supposed that the Arve had overflowed, that another mountain was threatening the valley of Servoz, that the Nant-Noir had never been so wide and so terrible, that the Saint-Martin bridge had broken, that all the rocks of Maglan had covered the woods with their ruins, suspended for so many centuries, that the formidable pass of Cluse had finally closed forever, for I had heard mention of those perils by voyagers and poets, However, a muleteer arrived, and then two. When the third had come I was no longer expecting anything. I thought that my destiny was accomplished. A week later, a letter from Eulalie was read to me. She had spent the winter in Geneva; she was going to spend the summer in Milan.

"My mother trembled for me. I laughed. I had expected it, and it is a great satisfaction to know the extent to which pain can go.

"Now, Monsieur, you know my entire life. That's it. I believed that I was loved by a woman, and I have been loved by a dog, Poor Puck!"

Puck launched himself at the blind man. "Not you," he said, "but I like you, since you like me."

"Dear child," I said, "Another will come who will not be her, and whom you will love because you will be loved by her."

"Do you know a young woman incurably blind?" said Gervais,

"Why not a woman who can see you and love you?"

"Has someone told you that Eulalie will come back?"

"I hope that she will come back, but you like Puck because he likes you. You would love a woman who tells you that she loves you."

"It's quite different, Puck hasn't betrayed me. Puck wouldn't have left me. Puck is dead."

"Listen, Gervais, it's necessary that I go away. I'll go to Milan. I'll see her. I'll talk to her, I swear it, and then I'll come back. But I too have dolors to distract, wounds to scar; you won't believe it, but it's true: in order to exchange for your suffering heart my own heart, with all its anguish, I'd like to be able to give you my eyes!"

Gervais sought my hand and pressed it forcefully. The sympathies of misfortune are so rapid!

"At least," I continued, "nothing is lacking that can contribute to your ease. The cares of your benefactor have enabled your little fortune to grow. The good Chamouniers regard your prosperity as their sweetest wealth. Your beauty will obtain you a mistress; your heart will obtain you a friend . . ."

"And a dog," said Gervais.

"Oh, I wouldn't give you mine for your valley and your mountains, if he hadn't liked you. I'll give you my dog."

"Your dog!" he cried. "Your dog! No, no, Monsieur . . . that can't be given."

See how Puck had understood me. He came to cover me with sweet caresses mingling love, regret and joy. It was the most urgent tenderness, but a tenderness of farewell, and when a sign that he was waiting for indicated the blind man to him, he leapt proudly on to his knees; and with one paw on Gervais' arm, he looked at me with the confident expression of a freed slave.

"Adieu, Gervais!"

I didn't name Puck; he would have followed me.

When I reached the corner of the esplanade I perceived him, ashamed, on the edge of the forest. I approached him quietly. He took a single step back, and then extended a humiliated head over his forepaws. I passed my hand through the undulating waves of his long coat, and, with a constriction of the heart, I said to him: "Go . . ."

He departed like an arrow, turned to look at me once, and then rejoined Gervais.

At least he would no longer be alone.

Insurrection

I had promised Gervais. A week later I was in Milan.

Don Pic de Fanferluchio went alone to the Bibliothèque Ambrosienne. Breloque and I would have given all the editions of the famous Lavagnia reviewed by the learned Boninus Montbritius,[1] for a representation of the heroic feats and tragic adventures of Polichinelle, and something cried to me:

"This is the hour, this is the moment. Enter, Messieurs, enter, Mesdames, there is a good and numerous company, and one only pays on the way out. It is here that the sole and veritable Polichinelle is shown. He is present, he is alive! You will see him as he moves his eyes; you will see him as he shows his teeth; you will see him as he makes the grimace while eating his hot macaroni . . . !"

"*O Polichinelle!*" I cried,

"O Polichinelle, original and capricious fetish of children!

"O Polichinelle, grotesque Achilles of the people!

"O Polichinelle, modest and powerful Roscius of the crossroads!

---

1 This book and its author are fictitious, but they are mischievously cited as if they were real in an article by the dramatist Étienne Cordelier-Delanoue, a member of the cénacle, in *Le Landscape français: Italie* (1833), a travel guide that also includes articles by other friends of Nodier, including Théophile Gautier, Lamartine and Anne Bignan.

"O Polichinelle, inappreciable Falstaff of unfortunate ages who has not known Shakespeare!

"*O Polichinelle!*" I said,

"O Polichinelle, animate simulacrum of natural man, abandoned to his naïve and ingenuous insticts.

"O Polichinelle, eternal type of truth of which the idle centuries have delayed too long in seizing the deformed but witty and pleasant style!

"O Polichinelle, whose original theme often enchanted the leisure of Bayle and reanimated once again the somnolent idleness of La Fontaine!

"*O Polichinelle!*" I repeated,

"O Polichinelle, inexhaustible orator, imperturbable philosopher, intrepid and vigorous logician!

"O Polichinelle, great practical moralist, infallible theologaster, skillful and sure politician.

"O Polichinelle, sole legitimate arbiter (it is necessary to agree once in the face of the nations), sole competent and irrecusable judge of Codes and Institutes, Digests and Pandects, Novelles and Authentiques, Constitutions and Charters, Extravagantes and Canons!

"O Polichinelle, you whose wooden head encloses essentially in its compact and inorganic mass all the knowledge and all the common sense of the moderns.

"*O Polichinelle!* Finally!"

I was at that point in that magnificent invocation (I shall not give it for that of Lucretius, especially in the translation that you know) when a long, somber and stormy rumor, like the *stridor procellae* of Propertius or the *tempestas sonoris* of Virgil came to die away in *smorzando* in my ear, after having passed through all the degrees of the frightful chromatism of hurricanes, in the place of Pozzo's dome.[1]

"Long live Polichinelle and Brioché!" cried some. "Malediction on Girolamo!"[2]

"Long live Polichinelle and Girolamo!" cried the others. "Malediction on Brioché!"

Eternal malediction on you, profane and stupid vulgar crowd!

Since you are in accord on Polichinelle, you, enterprising Girolamists, and you, obstinate Briochists, what does it matter which hand operates him and in which mouth the shrill and strident whistle is placed that will lend him a voice?

As for me, returned a little late from the insensate prejudice of the partisans, I have dropped the anchor of my resolutions on one invariable thought. I only make wishes any longer for Polichinelle.

---

1 Andrea Pozzo (1642-1709) was a painter famous for his ability to create the illusion of the interior of a three-dimensional dome on a flat ceiling.

2 Brioché was the pseudonym of a family of seventeenth- and eighteenth-century puppeteers whose real name was Datelin, who established their trestles at the south end of the Pont Neuf. He Frenchified a stock character of the Italian *commedia dell'arte*, Pulcinella, as Polichinelle (who gave rise in his turn to the English Punch). The Teatro Girolamo in Milan was the most highly-reputed puppet theater in Italy in the early nineteenth century.

Dissertation

Everybody knows, or everybody ought to know, that the marionette theater that makes our delight today was instituted by the immortal Brioché, tutor of Croque-Mitaine, and that, since the death of the great man (I mean Brioché, for the glory of Croque-Mitaine has never dazzled me) nothing has changed in the profile of its *proscenium*, the decorations of its *cella*, the costumes of its *comparsi*, the conduct of its *scenarium*, and the triple unity of its poem. The slightest infraction of the species of adoration that the professors have professed immemorially for Brioché was admonished by Universities, assessed by Parlements, investigated by Capitularies, challenged by Edicts, and fulminated by Bulls—not that Brioché was a very orthodox individual, nor that he had given great guarantees if his savoir-faire in the science of education, if it is necessary to refer back to Plutarch and Quintus Curtius; but because there is something genuinely frightening in his intellectual encyclism.

In politics, we owe to him those loaded dice that produce at will all the possible chances in the arduous science of government, in exchange for which, kings make use of them with dexterity and the people scarcely notice . . .

In morality, he has informed unoccupied sages of the art of passing the time innocently by cracking bladder-nuts between their fingers . . .

In statistics he succeeded (a difficult thing to believe, and which has never been repeated since) in weighing the shadow of a fake infallibly . . .

In optics, he determined, to an approximation that became insensible in common usage, the average visual range of a blind snail . . .

He was the only man of his time who split a hair into four isocolically, and who played peripatetically with Stagyrian goblets . . .

But he died of the regret of not having been able to explain the inconstant and multicolored hue of the waters of the Robec that pass through Rouen, because he was obstinate in following their course instead of going upstream to the door of the dye-manufacturer.

Brioché's successors were therefore in consecrated possession of making Polichinelle talk when Girolamo appeared.

It is true to say that Girolamo invented nothing, for nothing had ever been invented since Polichinelle was invented. But Brioché's theater was so narrow—Polichinelle crossed it in one stride . . . Brioché's boards were dressed in scraps of cloth so worn out, scarcely renewed from one century to the next, like the pirate vessel of Aeneas, by scraps so disparate and of such garish assimilation . . . Brioché's marionettes were so fatigued,

so truncated,
so whistled,
so criticized,
so attacked,
so antiquated,
so Gothic,
so masticated,
so implicated,
so complicated,
so ragged,
so flaking,
so dislocated,

so disconcerted,
so entangled,
so imbricated,
so intricate,
so skimpy,
so awkward,
so unclothed,
so broken down,
so worn-out,
so hirsute,
so furry,
so ludicrous,
so dirty,
so soiled,
so dissolute moldy,
so worm-eaten . . .

The story of Polichinelle was so monotonous; the play of Polichinelle's stick was so familiar . . . the great diabolical machine that carries all the characters away when no longer needed was so out of fashion . . . any in any case, Brioché was well and truly dead, and Girolamo so powerfully alive!

But I promised not to decide anything between Girolamo and Brioché.

What is certain is that Girolamo's theater is brand new;
That is because its motto is new;
That is because, its construction is new;
That is because, it is newly painted;
Newly varnished,
Newly decorated,
Newly furnished,
Newly waxed,
Newly polished,

And newly tricked out.

That is because it is very wide, very deep and very high;

It is because it brings together all the conditions that you would like to find united in your property, if by chance you have one;

It is because Polichinelle never risks falling into the prompter's hole or breaking his head on Harlequin's mask. Polichinelle appear there from head to foot—which is twice as tall as in Brioché's parallelogrammic box.

(Take note of parallelogrammatic, a picturesque adjective that says more than it is long, I only regret owing the construction of that geometrical figure to the classical Desreaux.[1])

Without Girolamo we would not know that Polichinelle wears clogs; and Polichinelle's clogs are one of the most special, most intimate and most complete characteristics of his original physiognomy.

Brioché's Polichimelle is, at the most, a bust. Girolamo's is almost human.

Abbé d'Aubignac[2] opines, in truth, that all would be lost in literature if the breadth of the compass that embraces the two extreme points of the diameter of Polichinelle's box were increased by a ligne. But Doctor Schlegel[3] replies to him, with his usual assurance, that the size of Polichinelle's box is irrelevant to the question, and he sees no inconvenience in making him dance in the great hall of a palace, provided that the strings are long enough.

The academy of the Eterni of Zeroniente, on the report of the committee of Sempiterni, cut through the difficulty abruptly; it had Schlegel's ears and Polichinelle's legs cut off.

That day, Girolamo advertised an intermission.

1 Gédéon Tallemant des Réaux (1619-1692) described Molière's auditorium as a long parallelogram.
2 François Hédelin, abbé d'Aubignac (1604-1676), author of *Pratique du théâtre* (1657).
3 The Romantic critic and dramatist August Wilhelm Schlegel (1767-1845).

Meditation

"By Popocambou!" I cried (that was the oath of Confucius), dropping Cruikshank's[1] *Punch* on my *somno*;

my spectacles into their case;

my eyelids over my eyes;

my *gourra* over my head;

my head into my hand;

my hand on to my pillow;

and the studious ball of Aristotle into an unsonorous cup in which it no longer resonated . . .

"By Popocambou," I repeated, in a loud voice, although I had no fear that it would awaken anyone on the Babelic floor on which my hostess had lodged me . . .

"By Po . . . po . . . cam . . . bou . . . it seems to me that the question would have been judged more sanely by the Institute of Timbuktu."

---

1 The illustrator and caricaturist George Cruikshank (1792-1878) made a minor contribution to the satirical magazine *Punch*, but it was not his property; he was far better known as the illustrator of the works of Charles Dickens.

Navigation[1]

Timbuktu, otherwise known as Tombot or Tumbut or Tumbuctu, is I know not what city in I know not what land under I know not what degree of I know not what latitude, and thus, if one can believe old wives' tales, at the perpendicular antipode of the capital of Sapience, which is Common Sense; and, in receiving notoriety and quidditative certainty, perforating our terrestrial capsule from here, neither more nor less than the practice, prompting you ociously to thread indicative unions and even seed-pearls; by means of which, if done dexterously and without circumbilivagination, you cannot fail, dunkers, to reach Timbuktu.

Of the Timbuktuans, nothing that is not garbled can presently be narrated to you in books of navigage of the marvelous and seigneurial history. Do not put any faith in that foolish geographical dreamer Claudius Ptolemy, who only disguises Timbuktu with gulfs, shores, deceptions, Lucianic absurdities and fantasies abhorrent to nature, such as cacomorphic and silenian humans with six-handspan tails. Mercy of God, what do you not have of supellative amplitude, you straw men of flatland, inasmuch as it is a fine thing to see, to the great profit

---

1 The original version of this brief chapter is extraordinarily rich in cacographic (deliberately misrendered) words, which only give an oblique suggestion of meaning, and is thus very difficult to transmute into an English equivalent, although "circumbilivagination," meaning to walk around in circles, really does exist.

of misnaming, as the sheep of Tartary can pertinently cognicize. But I assure you by Golfarin, who was the nephew of Carmentran[1] (by my share of paradise, I would not dare; I am so hypercritically overcooked!), that in order to transgress as far as the sad joyous and caudipotent nation, it is only necessary to walk westwards from the said Timbuktu for the range of thirteen blowpipes and the length of the bastonnet.

Timbuktuans are people likeable among all humans, smart, gallant and elegant, becoming in their manners, advantageous in the nose, fond of all pleasant games, good company and honest dealers, fine finders and flushers of hooded quail who would rather hear a hundred masses said than see wine drunk; furthermore, loyal subjects, good taxpayers, and as good Christians as any; but, blessed cowled elders of the ultimate council, you would fulminate at them and excommunicate them like snakes, because they make mistakes in babbling their prayers and meager suffrages regarding the number of hairs on the goat of Milord Saint Pascome. May God be praised everywhere! A matter of breviary.

---

1 The Carmentran is a scarecrow burned in southern France at the beginning of Lent—i.e. during the Carnival—to celebrate the end of winter. Golfarin [literally "glutton"] is one of the variants of the name adopted by the French guild of journeymen printers in the sixteenth century.

Apparition

I do not know whether you have remarked how the mysterious phenomena of dreams are accomplished. Artemidorus and Apomazar never suspected it.[1]

At the moment when those insignificant words "Institut of Timbuktu" died away slowly with the last of my ideas in the ever-increasing silence of slumber, I know not what vibratile and sonorous organ prolonged its reverberation further through the almost mute echoes of my soporific intelligence, and a few unknown keys made them echo in my ear like the confused notes of a distant voice

What is an Institute?

Does it exist?

Has anyone mentioned it?

Is there another institute than that of Timbuktu?

Why is there an institute in Timbuktu?

Are the inhabitants of Timbuktu savages?

What are the urgent circumstances and invincible necessities that have reduced them to inventing an institute . . . the Institute of Timbuktu . . .

---

1 The second-century diviner Artemidorus Daidanus wrote a five-volume *Oneirocritica* [Interpretation of Dreams], which scholars preserved, whereas most contemporary works, including his textbooks of divination by palm-reading and bird-watching, were lost. "Apomazar" is the mock-Arabic signature attached to a 1581 text on the interpretation of dreams.

There or thereabouts the first operation concludes of the man who is falling asleep; you can see that it is still sufficiently in conformity with the order of the dialectic; but the last act of reflection of rational thought is scarcely terminated than escaping perception falls into the domain of another sense, which is ordinarily that of sight. Your conversation with yourself is finished, but it has only changed form. The object of the discussion has become active and subjective. The judge of the discussion has become a passive witness. Deceived meditation has given way to a spectacle. An animate tableau develops in the eyes of your imagination. You see bored faces crowded on banquettes or sitting upright in armchairs, which are contemplating other bored faces, which dominate by a few feet other figures frightening in their importance and desolate in their nullity. Two ideas suddenly surge forth from your brain: Institute and Timbuktu.

Now the localities are known, the characters established and the costumes determined, as in a German drama; but I don't know how to make you understand the organization of the Institute of Timbuktu if I don't tell you its history.

And we shall not go far in seeking it, for I have it.

Exploration

"There as once a king who loved his people . . ."

"That commences like a *conte de fée*," said Jalamir.

"It is one," replied the druid.

But I don't know why I have stolen that magnificent debut from Rousseau.[1]

Would you prefer Tacitus?

"For a long time, Timbuktu had been governed by kings . . ."

Or would you prefer that we enter into the matter with Suetonius?

"Popocambou the Hirsute had scarcely attained his sixteenth year . . ."

What is certain is that of all the sovereigns in the world (there is no question here of Caesar, Galba or Charles the Bald) the hairiest that ever existed was Popocambou the Hirsute.

And that favorable hazard had inspired him sympathetically with such a pronounced taste for ample tresses, and for academic, scientific, philosophical, sophistic, doctoral, medical, theological, judiciary and universitarian hairpieces that he had formed a collection of wigs unique in all the nations, which is essentially lacking to our royal museum.

Apart from that innocent mania . . .

---

1 Specifically, from Jean-Jacques Rousseau's "La Reine Fantasque" (1769; tr. as "Queen Fantasque" in the showcase anthology appended to *Tales of Enchantment and Disenchantment, A History of Faerie*, Black Coat Press 2019).

("That of Dionysius, tyrant of Syracuse," said Breloque, "was metricating verses and spouting them inhumanely to all comers; that of Nero was singing and miming on stage with mimes and strolling players; that of Commodus Hercules was boxing in the arena with gladiators; that of Henry V of England was occasionally raising a large number of tankards in the taverns of London with roisterers and joyful companions; that of Henry VIII of controversing in the schools with preachers in a rage of argument . . .)

Apart from that passionate but inoffensive taste, Pompocambou the Hirsute was a sage of sorts—and that, according to Marcus Aurelius, is the greatest eulogy that one can make of a man, especially when the man is a king, and he is the king of Timbuktu.

Pompocambou, weary of flatterers—the worst of the ennuis of royalty—and even weary of his delights and his glories, had shut himself away in his favorite museum, as if in a seraglio. He lived there as a contemplative philosopher in the midst of his wigs; he rejoiced in his wigs as Solomon did in his works; he meditated on his wigs, he consulted his wigs, and he sometimes quit them with the sentiment of mild satisfaction that a verity acquired procures—which he had very rarely taken away from his Council of State.

In the meantime, the government marched on, and the people had never been as happy to submit to the influence of wigs as when they no longer had heads inside them.

Like thought, speech and the press were free in Timbuktu. Popocambou the Hirsute, who no longer saw anyone but who read everything, understood that he was not far from arriving at the most perfect form of government possible.

"And yet," he said, "what if I were to put an idiot under that scholarly wig? A cruel and insidious man under that judiciary wig? A cunning and avid man under that administrative wig? A cowardly or irresolute man under that martial wig? A perverse hypocrite under that chaste and modest wig called confidence and respect?

"Oh my God!" cried Popocambou pulling his long hair down over his eyes, "how difficult it is to govern!"

And after a moment of reflection, he invented wig-heads.

Procreation

Timbuktu possessed then one of those great men whom peoples ordinarily only appreciate when they have lost them. He was a mechanican, a philosopher and perhaps a necromancer, whose name was Mistigri, either because he had chanced to receive that name patronymically—which is, in truth, a name as common as any other—or because it had been given to him by allusion to some fortuitous resemblance to the Jack of Clubs.[1]

That powerful genius, long flattered by the two religious factions that split the empire and ardently sought his support, had ended up rejecting both of them, because he had refused to pronounce upon the dangerous question that divided them. He preferred to condemn himself to exile than decide whether the sacred cockchafer that had founded the isles of the sea—as no one doubted—was male or female.

Popocambou the Hirsute, whose excellent education and the solemn direction that his royal studies had taken for some time, raised him, as I have said, far above the vulgar, was entirely of your advice and mine regarding that scabrous controversy. He was marvelously well aware that the great cockchafer was hermaphrodite, but he did not say so.

---

1 There was a French trick-taking card game called Mistigri [approximately, Pussy-Cat], in which the Jack of Clubs often featured as the highest trump or as a wild card.

Popocambou had, therefore, regally abandoned Mistigri to his enemies, while reserving the memory of him when he had an urgent need for him.

On the occasion of which we speak, he placed an enormous order for wig-heads.

The affair of the wig-heads brought Mistigri back to court. Preceded by the renown of his wig-heads, he entered it as if he had never left. The question of the sex of the great cockchafer was still agitated in a few recalcitrant and backward gazettes, but positive men, who are always in the majority in affairs, settled for wig-heads and Mistigri was appointed Minister of State.

"It's astonishing," said the king, "but I recognize them! One might think that they were posed."

(Mistigri smiled.)

"Finally," said Popocambou the Hirsute, "I shall have ministers in perpetuity, an immovable council, and, so far as possible, an immortal academy. In truth, they only lack speech."

"My wig-heads will speak when your majesty orders it," replied Mistigri, bowing with a respectful dignity.

"When I order it!" cried the king. "I'd like to hear one right away, even if it costs me the best of my wigs!"

"Your majesty," said Mistigri, "only has to lift up the wig of the head that it would please him to hear, and tap with his finger one of the protuberances that he will remark there, which are more or less pronounced in proportion to the degree of mechanical intelligence that I thought it appropriate to give to my wig-heads."

Popocambou the Hirsute had not waited for the end of the sentence. "But there isn't the slightest protuberance, my dear Mistigri. I wouldn't give a kopek in exchange for the wooden head of the commander-in-chief of my army. It's as smooth as an egg!"

"It's true," said Mistigri, but your majesty's wisdom will easily find employment for it. You'll make him a great lord, assiduous at your *petit lever*, a dignitary by birth, a counselor in favor, a fortunate academician, a transitional minister, an official journalist. Pass on."

"Here's a head charged with little protuberances in infinite abundance."

"A superficial mind that touches everything and is good for nothing, what fools call a universal man."

"What does this unique protuberance signify?"

"A trenchant and absolute mind that has concentrated all its faculties on one idea, for want of the ability to combine two—what simpletons call a philosopher."

"And this other one, so remarkable, on this head."

"Cupidity. It's a philanthropist.

"And this monstrous bump?"

"Ambition. It's an independent."

"I have a desire to make one of my wig-heads talk," said Popocambou, imprinting his thumb forcefully on a protuberance that had been worn away by usage,

"Sire, it's a great and fine day for us," said the wig-head.

"Oh, divine Popocambou," cried Mistigri, "release the spring. I know that head. It always says the same thing, and never knows what it is saying."

The joy that Popocambou experienced in that experimental session is unimaginable. He was finally able to conciliate his tender esteem for wigs with his old amour for society, and rediscover whenever he wished the docile conversation and obsequious ceremonial of his palace, among his wooden courtiers.

"Sublime man," he said to Mistigri, with a profound expansion, "how can I recompense your genius?"

"By asking me for the truth when you need it," said Mistigri

"And will you tell me whether the sacred cockchafer is hermaphrodite?" cried Popocambou.

"I have never seen or known the sacred cockchafer," Mistigri replied.

"Well," said Popocambou, "palpate my royal head without fear, and tell me with security what my dominant protuberances signify."

Mistigri exposed his astrolabe, unrolled his sibylline scrolls, interrogated his tarot cards, summoned the spirits of Etteilla, Decremps and Spurzheim; Apollonius of Tyana, Cabanis and Simon Magus, Agrippa, Pinetti and Lavater, Comte, Gall and Cagliostro.[1]

He threw his fateful dice, launched his toe- and knuckle-bones, made his top pirouette, made his rhombus whine, and applied his hand to the frontal protuberances of the good king of Timbuktu.

"They signify," said Mistigri, "that the first princess who will be honored by your majesty's good graces will be very fond of dancing."

"Alas!" sighed Popocambou the Hirsute.

(It is well-known that I have always sought to place some trait of sentiment in my most serious writings.)

"Alas," he continued, sobbing, "she couldn't dance. Her pantoufle was too tight."

---

1 "Ettailla" was the pseudonym of Jean-Baptiste Alliette (1738-1791), who popularized tarot reading in France after reading Count de Gébelin's scholarly fantasy; Henri Decremps (1746-1826) was a conjurer who became celebrated for exposing charlatans by explaining their trickery; Johann Spurzheim (1776-1832) was the chief popularizer of phrenology, following the theory of Franz Josef Gall (1758-1828), based in Lavater's theories of physiognomy. The insertion of the name of the materialist physiologist Pierre Cabanis (1757-1808) between those of the two legendary magicians is a trifle mischievous. Giuseppe Pinetti (1750-1803) was a stage magician, who started out as a charlatan but changed his stance after being exposed by Decremps; he survived being Louis XVI's court magician to perform under the Directoire and Napoléon as "Theophrastus Paracelsus."

Distinction

"You're decidedly a sorcerer, then?" said Popocambou the Hirsute.

"No, sire," Mistigri replied. "I'm a craniologist."

"It's quite different, then," said the king.

Remuneration

However, the good Popocambou, enthusiastic to recompense Mistigri magnificently, because he was naturally more generous and more grateful than people are ordinarily inclined to be in the genteel métier of autocrat, awarded him the right to blazon his coat of arms with a wig-head, which was held in reserve in the heraldic constitutions of Timbuktu for hyperbolic royal favor . . . and, in addition, the exclusive and privileged freedom to hunt, throughout the extent of the empire, every species of farfallesque and culiciform flying creature bearing mouths, teeth, claws, talons, jaws, mandibles, pumps, trunks, suckers, beaks, proboscis, stings, tongues, ligulae, palps, lips, siphons or other intussusceptive instruments, which little beasts are vulgarly known as butterflies or moths, and urban, rural, paludal or sylvan flies, to wit:

Sphinx-moths,[1]

Night-moths,

---

1 Many of the names included in this list are taken from the survey of entomology contributed to Georges Cuvier's *La Regne animal* (1817; revised 1829-30) by Pierre Latreille (1762-1833); some produce no hits at all on search engines. Many of Latreille's names were improvised by him for the purpose of taxonomic distinction, and were not taken up as generic descriptions by other taxonomists, making it difficult to ascertain which modern terms would be closest in meaning, especially with reference to obscure types of wasps and flies; I have left many as they appear in the original, where the author could not have expected them to convey any meaning to any of his readers.

Bat-moths,
Owl-moths,
Silk-moths,
Grass-moths,
Burnet moths,
Fungus-moths,
Clear-wing moths,
Ghost moths,
Cabbage moths,
White plume moths—which have daintily feathered wings like those of birds, sliced up into thin oars like the fans of our young women;
Dragonflies,
Damsel-flies,
Owl-flies,
Grasshoppers,
Ant-lions,
Mayflies—such as you might have seen on the river Hypanis,
Lacewings,
Caddis flies,
Ground pearls,
Scorpion flies
Tenthredons,
Ichneumon flies with bifid and trifid tails—which are vampires of caterpillars, larvae, nymphs, chrysalides and aurelias,
Ensign wasps,
Sand-flies,
Scolid wasps,
Cuckoo-wasps,
Ruby-tailed wasps,
Mason-bees,
Andrenes,
Mellifluous bees,

Hornets,
Crabrons,
Bumble-bees,
Gall-wasps,
Diplopes,
Uroceres,
Crypt-keeper wasps,
Allantes,
Nemates,
Pterones,
Cephaleies,
Orysses,
Trachetes,
Sireces,
Tremeces,
Aulacids,
Fenes,
Stephanes,
Anomalons,
Braconids,
Anteons,
Ceraphronids,
Spider-wasps,
Digger-wasps,
Fig-wasps,
Honey-bees,
Larra wasps,
Hover-flies,
Sapygid wasps,
Myrmosid wasps,
Bembeces,
Masarides,
Simblephiles,
Arpactes,

Alysons,
Nyssons,
Philantes,
Cerceres,
Gonies,
Miscophes,
Dinetes,
Cemones,
Helores,
Oxybeles,
Prosopes,
Nomades,
Pasites,
Epeoles,
Certatines,
Belytes,
Lasies,
Crocises,
Trigones,
Trachuses,
Xylocopes; in your days you will not find ruder laborers in old tree-trunks,
Doriles,
Labides,
Figites,
Chelones,
Cleptes,
Omales,
Codres,
Cinetes,
Chalcides,
Psiles,
Myrmes,
Winged ants,

Termes,

Termites,

Mutilles,

Bremedes,

Attes,

Maniques,

Tipules,

Bibions,

Rhagions,

Syrphes,

Asiles,

Conopes,

Stratyomes,

Stomoxes, which sting outrageously in stormy weather,

Maringouins

Cousins; it was one of these that buzzed tempestuously in Uncle Toby's bedroom when the latter opened the window; "Go, poor beast," he said benignly. "The world is big enough for both of us."

Mosquitoes: I never saw as many as in Tarascon at the Pont du Gard, but Mistigri never passed that way;

Ceroplates,

Ctenophores,

Chironomes,

Hirtees,

Scatopses,

Lertes,

Mydes,

Siques,

Sciarres,

Hermeties,

Xylophages,

Atherices,

Nemoteles,

Pangonies,

Heptatomes,

Heptatopotes,

Chrysopes; what blessed and cheerful color they have in their eyes!

Cytheres,

Volucelles,

Anthraces,

Bombyles,

Ploades,

Empides,

Tachydromies,

Hybotes,

Damalides,

Dioctries,

Laphries,

Dasypogons,

Ceries,

Myopes,

Mulions,

Milesies,

Merodons,

Bacques,

Diposes,

Loxoceres,

Scatophages; Ugh, the villains!

Psares,

Lauxanies,

Oscines,

Thereves,

Rhingies,

Oestres,

Tabans: the midge that stung Aesop's lion so vehemently was of that species;

Eristales,
Achiades,
Scaeves,
Sargues,
Vappons,
Calobates,
Neries,
Dolichopes,
Daques,
Tachines,
Ocypteres,
Tephrites,
Dictyes,
Acroceres,
Henopes,
Scenopins,
Trineures,
Hippobosques, and innumerable other unnamed animac-
ules that you can see dancing, singing, chirring, murmuring,
whispering, whirring, droning, baritoning, buzzing and hum-
ming in rays of sunlight on beautiful autumn evenings.

But the nobility of the land, grievously irate and chagrined
that a simple clerk could hunt to his heart's content in the
best part of their prerogatives, took advantage of a new reign
that followed shortly thereafter and the license of that joyous
event to hook milord the great hunter and have him hung well
and truly from the corner of the great pyramid facing toward
Villers-Cotterets, where the unfortunate Mistigri was misera-
bly devoured by the aforementioned flies. And that happened,
if the chronicles are not misleading me, on a certain day of a
certain week of a certain month of a certain year of a certain
Olympiad of a certain lustrum of a certain indiction of a certain century of a certain hegira of a certain era that went by
long before the first usage of wooden watches—so I do not
know the hour.

But that, whatever those damned liars of Hellenes might have scribbled in their poetic wads of paper, is what lies behind the creation of humans by the Titans and the punishment of Prometheus. Always understand by that, I beg you, the invention of organic wig-heads and the deplorable end of Mistigri, delivered to the flies.

And that is how the greatest difficulties are simplified when one imports a little philosophy into history.

Precaution

And I ought to add that in that state—I mean the state of the sleeping human (isn't that you?)—there only remain of acquired ideas a small number of salient and characteristic aspects, which suffice for naming them, but the veritable expression of which soon vanishes under a host of capricious forms. Those slight superficia of real existence, gone astray in the vague breath of the imagination, intersect, mingle and are confounded, varying in color and brightness in accordance with the bizarre play of the dazzling prism of dreams. Slumber, the blind tyrant of thought, amuses itself in deceiving our most familiar impressions and disconcerting them, like a skillful charlatan, by means of opposed impressions.

Scarcely have the fingers made a harmonious and fantastic string vibrate, than it is already embroidered over the majestic notes of a gross bacchanal or a ludicrous vaudeville. Scarcely has the changing decoration that obeys it offered to your gaze the veritable pulpit of the scholar than it allows to appear the grotesque stages of Mondor and Gratelard;[1] for it is the nature of the irrational soul that awakens within us when we sleep, not to allow a sublime perception escape without spoiling it with some imprint of the ridiculous; and that is what caused a wise man to say that dreams are a parody of life.

---

1 Two characters invented by a famous Parisian double act of street-performers, Antoine and Philippe Girard in the early seventeenth century; several printed farces signed "Tabarin" were probably theirs.

Go on, go on, my dear Breloque, veritable science is too indulgent to be offended by the assaults of your stupid fool's bauble. It knows that the discoveries that push back its limits sometimes have a humorous side, and it forgives slumber, because slumber is a buffoon.

Installation

After the death of Popocambou the Hirsute his wigs had been forgotten in his wardrobe for a long time. They were no longer shown except on extraordinary occasions, like the clothes of Charles the Bold in the great jubilee of Berne, and the springs of the protuberances had rusted irreparably even in the best heads. It is painful to admit that three-quarters of the Institute of Timbuktu only served to make tapestry; but people always came back to it, because there was really something marvelous in the industry of the mechanician, and in addition, of all the cities of the world, Timbuktu was the one that had the most time to waste.

Mistigri had been so fortunate in the expression of his fig-ures that there was not one that did not appear to be occupied with an object or given to a study, as if it had been organized in the manner of rational creatures, and that is something that had only ever been seen in the Institute of Timbuktu.

There were some that filtered the words of the language through a great academic sieve.

There were some that filtered them sophistically, and obtained a great profit from selling the filtrate to ill-favored idlers in order to make a few mouthfuls of them.

There were some that plucked the pronouns, selected the conjunctions, winnowed the particules and scotched the adverbs.

There were some that passed the ideas of great writers through a classical filter two or three times, and spun them properly on an endless bobbin.

There were some who extended them on a rolling-mill or crushed them under a cylinder until they reached the most perfect degree of possible platitude.

I saw one that crumbled Latin etymologies grammatically in a fine Despauterian[1] mortar—God, what a rich operation!

I saw another who had succeeded in making a ruby spinel thicker by half than the block of insectile amber from which the colossal statue of Popocambou was extracted, without employing any other ingredient than a carefully elaborated pimpernel seed; but I found him later selling rosaries in order to make a living and crying *corone, corone* on the parvis of Saint Anthony of Padua.

The most skillful of all proposed a magnificent enterprise to me: that of a suspension bridge between Timbuktu and the Rue Folie-Méricourt, under Victorine's entresol, and that of a no less ingenious tunnel that would open after a few billion millimeters in the exact center of Fanny's bedroom, but he could never raise its initial foundations more than two English feet above the terrain because of the great ultramontane winds that blew in that country.

The doors were opened to a venerable scholar well known for the meritorious patience with which he tried for fifty years to weigh matter and spirit in two spider-web basins that had not resisted the experiment once. He entered proudly with his empty balances, but lost nothing in the event; he had not dropped a single idea on the way.

I noticed among them a dozen young men of good appearance who were shuffling rather industriously sheets of paper

---

1 Related to the Flemish Humanist Joannes Despauterius (Jan de Spauter, c1480-1520), who published books on Latin grammar that became standard textbooks.

on which were figures of kings, queens and knaves, and who distributed them very elegantly in five packets, as in a game of brelan. I was assured that they believed that they were writing tragedies.

The session was opened, as was customary, by an item of pageantry that had been requested of the most oratorically organized head in the Institute of Timbuktu. It began with the distribution before the orator of a number of phials industriously prepared by the great abstractor of verbal and grammatical quintessences, on which could be read: *verbs, adverbs, conjunctions, particules, subtantives* and *adjectives*. The last-named was the most replete, and, let it be said in passing, the one with the finest appearance. He mingled all of that delicately in a measuring-glass, and then sprinkled it with a mixture of an immense quantity of vowels, tropes and exclamation marks. Then, striking his wooden head with a wooden hand and leaning backwards in such a manner as to describe an obtuse angle of a hundred and thirty-five degrees relative to the foot of the machine, he ingurgitated the sonorous potion, and gargled sonorously for a full hour on the clock, in accordance with the formula, to the reiterated applause of the audience. It is true to say that it was the most harmonious gurgling that it is possible to imagine, and that you would have obtained great pleasure from it, almost as much as the son of the enchantress Craca,[1] who understood the language of animals like his own but only grasped, in the succession of the centuries, the most minimal portion of meaning—which caused several ladies in the assembly to faint by virtue of excessively powerful mental contention.

---

1 The sorceress Craca, who cooks a magic food for her stepson Ericus, can be found in the twelfth-century *Gesta Danorum* of Saxo Grammaticus; Nodier probably found the reference to her in Pierre de Lancre's history of witchcraft.

Someone assured me that the majority of those heads only lived to gargle like that in public three or four times a year, so I can swear to you on the pantoufle of Popocambou that they were all emaciated, anhemic and chlorotic, neither more nor less than the invalids cured by Doctor Sanguisorba.[1]

---

1 Sanguisorba is the Latin name of a genus of plants commonly known in English as burnets. It is conceivable that the remark is an oblique reference to the famous physician Thomas Burnet (1638-1704).

Dentition

A curtain was then drawn, behind which two individuals were sitting at antidotal and charlatanesque tables, whose attitude reminded me of the merchants of catholicon whom we saw in 1593 in the States of the Ligue.[1]

The table of the former was covered in tall, stout, long, broad and profound bottles in which were floating, in a limpid liquid, a multitude of animals that I had only ever encountered in lands of tapestry, such as:

hare-like wolf-dogs;

horned squirrels;

feathered rabbits;

prickleless hedgehogs;

lepidopteran snails;

quadrumane eels;

inoculated lampreys;

locusts with hands, saddles and stretchers;

July cockchafers caparisoned in the Moorish manner;

acrobatic tortoises; vertebrate oysters, and other rare marvels.

"Messieurs," said the young professor, ...
. . . .
. . . .
. . . . "what I have just reminded you of our academic

---

1 "Catholicon" became a generic term for supposed panaceas hawked by charlatans.

theories," he resumed, after a momentary pause, will dispense me of insisting on the motives that have determined me in the classification of Anomalata, or animals with jaws improperly called monstrous. You know that after having recognized the sublime action of nature in these extranormal creations, which do no less honor to it than more regular jaws, we have divided the Anomatala into three great families, to wit:

"Firstly, the Polyodontes, or jaws with multiple rows of teeth. The magnificent jaw that I have the honor of submitting to you is that of the ancient Hercules, who ought not to be confounded with the host of Hercules of new fabrication that you find in the Mythographers. This one is easily recognizable by his three rows of teeth, which are so curiously described in Apollodorus. That particularity has only been renewed since in a good man of Cleves, whose mandibles have kindly been communicated to us by the savant Mentzelius.[1]

"Secondly, the Monodontes, or jaws with a single tooth. That genre furnishes us with two very remarkable species. Here, Messieurs, in my right hand, is the jaw of Pyrrhus, king of Epirus, and in my left hand, that of Prusias, son of the king of Bythinia, who was born monodontal, in the upper jaw, as is written in Plutarch. The jaw of Pyrrhus is all the more interesting because it was found under a shard of pottery that apparently came from the earthenware pitcher with which he was killed by an old woman on the day of the taking of Argos.

"Thirdly, the Anisodontes, jaws defective by virtue of ex-cess of default, which it has not been possible to categorize in the first two divisions, notably the broken-toothed."

(I was listening with all ears.)

"What is most extraordinary in this genre, and perhaps in all that we know and all that we can conjecture regarding past, present and future jaws is the jaw of Popocambou the Broken-toothed."

(I breathed out.)

1 The German botanist Christian Mentzel (1622-1701).

"Popocambou the Broken-toothed," he continued, opening respectfully a gold reliquary inlaid with silver, like the necklaces of the Shulamite, in which he exhibited I know not what mandibular form, which has no name in any language, as Tertullian might have put it. "This is the jaw of Popocambou the Broken-toothed."

Applause burst forth,

"Everyone can observe the absence of one of the upper incisors, and as that particularity is often encountered in vulgar jaws, as a consequence of certain maladies or percussions, I beg you to observe that it is not accidental in Popocambou the Broken-toothed. It results from the conformation of the maxillary bones of the great prince—which is to say, from a fault of the alveolae in that part of the august jaw, in which you would search in vain even for the dentiform verrucosity of oviparous quadrupeds and the dentivacal stria of birds."

(Movement.)

"If there were ever anything pleasant and honorable in our research, Messieurs," said the orator, in conclusion, with an expression of modest satisfaction, "it is, above all, having been able to observe that the adored monarch of whom Timbuktu conserves the memory so preciously belonged, by virtue of his jaw, to our class of Anomalata."

(Here the enthusiasm attained the highest degree.)

And I turned over in my bed.

Exhumation

I had turned toward the second table, which was occupied by a little old antiquarian, dry, pale, shrunken, defaced, eroded, furred, rusty, worn, pasty and unpolished, who had been found between two amphorae in an antediluvian crypt, while rummaging in the foundations of the great pyramid, and who owed to his mummiesque eternity the privilege of figuring in perpetuity as a stand-in for all the mummies that can be encountered on the globe, from the narrow sheaths of the Guanches to the profound caves of the Egyptians. His desk was flanked by four proud mummies, which stood upright, supported at the hip, their noses to the wind, their legs tense and alert: princely and royal mummies.

There was another mummy in front of him, so gracious, so slim and so dainty!

So much candor shone on her ingenuous forehead
So many amours played over her semi-naked breast! [1]

How softly those voluptuous arms must have embraced the body of a lover! How that supple and delicate body must have flexed with abandon on the arm of a lover!

---

1 The lines are improvised from an ode by the prolific François-Thomas-Marie Baculard d'Arnaud (1718-1805).

I know not what invincible power drew me to that mummy! I would have flown to it if respect had not stopped me.

"Messieurs," said the antiquary, "the young person you see is the grandmother of Popocambou."

Operation

"Gentle and touching model of all the virtues," the antiquarian continued, addressing the mummy, "is it necessary that you were stolen, in the flower of your youth, from a great nation of which you were the ornament and the hope?

"Dire and incomprehensible destiny, which only shows on earth the rarest perfections in order to teach us that nothing is durable down here and that the divine types of the most perfect human organization are those that are effaced most rapidly . . .

"Let it at least be permitted to us, chaste and glorious stem of our masters, to shed undrying tears over your fate and to sow new flowers every year over your tomb! Daughter and ancestor of kings, may the earth be light upon you . . ."

After that pathetic allocution, he armed himself with a freshly molded scalpel, introduced it profoundly into the throat of the queen mother between the two clavicles and opened her longitudinally all the way to the navel.

The purpose of that operation, which chilled Breloque and me with a holy horror, was to verify whether the subject of the demonstration was, as had been supposed, the young and beautiful princess, the Isis, the Astarté, the Venus of Timbuktu, the Alma Popocamba of I know not what Wolof griot—and no one is unaware that an old law of the land obliged people of quality to carry their death certificate in the stomach for the convenience of scientific research.

"It's her," said the antiquary, presenting to the expectant
assembly in the tips of his fingers a small scroll of vellum . . .
knotted with a white ribbon,
gilded on the edges,
and so neat,
so tightly
and so tidily wound . . .
And so white,
so elegant,
so genteel,
so subtle,
so pretty,
so polished,
so pink,
so curly,
so crammed,
so playful,
so dear,
so florid,
so unified,
so brown,
so painted,
so cared-for,
so bound,
so folded,
so smooth,
so creased,
so embroidered,
so bordered,
so guarded,
so powdered,
so cheerful,
so fond,
so brilliant,

so valiant,
so pleasant,
so shiny,
so bold,
so dainty,
so silvery,
in the sunlight,
so adorned,
so waxed,
so ambered,
so silky,
so well-wrought,
so honored,
so decorated,
so colored,
so iridescent,
so gaudy,
so multicolored,
so illustrated,
so figured,
so miniatured,
so overpainted,
that you would have sworn
that he had taken it,
from his sleeve.[1]

"It's her!" he repeated, ecstatically, with an indescribable mixture of joyful astonishment and astonished joy.

But it would be necessary to have seen, in order to judge it, a guinea-fowl that has turned over a ruby bracelet in its trough, or one of our chickens that had just found a knife with a mother-of-pearl handle.

---

1 This list, which is rhymed in the original, thus forming a poem of sorts, loses its effect in literal translation, where the paired rhymes cannot be preserved.

"You can be assured," he continued, "by deciphering this rebus with me, for the explanation of which the royal society of tented unearthers of hieroglyphs would give you a large bonus, payable at your choice on a zodiac or on an obelisk, on a sphinx or on a pyramid, first-class merchandise.

(Oh, how I gazed at it!)

But may the devil carry me away if I saw anything there other than:

Syrian cobras,

Mystifrised flowers,

Hooded geese,

Statipedal storks

Globiferous scarabs,

Death's-heads with the rump of a lioness,

Crouching apes with the faces of dogs,

And other Isiac and Osiriac nonsense, which our antiquary deciphered as fluently as you would have done your *pater noster* written in molded letters.

Unfortunately, it was in such a low voice . . .

And note that I had sworn to forget my acoustic funnel every time I attended a lecture!

The assimilation of the orator's ideas was, in any case, so compact, their filiation so abrupt, their consanguinity so intimate, their concatenation so tight, their collusion so adherent, their isology so indestructible, and their conclusion so laconic, that anyone would have lost . . .

I don't say a paragraph!

But a sentence. . .

I don't say a sentence!

But a phrase . . .

I don't say a phrase!

But a full fraction, significative and complex, like the substantive and the attribute, or the pronoun and the verb . . .

I don't say a fraction of meaning!

But a word . . .
I don't say one of those essential words that stand alone!
But a simple verbal root . . .
I don't say a verbal root!
But a syllable as trivial as one can imagine . . .
I don't say a syllable!
But a characteristic letter . . .
I don't say a characteristic letter!
But a euphonic letter,
An etymological letter,
A mimological letter,
A phraseological letter,
A battalogical letter,
An anagogical letter,
A diagogical letter,
A paragogical letter.
I don't say any of those parasitical letters!
But a cedilla,
A tilde,
A trema,
A closure of parentheses,
An apostrophe,
An accent,
A comma,
A sigh,
A spirit,
A zephyr,
A dot . . .
Anyone, I say, would have lost in that lecture the most
infinitely petty division of human thought that it is possible
to submit

        To Bacon,
        To Leibnitz
        And to me,

and would not have known any more about the grand-mother of Popocambou than the good Mistigri ever knew about the equivocal sex of the great cockchafer . . .

See, then, what little use science is!

Poor Mistigri!

I admit that, tormented by a curious inquietude, by the studious need to simulate the intelligent organ that contains the soul, and which nevertheless sleeps like the body when it is fatigued, I had recourse to my Spanish tobacco . . .

But I was preoccupied by an attention so forceful . . .

The springs of my intelligence were tightened with such an unusual vigor . . .

My faculties, absorbed by the contemplation of that mummy and by the development of its mystical history, were so incapable of ubiquity . . .

My intellectual self and my material self had suffered a divorce so abrupt and so complete . . .

And it resulted naturally that the spontaneity of my physical movements was so poorly regulated by the operations of my mind . . .

That what has probably sometimes happened to you on similar occasions finally happened . . .

After having slid ten times under my fingers the light boards of polished laburnum, the imperceptible hinges of which are fitted so tastefully in the accursed village where the English captured Wallace . . .

(That episode could take me a long way, and I believe, in any case, that it is sovereignly futile.)

What is certain is that I opened my box the wrong way and that the caustic powder spread into the scholarly atmosphere with a frightful suddenness. Several thousand wig-heads, surprised by its numbing vapor, pirouetted on their pivots, and the four great mummies at the demonstration table sneezed so loudly that everybody woke up.

Position

And I found myself in the middle of my bedroom, with one leg shod and the other bare.

Distraction

But that did not get my toilette much further forward. My silk stockings were the wrong way round and I had put my left foot into my right pantoufle.

Reception

You might perhaps accuse me of having wasted a lot of time before acquitting Gervais' commission, for, since I have been in Milan, we have had a digression in Girolamo's theater, a voyage to Timbuktu, an excursion of sorts to Egypt and a session at the Institute. That was very long. Fortunately, I am able to respond to you in complete surety of conscience, my Breguet watch in hand, that I have arrived in Milan at sunset, that I have not slept for more than twenty-seven minutes, and here I am, ready for the soirée of the Marquise de Chiappapomposa, the idol of those infantile days when a coquette alarmed Amour by showing him a bell-cord.

At the moment when I went into the drawing room, my gaze fell upon the bell-cord. I blushed. It had been eighteen years since I had been in Milan. I approached the marquise with a sentiment of compunction that contained even more shame than regret, and only raised my eyes to her tremulously. I hardly recognized her.

"Not so stupid," said Breloque . . .

Oh, young reader, whoever you are (but how old are you, if you please? Let's say twenty-three years on Saint Sylvester's Day; it's take it or leave it, and I believe I can treat you as a friend . . .)

Oh, young reader, if you are condemned to grow old, if your cheerful forehead must one day be veiled by borrowed hair—and I sympathize with your misfortune, even if it is fitted with more art than the gallant wig of an academician of Timbuktu—if some memory of youth still finds a place in your chilled brain . . . dream, dream often of your first mistress—there is no sweeter pastime—but refrain carefully from seeing her again!

Everyone knows what a soirée in Milan is like, from the embarrassment when one enters to the curiosity when one has entered to the timidity when one is known to the embarrassment when one is not; young women who peep anxiously, young men who look you up and down boldly; slightly mature women all plumed, all tittivated and all illuminated, who mount assaults against one another with cunning lies and, each for her own part, clandestine gossip; important figures wearied by their life of representation, who nevertheless believe themselves to be obliged to display their magnificent ennui every evening in a new circle; the fashionable poet, finally, spouting, with his eyebrow raised in a sign of inspiration, flaccid and cold verses that inspiration has betrayed, listening to them without rivals, proud of hearing them resonate under the vaults of the palace, by courtesy of an echo that they will not find either in the public or in posterity.

But above all, what is never lacking in a circle, what you will infallibly find in Inverness as in Ragusa, in Cadiz as in Tobolsk, at Odessa as in Cairo, what you will perhaps find today even in Timbuktu, is a brilliant and bold young man with a fashionable cravat, windblown hair, a top hat lined with cherry-red satin, an orange waistcoat, pearl gray stockings embroidered with hoops, a scrutatory lorgnon, imperturbable self-assurance and a loud voice, whom you encountered once at Tortoni's, or next to whom you yawned one evening at Favart's, and who, without asking whether or not you are traveling at the behest of Monsieur Metternich, throws you a familiar salute from the other end of the drawing room.

"But it's him, it's Théodore, the most amiable prince in the confederation! Oh, dear friend, let me embrace you!"

"Damn you!" said Breloque

"What a fortunate event," he continues, linking arms with you familiarly, putting his hand on your shoulder and making you pirouette in a cavalier fashion in front of everyone, in order that no one can be in any doubt as to the intimacy of that sudden and inevitable amity.

"But," he goes on, in a lower voice, "you're newly arrived here. You need a cicerone, and as I've been in Milan for five days, you couldn't have found anyone better to bring you up to date with the local gossip . . ."

He had not stopped talking, but while his phrases came to die in my ear, like the confused buzz of an importunate insect, my eyes had paused on a young woman of the rarest beauty and the most dazzling adornment, who was there, alone, pensive, and melancholy, leaning against one of the pillars of the colonnade.

"Oh, I understand," he said. "It's there that you want to commence, and that really isn't bad. I recognize the exercised taste that distinguished you among all amateurs; it's an affair to attempt. In her position, one belongs to the first comer, and a man who arrives with your advantages . . . I thought about it, but I've been taken higher."

"In truth," retorted, measuring him, "that's possible."

"All right! The heart is occupied. You only have attentions for her. Agree that it would have been unfortunate if those lovely dark eyes had never opened to the light."

"What do you mean?"

"What do I mean? That she was born blind. She's the daughter of a rich businessman from Antwerp who only had that child from a wife who died young and left him with profound regrets."

"You think so?"

"It must be the case, since he quit his house, which was, it's said, more flourishing than ever, and left Antwerp, after having distributed magnificent presents to his employees and pensions to his domestics."

"And then what became of him?" I said, with the impatience of a curiosity that was gradually increasing.

"Oh, that's a romance, which would bore you . . . but then, what do I know? The fellow went where we all go once, in order to say that we've been to the cold valley of Chamouny, whose bleak marvels I've never understood, and, astonishingly, he stayed there for several years. Haven't you heard mention of him? A bourgeois name . . . Monsieur Robert, that's it."

"And then?" I said.

"Finally," he continued, "an oculist restored the little girl's sight. Her father took her to Geneva, and in Geneva she became smitten with an adventurer, who abducted her because her father refused him as a son-in-law."

"Her father had judged the wretch accurately."

"He had judged him all the better because the adventurer disappeared with all the gold and diamonds he had succeeded in taking. It's said that the gallant fellow was already married in Naples, and had been sentenced to capital punishment in Padua. The law has reclaimed him."

"And Monsieur Robert?"

"Monsieur Robert died of chagrin, but that event made no great impression. He was a species of visionary, a man with bizarre ideas who, among other extravagances, had conceived for his daughter the most ridiculous establishment. Can you imagine that he wanted to marry her to a blind man?"

"The poor woman!"

"Not so unfortunate, my dear. Little considered, in truth; it's the necessary consequence of a fault among those poor creatures; but consideration only serves the poor."

"Is that true?"

"As I tell you. Look, rather! Oh, my friend, one has many privileges with an income of two hundred thousand francs a year and eyes like those!"

"Eyes, eyes! A curse upon her eyes! It's them that have given her to Hell!"

Retribution

There is a horrible leaven of cruelty in my heart. I would like those who have made others suffer to suffer, once, all the suffering they have caused. I would like that impression to be lacerating, and profound, and atrocious, and irresistible; I would like it to grip the soul like a red-hot iron; I would like it to penetrate the marrow of the bones like molten lead; I would like it to envelop all the organs of life like the devouring shirt of Nessus.

I would like it, however, to be of short duration, and to finish with a dream.

I had fixed on Eulalie one of those gazes that make women feel ill when they do not flatter them—I don't know where I had learned it. She got up from the pedestal that she was embracing so sadly and stood before me, motionless and almost frightened.

I approached her slowly. "And Gervais?" I said to her.
"Who?"
"Gervais!"
"Oh, Gervais," she said putting her hand over her eyes.
That scene had something strange about it, which would have astonished the most assured soul. I appeared there as an unknown intermediary: penitence or remorse.

"Gervais," I said, vehemently, seizing her arm. "What have you done about him?"
She fell down. I do not know whether she was dead.

Equitation

"As long as the womanly species exists, as long as it dances, as long as it turns, as long as it fidgets, as long as its strives, as long as it hops, as long as it flutters, you will see everything finish, by virtue of the male desire to be charmed or by virtue of the rage of vanity," said Breloque. "That is what doomed Patricia, Patricia herself, a mare of such rich coloration and such a beautiful coat, a thoroughbred mare, a château mare, a titled mare, a very noble mare; the mare of officially entitled madmen and the Prince of Fools.

"Oh, she was, trust me, a grandiose, beautiful, energetic and vigorous mare. That is because she had earned her litter in battles. It is because you would not have read a pamphlet of those times in which there was no mention of Patricia.

"*Hic*, Fredegarius;[1]

"*Illic*, Gregorius Turonensis;[2]

"*Qui* Ariosto;

"*Qua*, Tasso;

"*Ci*, Mézeray;[3]

"*Ça*, Daniel:[4]

"*And* Shakespeare himself.

---

1 Fredegarius is the name belatedly attributed to the author of a Frankish chronicle of the seventh century, subsequently augmented by other hands.
2 The historian and legend-monger Gregory of Tours (538-594).
3 The historian François Eudes de Mézeray (1610-1683).
4 The Jesuit historian Gabriel Daniel (1649-1728).

"And God knows, said Monsieur Voltaire, whether she would have been a marvel at Fontenay . . ."

"Did you know Patricia, Breloque?"

"I should think so. I nearly mounted her. And why should I not have mounted her?

"Triboulet mounted her.[1]

"Caillette mounted her.

"Brusquet mounted her.

"Thoni mounted her.

"Sibilot mounted her.

"Angoulevent mounted her.

"Molinet mounted her.

"Taupin mounted her.

"Patz mounted her.

"Jouan mounted her.

"Drumoinet mounted her.

"Tabarin mounted her.

"Monsieur Guillaume mounted her.

"Bluet d'Arbères, Comte de Permission, mounted her.

"Polyte mounted her, Polyte, the wisest of fools, who remonstrated so much with Abbé de Bourgueil.

"Pape-Them mounted her, who had the honor of being, while he was alive, the jester of Emperor Charles Quint.

"Maretz mounted her; Maretz, who flattered himself with having made the sad Louis XIII smile, who disputed royal favor momentarily with the brilliant Cinq-Mars and little Baradas.

---

1 This name and the five that follow are those of the most famous *fous* [court jesters] in French history; the other figures are more esoteric and some are probably improvised, although Bernard Bluet d'Arbères, "Comte de Permission," who was in service with Charles Emmanuel I, Duc de Savoie in the early sixteenth century, achieved some notoriety. Although the list was published long before Joseph Oscar Delepierre (1802-1879) published his definitive *Histoire littérare des fous* (1860) Nodier would have been familiar with Delepierre's work on macaronic language, his work as an archivist and his activity as an avid book-collector, and it is possible that the list owes something to him.

"Langeli mounted her; the unfortunate Langeli whom Boileau so unjustly reduced to the level of Alexander.[1]

"Oh, how I would have mounted her if I had wanted to!

"When I saw her, although a trifle decrepit, she still had the scent of a high-class mare. She still whinnied with impatience and courage; she sought the skirmish, summoned combatants. She scraped the ground with her foot, she took the bit between her teeth *ut dicitur ubiquaque.* She was a proud mare.

"But Patricia ended up growing old; and Patricia, I have to say, had never been noted for her intelligence. The habitude of the court ended up dooming her, and when it was permissible for her to replace her burning and dusty irons with morocco leather heels she became what you have seen: prudish, bigoted, precious, pretentious and disagreeable, like a stupid mare. She started employing her time making passes and passing wind, in masquerades and fanfares; running in the circus to show off her graces; gilding her curb-chain, talking her bells and offering her curtseys for admiration; to follow, contrary to the sun, the stupid beast, the shadow of her large plumes. She ran, she trotted, she galloped, she flew, she gamboled and she pranced, and it's lucky that she didn't break Triboulet's neck.

"Then, one day, Malotru, the head groom, came to say to us, while turning his giant, gross, gray, greasy, vile cap in his hands: "With respect, Messieurs, it's no longer worth the trouble of sorting out Patricia's straw, of sieving her oats through silk, brushing her with fine silver curry-combs and spending ten times as much on the embroideries of her blanket than it takes to maintain the stables of our men-at-arms.

"Patricia is finished.

"Patricia is going blind.

"Patricia is lame.

"Patricia is worn out.

---

1 The fool in question, who served Louis XIII, was actually named Angeli, but Nicolas Boileau-Despréaux referred to him in a poem as "L'Angeli."

"Patricia is coughing.

"Patricia has broken teeth, like Popocambou.

"Patricia is no longer good for anything.

"Patricia has had her day.

"Patricia's life is over."

"Did you see Patricia die, Breloque?"

"Wait a little. 'How painful it is,' she said to me, turning her worn velvet blinkers away with a languid gesture, 'how cruel it is to see oneself abandoned by everyone, including Triboulet, when one is descended from Job's horse and Gargantua's mare, or a few illustrious individuals of the same species. You can see that in my genealogy!'

"'Madame,' I replied to her, kissing her hoof respectfully, 'everything finishes in this transitory world. Triboulet, whom you have done me the honor of mentioning, went to join his ancestors a long time ago, who had believed him to be immortal; and the lodge of the Prince of Fools—the last was named Nicolas Joubert[1]—has been closed for more than two hundred years at the Hôtel de Bourgogne, in spite of the edict of Parlement, which conformed his possession of it on the nineteenth of February 1608, on the plea of Master Julius Peleus, so Don Pic de Fanferluchio tells me.'

"'What do I care?' she replied, impatiently. 'I'm none the less, by virtue of ordinances and letters patent, the young, beautiful and spirited mare of the Prince of Fools . . .'

"So young, so beautiful and so spirited that you would have given a hundred like her for the milkmaid's donkey!

"And that's the vanity of women and mares!"

---

1 The self-styled Nicolas Joubert d'Angoulevent, one of Henri IV's *fous*, did declare himself the last Prince of Fools, but the title was not uncontested.

Imposition

What I wanted to know—for I was convinced that Triboulet's mare had to die, neither more nor less than Charlemagne's nephew . . .

What I wanted to know . . . but that's not putting it strongly enough . . .

What obsessed me day and night, what devoured my life for weeks, months and years, what transformed into cruel sufferings the joyful forgetfulness of my flourishing youth . . .

And what the devil had I to sort out, I ask you, with Triboulet's mare?

It was the invincible need, the determined will to verify whether that unlucky squire succeeded in mounting his mare or in mounting another . . .

"It's true," said Breloque, more emotional than is characteristic, "that when you've mounted a good mare for a long time,

"You've put her through her paces;

"You've made her walk;

"You've made her amble;

"You've made her stride out;

"You've made her trot;

"You've made her gallop.

"You've stretched her, sustained her, retained her, made her rear up;

"You've made her turn, paw the ground, dance, jump, prance, pirouette, and spin, with a gymnastic kiss or a cavalieresque command.

"But what do you expect to do with a dead mare?"

"Do you believe," I said, interrupting Breloque with a concentrated emotion, "that he was ever able to find such a mare again?"

"He found several," Breloque replied. "I saw him recently astride a grand mare from England, a cousin of John Bull's mare—John Bull is Triboulet's cousin. She was, in truth, a brisk and agile mare, vivacious and bold, broad in the rump, trenchant in the saddle, strong in the neck, supple in the hindquarters, solid in the pastern, as good to mount and dismount as the Bucephalus of King François, which accommodated everyone, although she was a trifle restive to her rider, and neither you nor I could have mounted her."

"And why couldn't I mount the banal mare of that madman with innumerable faces whom you call the Prince of Fools?"

"If Your Highness will permit, dare I ask him first how he pays his personal contribution, fundamental and variable, direct and indirect, over the extent of his principality?"

"The exact sum at which the infamous Judas Iscariot of criminal memory dared to evaluate the life of the Man-God—thirty deniers of bell-metal, minus my legal rebate. But what does that have to do with it?"

"Everything, and that's hit the nail on the head. All that wealth wouldn't be sufficient to discount your patent as a gentleman or your license as a prince if they weren't already endorsed in Timbuktu, for nobility is beyond price, and so are mares. No one any longer bestrides a household mare—except for horse-dealers—unless he pays the treasury at least fifty genuine gold coins, heavy, shiny, with a fine ring and a full weight, and one wouldn't mount a political mare of high quality when one comes out freshly molded from the Hippodrome. As with the tax, so with the squire."

I was suffocating with indignation.

"What!" I said. "It will be said that I've passed the days of a robust adolescence trotting on the flat, pressing the bare flanks of recalcitrant Andalusiam mares, overworking barbaric mares that have never felt the bit, rivaling the proudest professors of equitation and hippiatrics, and I'm banned with impunity from mounting Triboulet's mare like anyone else!"

"It's only too true," said Breloque, in a resolute tone. "You unite in yourself alone

"Grison,

"Fiaschi,

"Vargas,

"La Broue,

"Malateste,

"Pluvinel

"Tapia de Salcedo,

"Menou,

"Cavendish,

"Imbotti,

"Winter,

"Ridinger,

"Eisenberg,

"Ruzé,

"Laguérinière,

"Saunier,

"Garsault,

"Solleyzel,

"Drummond de Melfort,

"Dupaty de Clam,

"Montfaucon de Riogles,

"Mottin de la Balme,

"Astley,

"Pembroke,

"Thiroux,

"Mazzuchelli,

"Gambado,

"Viter,

"Amoreux,

"Bourgelat,

"Robinet,

"Cabero,

"La Fosse,

"Flandrin,

"Huzard,

"Chabert,

"And Franconi . . .[1]

"I'll say more; you could jump the ribbon and the hoop with Don Quixote's Rosinante or Don Japhet of Armenia's Criquet, but you'd never receive in the arena where she maneuvers quadripedally the financial mount of the Prince of Fools if you hadn't succeeded, by means of some rich heritage that you scarcely expect, or some rare industry that you don't know, in exhibiting one day at the door the invoice of a good eligibilifying contribution."

"I'd rather, Breloque, I swear by the finest of the chargers of the sun, whose name in Phlegon, that I'd rather mount all my life a broken-down, worn-out old horse, curded, curved, smitten, crooked, rickety, sick, knock-kneed, spiked, crowned, unshod, blunted, short-legged, bow-legged, with corns on its feet, bandaged, wheezing, squinting, cringing, foundered, coughing, varicose, eaten away by figs, bristles,

---

1 This list includes the names of several famous riding-masters and cavalry officers, along with veterinarians such as Claude Bourgelat (1712-1779), a contributor to the *Encyclopédie*; some of the names might have been improvised in order to inflate it. The inclusion of the contemporary veterinarian Jean-Baptiste Huzard (1755-1838) is significant, as Nodier would certainly have known of him as a notorious book-collector. He would certainly have seen the sons and grandsons of the famous equestrian Antonio Franconi (1737-1836) performing in the Cirque Olympique.

combs, nails, rasps, spindles, tumors, splints, ulcers, osselets, spurs, knots, swellings, furrows, caps, splits, boils, carbuncles, inflammations, spavins, anthrax, buboes and blisters than that capricious and interested mare!"

"Alas, Monseigneur, she's scarcely any better than that at present," replied Breloque, uttering a long sigh and wiping his eyes with the sleeve of his doublet. "Also, Monseigner," he continued, "if you knew how her grooms have labored her!

"How they've squabbled with her!

"Hoe they've pestered her!

"How they've squawked at her!

"How they've battled her!

"How they've braced her!

"How they've shoed her!

"How they've herded her!

"How they've clung to her!

"How they've searched her!

"How they've ragged her!

"How they've taken her slumming!

"How they've harnessed her!

"How they've dressed her!

"How they've curry-combed her!

"How they've spun her!

"How they've mucked her out!

"How they've wasted her!

"How they've grasped her!

"How they've nibbled her!

"How they've dotted her!

"How they've twisted her!

"How they've stripped her!

"How they've deprived her!

"How they've confounded her!

"Hoe they've muddied her!

"How they've charboiled her!

"How they've triboiled her!

"How they've soiled, foiled and spoiled her!

"How they've buried her!

"How they've let her loose!

"How they've set her loose . . ."

"In truth, Breloque?"

"So that you wouldn't recognize the figure of the mare from top to toe."

"The poor beast!"

Dotation

"Oh, my God," said Breloque, "with such a schedule of contribution, with what do you propose, Monseigneur, to constitute our dotation? On what will you found the noble Théodorian right of primogeniture, which is, between us, and without it surpassing us, the most solid hope of future aristocracies?"

"On what? Breloque! Have you seen an errant spider at the end of its thread, blown through the air? Ask it where it is going to attach itself? To a tree that the wind has planted in the corner of a wall ruined by time, which unfortunate shepherds have built in order to shelter from the storm, on the far side of a ditch hollowed out by the first comer? Is that nothing for an organic and sensitive being but the destiny of a spider? Is a six-foot grave nothing for a dead man? Apart from the giants that are shown in fairgrounds, almost all men would be at ease there. Oh, Breloque, if all the creatures that had crawled on this pile or this lump of mud[1]—for that variant of *Télémaque* is still in question—if some Gracchus of the dead came to demand in their name a proportional share of the earth's surface, an agrarian division of the common cemetery, in order to sleep there eternally, dear Breloque, the grave of an ant would acquire a higher price in the tariff of burials that the funeral of an Emperor has today!

---

1 The suble contrast between *monceau* [pile] and *morceau* [lump] loses something in translation.

"And you want a fallen prince, only too happy a hundred times over to have a grave for which to hope . . .

"It is at least dubious, at the point things have reached, that the Holy Alliance has the leisure to occupy my principality, although my principality is, in conscience, just as real, just as essential, just as substantial and just as plenipotential, as a good number of the principalities that the Holy Alliance has recognized in the last eight or ten months . . .

"Besides which, the kings of the earth have been so miserly for some time with their landed privileges that I cannot see, to tell the truth, a corner of the political map of Europe that can be given to me henceforth as an indemnity for my lost principality, a space where one could fit a poor little boy from Barcelona or the valley of Argelès, in order to enable Pierre de Provence and the beautiful Maguelonne[1] to dance on a thin piece of fir-wood:

"Pierre with his Spanish toque heightened by a glass bead, his worn red coat braided with fake gold and his tanned boots of an equivocal color, beaten by a floating tassel;

"Magdeleine with her little black fur hat, with a cockerel feather over her ear, her old green satin camisole and a fustian skirt . . .

"So I have no more of which to dispose than remains to me, Breloque, and I make you my testimentary executor . . ."

"Oh, what jewels!" cried Breloque.

---

1 *Pierre de Provence et la belle Maguelonne*, is the title of an eighteenth-century "Bibliothèque bleue" chapbook recycling a Medieval romance, which prompted the German Romantic Ludwig Tieck to write a new version in 1797.

Donation

"But if I proceed, Breloque, with the inventory of my wardrobe, don't suppose, in your foolish confidence, that it's to compete in magnificence with Jacques Coeur of Bourges or the rich Ango de Dieppe, our the Fourques of Augbsurg, or Nicolas Flamel of the parish of Saint-Jacques-la-Boucherie, or the honest lunatic who collected so many billions in diamonds in Cayenne. The imbecilic pride of fortune has never seduced me.

"I only want to leave to those I have loved a pledge more durable, alas, than this existence which is escaping me, of the inextinguishable tenderness that inflamed my heart before death will have made a cold ember of it:

"To Victorine, the sole lock of hair that my despair has spared, in the tribulations that her coquetry and her caprices have made me suffer. Oh, that the least of the wigs of that good trichomaniac prince might come to me now!

"To Diocles of Smyrna, a very exact median proportionality between the judgment of an ideologue and the imagination of a commentator . . .

"To Henry Dodwell, a beautiful map of my lordly rights, fiefs and freeholds, to be added to the next edition of the *Petits geographes* . . .

"To Doctor Abopacataxo, the dregs of my ink-bottle . . .

"To the Marquise de Chiappapomposa, a felt-lined bell without a clapper . . .

"To Patricia, a bit worn in the middle, incomplete in its two studs, against which I had the stupidity to exchange, on the Quai de la Feraille, the stem of an old pipe that I had smoked at Wagram . . .

"To the sublime Mistigri, a little godenot[1] in elder-wood, two inches and three lignes tall, with his coat of green paper, to make him an academician of sorts . . .

"To Popocambou, the better of my two pantoufles; but who the devil will give him the sole?

"You may distribute the rest as you wish, my ear Breloque: *scilicet*, or *si licet*, or *sic licet*. (What vivid ecstasy those beautiful variants would have procured my old and great friend Joseph Scaliger![2])

"The dried rose that I detached from its stem by striking it with my foot in a movement of romantic sensibility near the Rock of the Blind . . .

"Item, a few plumes of the last molt of the famous red and green lory that knew four pages and half a dozen rubrics. If it had not died in a fashion untimely for its glory and mine, it would have eclipsed all barristers of renown a long time ago . . .

"Item, the perch of which I made use to bring up Jeannette's surprising blackbird, which said 'I love you,' like Jeannette, and forgot it less promptly than she did . . .

"Item, three reseda seeds that Lubin had given to Lubine,[3] which she watered with her tears, our sweet Lubine, while gazing from her mansard in the Rue Saint-Martin-bleu-d'yeux to see whether he had returned from Flanders, the friend who had died at Walcheren!

---

1 A godenot was a grotesque human figurine made of wood or ivory, frequently used by street performers in tricks of sleight-of-hand.
2 The historian and chronologist Joseph Scaliger (1540-1609).
3 Probably the central characters of *Lubin ou le sot vangé* (1661), a farce by Raymond Poisson.

"Item, the straw that was to have rounded out the nest of my swallow, but which she no longer wanted for her nest. The storm that broke our last window, Breloque, had killed her chicks!"

"Item, a pip from the pear that my dear Thérèse bit into a moment before expiring, saying to me: 'Théodore . . . I'm still thirsty . . .'"

"Item, the pin with which Justine pricked herself in order to write in her blood that she still loved me (the wound inflicted by the pin had not healed before she had deceived me three times) . . .

"Item, a denier of worn fabric that she left me as a ledge of engagement . . .

"Item, the onion-skin of a pierced mirliton on which I played at sixteen: *As soon as our hearts love* . . . , and wore away for a long time playing: *Past felicity*, etc . . .

"Item—this, Breloque, merits attention! The numerivorous pencil of the great logarthimist, and all his works, into the bargain!

"Item, finally . . . . ."

"Item," said Breloque, in an anxious manner, "something will come from so many treasures to your faithful steward . . ."

"I'm coming to that, Breloque. I give you—listen carefully—first of all, my library."

"Good," said Breloque. "A thin book that has neither a beginning, nor an end, nor a middle, of which rats have eaten the edges!"

"I scarcely remember what it contains."

"Inconsequential pages, in which one discovers, with difficulty, under the mildew, a few disconnected phrases: *To philosophize is to learn to die* . . . *The soil over the head, and that's it forever* . . . *Where are you going, wedding guests?* Wait, wait, Monseigneur, what's this? *Chitterlings are not to be scorned between humans* . . . Damn! Beautiful words!"

"Enough, Breloque. You have in there all the verities necessary to the moral conduct of life. Don't seek to penetrate any further into the secrets of our infirm and wretched nature. It's not, however, to that gift that my benefits are limited."

"Good!" said Breloque.

"I give you, Breloque, all my rights, immunities and privileges over the principality of Nihil-no-not-night."

"Thanks!" said Beloque.

"Plus the net product of the second edition of our *Story of the King of Bohemia and his Seven Castles.*

"Thanks!" said Breloque.

"Plus, Breloque, our four brevets of the Order of the Lily, the Order of the Holy Sepulcher, the Order of the Phoenix and the Order of the Golden Spur."

"Thanks!" said Breloque

"And then . . . ?" added Breloque, nonplussed

"And then . . . ?" he repeated, in a peevish tone.

"For, in sum . . ." he growled, between his teeth, while recapitulating all of that on his fingers . . .

"And then, something even more precious."

"Aha!" said Breloque, breathing out.

"I give you my carriage, Breloque, my pretty traveling carriage, which took us to Timbuktu and will perhaps take us one day to Bohemia."

"Dare I ask Monseigneur where the carriage is garaged?" said Breloque, sniggering.

"Everywhere, Breloque, and that is what makes its convenience. I can make it descend into the entrails of the earth with the sound of an artesian well. Do you know, Breloque, the layers of the six creations? Have you discovered in the quarries of Montmartre the vegetal skeleton of a juncacea higher than the peak of Tenerife? Have you sometimes dreamed of saurians with immense wings that could have swallowed armies of elephants and hippopotamuses in a single gulp? What would you say about an insect whose weight would have crushed on its immortal base the inverted pyramid of Timbuktu? That's nothing. My carriage can take you into abysms where the hazardous bucket of the minor has never plunged, and where we leave far behind the futile hypotheses of the Vulcanists and the Neptunians. I can suspend you, Breloque, at the central point of the diameter of the earth, where isothenic force of the ambient atmosphere equilibrates so absolutely with the gravitation that the heaviest and most imponderable body you can imagine—an inauguration speech, a circumstantial epistle, a lesson in metaphysics—would remain there, difficult as it is to believe, eternally motionless between its eternal poles."

"I don't want to go there," said Breloque.

"Have you sometimes seen, on the stream of our village, the valve of a dry nut fleeing like a pirogue, carried away by the current, sometimes pirouetting on a little swirling wave, sometimes running into a reef between two iris stems or two water-lily leaves, drifting like the old hull of a ship after a desiccation, set afloat again by a downpour, without a mast, oars or a flag, at the whim of the wind and rain? That is the nautical vessel in which I travel the immense folds of the world's girdle! I descend the long courses of rivers, between banks enriched by pompous vegetation; I see cities repeating their magnificent panoramas in the immense crystal that I labor with my assured keel. I arrive at the seas on my deck soaked by the silvery foam of a favorable tide, or drops of water that fall in pearls from the quivering wings of cormorants. Soon the birds disappear. I can scarcely still see some flying fish closing its membranous fins, dried by a ray of sunlight, falling from a height into the sea, or some stray bonita leaping. The ocean is open to me, with its isles and its worlds. Would you like, Breloque, to head for the northern passage of America, or shall we trouble, on the enchanted shores of Tahiti, the slumber of some young queen?"

"Damn," said Breloque.

"If, however, you prefer, you can see the north wind carrying away the wing of a dead butterfly, or the impalpable down that it has expelled from a newly abandoned nest, or the spinning leaflet of a linden seed; or the silvery feather of a floccular seed rising and swaying like an aerostat, and fleeing in order to drop its light silken anchors on the other side of a mountain; or, better still, the flakes of white snow that a planetary virgin has allowed to fall from her hair, and which the lightest emanation of her breath send back to the sky from which they have descended? Behold my aerial carriage, the one with which I visit the Suns . . .

"And if you wanted to voyage in the nearest gutter . . ."

"In truth, no!" said Breloque.

"I would have at your service the invisible equipage of the rotifer, and we would visit with it a microcosm incomparably vaster than the universe given to science by Herschel's telescope."

"Go for your carriage," said Breloque, leaping aboard. "Roll on, and at the end of the ditch is the crash; but if Doctor Abopactataxo were here, he would demonstrate to you, by arithmetical reasoning, Monseigneur, that all your capital isn't worth a handful of loose change."

"It is, however, my dear Breloque, all that remains in this old pine dresser that our hostess has lent us."

Supputation

"What if I were to go in one jump to Bohemia," I said, when I woke up in the morning. "The calculation isn't difficult!"

My adventures in the amphitheater of Verona demand at least one volume;

My sentimental and romantic promenades on Lake Como, one volume;

Breloque's escapade with the spirited novice nun of the Torre dei Confizzi, one volume, unless I keep my confessions to myself; but the public is so demanding!

I cannot in all conscience meditate as little as one volume on the ruins of Venice. I know a publisher who would make six of them.

Only employing thirty-two volumes in the conscientious description of the whole country, from the low lagoons to the counterscarp of Koenigsgratz—if I only leave from Treviso and the fish market—I'd need thirty-six preliminary volumes.

I ought to declare that this one isn't included in the count.

Now, if I give one minute a day to sensation,

One minute a day to perception,

One minute a day to apprehension,

One minute a day to comprehension,

One minute a day to reflection,

One minute a day to discussion,

One minute a day to intuition,

One minute a day to meditation,
One minute a day to invention,
One minute a day to disposition,
One minute a day to distribution,
One minute a day to execution,

And fourteen hundred and twenty-eight minutes to distraction and sleep (that is really the smallest measure of relaxation and repose that one can dispense in a life occupied with such vast and serious labors) . . . that makes fourteen hundred and forty minutes from which I could depart daily in favor of *The Story of the King of Bohemia and his Seven Castles.*

But, the composition of the first volume having cost me thirty years, three weeks and a few hours—we'll only count thirty years, in order to avoid the calculation of fractions—I can scarcely furnish my last book before the month of March in the year 1909.

And between now and 1909? My word, I'll see Gervais beforehand; From Milan to Chamouny you only have a short stroll, especially by traversing the Sea of Ice via the land of Aoste, like Lady Very-Mad and Miss Frolicsome. And you're almost sure, at least, of not finding the agents of the treasury or the policemen of the alliance.

Desolation

It was the time; it was the place; it was the rock. But Gervais was not there.

The sun was shining brightly; all the daisies were blooming and all the violets were perfuming the air. Only the Alpine roses had not grown back.

But Gervais was not there.

I approached his bench. He had forgotten his long laburnum staff there, knotted with a green ribbon with characters printed in relief. That circumstance worried me.

I called Gervais. A voice replied: "Gervais." I thought it was an echo. I turned in that direction and I saw Marguerite coming toward me leading a dog on a leash. They stopped. I recognized Puck, but Puck did not appear to recognize me; he was tormented by another idea, an indefinable idea. He had his nose in the air, his ears raised, his paws immobile but tense, as if preparing to run.

"Alas Monsieur," Marguerite said to me. "Have you seen Gervais?"

"Gervais?" I replied. "Where is he?"

Puck turned toward me as if to look at me, because he had heard me. He approached me at the full extent of his leash. I stroked him with my hand; he licked it—and then he resumed his station.

"Monsieur," she said to me. "I can thank you now; it's you who gave him that spaniel, which he loved so much, to console him for the loss of his barbet, which he loved so much. The poor animal had not been in the valley for a week when he was struck by a malady of the eyes like his master. He's blind."

I lifted up the silky hair on Puck's head. He was blind. Puck turned his head, licked my hand again, and then howled.

"It's for that reason," Marguerite continued, "that Gervais hadn't brought him yesterday."

"Yesterday, Marguerite? He hasn't been home since yesterday?"

"Oh, Monsieur, it's incomprehensible, and has astonished everyone. Can you imagine that there was a big storm on Sunday, and that a seigneur arrived at our house; I could have sworn that it was an English milord who had come down the Burt with a straw hat, all beribboned, and a glacier-staff with a chamois horn handle, but wet, wet, wet!"

"What does that matter?"

"While I went to search for faggots to dry him off, Monsieur de Roberville remained alone with Gervais."

"Monsieur de Roberville!"

"That was his name, and I don't know what he said to him, but yesterday, Gervais was very sad. However, he seemed more in haste than ever to go to the esplanade, so hasty that I hardly had time to throw his blue mantle over his shoulders, because it had rained a great deal the day before, as I said, and the weather was still cold and damp. 'Mother,' he said to me when we went out, 'I beg you to keep Puck here and care for him. His petulance inconveniences me slightly, and if I drop the leash, we might not be able to find one another again.' I brought him here, but when I came to look for him, I couldn't find him."

"Gervais!" I cried. "My good Gervais!"

"Oh, Gervais! My son Gervais! My little Gervais!" said the poor woman.

And Puck! He was biting his leash, and bounding around us impatiently.

"If you let Puck go," I said to her, "perhaps he'll be able to find Gervais?"

I don't know whether I had reflected on that means, but the leash was cut.

I scarcely had time to perceive it. Puck gathered himself, made four bounds, and I heard a noise like that of a body falling into the gulf of the Arveyron.

"Puck! Puck!"

When I got there, the little dog had disappeared, and I saw a blue mantle floating over the turbulent gulf.

Humiliation

Since Don Pic de Fanferluchio had opined that all the questions of verbal criticism that my narration could raise were reduced to the famous catachresis of the green ribbon, he had rested his head on the back of the chair and was asleep, his slumber slightly agitated because he was dreaming about the three etymologies on which his opinion was not yet fixed, that of *baccara*, that of *farandole*, and that of *calembredaine*.

I therefore searched with my eyes for Breloque, who formed my entire audience on his own (Victorine was in the bath, or elsewhere); and I remarked with pleasure that he was probably not asleep. He was standing up.

I was about to interrogate him regarding the impression that the story of the amours of Gervais and Eulalie had produced on him, but I surprised him in one of his characteristic attitudes, which spared the expense of a question to an interrogative yawn of *L'Ingenu*.[1] His right arm was wound in a quarter-circle at head height, his hand extended and widely deployed; his mouth was rising convulsively in the opposite direction—which is to say, from right to left—as if to stifle a yawn under a grimace; and his left shoulder, which is naturally somewhat deformed, approached his ear spontaneously, in such a manner as to express almost as distinctly as speech an idea that you could translate into vulgar language as:

---

1 A 1767 novella by Voltaire, known in English as "Master Simple."

What a Pity

I don't know if you know the physiognomic symptoms of it, but when you see a man in a similar position, you can bet boldly that he is bored to death. I would gladly take half your bet.

I have said that the phrase that I was preparing was a kind of interrogation, and you know that there are affirmative integrations that testify to an imperturbably self-consciousness, to which one cannot respond negatively without offense. "Great God, do I have wit, my dear Breloque? Don't you find that story admirably recounted?"

It was in that mold that I had cast my question. When I perceived Breloque, I launched my mold into the garden of an excellent Toulousan poet of my acquaintance, who has often served since.

The second of the molds between which I had to choose was the dubitative mold in which one pretends to throw out an uncertain thought in order to produce the response one desires. "Between us, is it good or bad? Tell me, my dear Breloque, whether you like the story a little?"

But those concessions were repugnant to my dignity. In any case, Breloque's dispositions were so manifest, and the mold of an ironic question is so fitting to the chagrin of a wounded author.

"It appears that Monsieur Breloque is not extremely satisfied?" I said, in a bitter tone.

Breloque removed with a nod of the head his Basque cap surmounted by a stork feather—that was his ceremonial costume that day—drew his legs together, brought his arms close to his body, opened his hands on an exactly horizontal plane, and with the voice of a street singer intoned the following verses:

> *Of two lovers of Aiguperse,*
> *Learn the piteous case.*
> *They were born to great distress*
> *Blind in both their eyes . . .*

"I understand you, Breloque; you mean that the subject isn't new, and I wish it were even less so. The productions of the mind only live by means of form. Would you dare to compare a bad village song . . ."

"Why not," said Breloque. "A bad village song that says what it has to say is worth as much as a mannered romance . . ."

"Mannered!"

"That's the word. Affectation for grace, the sentimental for the tender, declamation for eloquence, the commonplace for the naïve . . ."

"Breloque!"

"I'm telling you the truth, Monseigneur. I'm not your highness's fool for nothing. If you're not content, wake Don Pic and talk to him abut catachreses . . ."

"I've never seen you in this mood! What, even my pretty dog . . . ?"

"That spaniel with long ears? He has fluffy fur, as if he descended ready varnished and glazed from a painting by Watteau. Oh, he's a long way from Brisquet's dog . . ."

"And what, in God's name, is Brisquet's dog?"

"Brisquet's dog?" said Breloque. "Alas, he's only a dog; but he's a dog, a veritable dog, whose story contains neither unnecessary descriptions, nor speeches with sonorous periods, nor dramatic combinations, nor verbal artifices. His story is simply that of Brisquet's dog . . ."

"And that story?"

"Here it is," said Breloque.

Opposition

The Story of Brisquet's Dog

Monseigneur,

In our forest of Lions, near the hamlet of Goupillière, very close to a large well that belongs to the Chapelle Saint-Mathurin, there was a good man, a woodcutter by estate, whose name was Brisquet, or otherwise, the splitter with a good ax, who lived poorly on the produce of his faggots, with his wife, whose name was Brisquette. The good God had given them two pretty little children, a boy seven years old who was brown-haired, and whose name was Biscotin, and a blonde girl six years old, whose name was Biscotine. Apart from that they had a mongrel dog with curly hair, black throughout its body except for its muzzle, which was the color of flame; it was the best dog in the region for its attachment to its masters.

They called it Bichonne, because it was probably a bitch.

You will recall the time when a great many wolves came to the forest of Lions. It was in the year of great snows, when poor people had great difficulty living. There was a terrible desolation in the land.

Brisquet, who always went to work and had no fear of wolves, because of his good ax, said to Brisquette one morning: "Wife, I beg you not to let Biscotin and Biscotine out

213

until the great wolf-hunter has come. They would be in danger. They have enough walking between the hill and the pond, since I planted pickets along the pond to preserve them from accidents. I beg you, too, not to let Bichonne out, who only asks to run free."

Brisquet said the same thing to Brisquette every morning. One evening he did not arrive at the usual time. Brisquette went to the doorstep, came back inside, went back again, and said, putting her hands together: "My God, how late he is!"

Then she went outside again, shouting: "Hey, Brisquet!"

And Bichonne leapt up to her shoulders, as if to say: "Can't I go?"

"Peace!" Brisquette said to him. "Listen, Biscotine; go as far as the hill to see whether your father isn't coming back. And you, Biscotin, follow the path along the pond, making very sure that there are no pickets missing, and shout very loudly: 'Brisquet! Brisquet!' Peace, Bichonne!"

The children went, and when they met up at the place where the path along the pond intersected the one to the hill, Biscotin said: "Damn it, I'll find our poor father, or the wolves will eat me."

"Well," said Biscotine, "they'll eat me too."

In the meantime. Brisquet had come back by the high road to Puchay, passing by the Croix aux Anes at the Abbaye de Mortemer because he had a bundle of firewood to deliver to Jean Paquier.

"Have you seen our children?" Brisquette asked him.

"Our children?" said Brisquet. "My God, have they gone out?"

"I sent them to the hill and the pond to meet you, but you took another route."

Brisquet did not put down his good ax. He started running toward the hill.

"Should you take Bichonne?" shouted Brisquette.

Bichonne was already far away. She was so far away that Brisquet soon lost sight of her.

He had shouted "Biscotin! Biscotine!" in vain; no one replied to him.

Then he started to weep, because he imagined that his children were lost.

After having run for a long, long time it seemed to him that he recognized Bichonne's voice. He marched straight into the undergrowth at the place where he had heard it, entering it with his ax held high. Bichonne had arrived there at the moment when Biscotin and Biscotine were about to be devoured by a huge wolf. She had thrown herself forward, barking, in order that the noise would warn Brisquet. With a blow of his good ax, Brisquet felled the wolf, stone dead, but it was too late for Bichonne, She was no longer alive.

Brisquet, Biscotin and Biscotine rejoined Brisquette. There was great joy, and yet everyone was weeping. There was no gaze that was not searching for Bichonne.

Brisquet buried Bichonne at the bottom of his little yard under a large stone on which the schoolmaster wrote in Latin:

Here lies Bichonne, Brisquet's poor dog

And it is since that time that people have said, as a common proverb: "As unlucky as Brisquet's dog, which only went into the forest once and was eaten by a wolf."

Argumentation

Breloque did not believe himself to be obliged, like me, to the embarrassed circumlocutions of a timid author who is trying out his first composition before an imposing audience. He stood there, straight-legged, his fist on his hip, his head held high and his eye assured, like a tragic actor in the First Theater who seemed to be proffering the *Plaudite, Cives!* His sufficiency nonplussed me so much that I searched in my pocket for my Lumloch snuff-box in order to give myself countenance; but I had thrown it away indignantly on the fatal day when, as you know, it had caused me to miss the interesting lesson of the demonstrator of mummies.

"What does Monseigneur think of it?" he said.

"Can you, Breloque . . . ?" I said, blushing. "It's good, for a nurse's tale."

"What does it lack, in your opinion? I would gladly report it to Don Pic de Fanferluchio, if he were not asleep. (The good fellow does nothing else since you have taken him to the Institute.) The subject is simple, but interesting. The episodes are connected to it easily, or, rather, make an essential body with it. The narrative twist is striking and natural, the denouement pathetic and unexpected, and there emerges from it, as in an antique fable, a kind of adage that is engraved profoundly in the memory.

"Shall we talk about the characters? They are traced with so much skill that the exiguity of the frame takes nothing away from their development, and that there is no one, after having heard the story of Brisquet's dog, who does not know Brisquet, his wife his children and his dog as perfectly as after three months of residence in Goupillière. You wouldn't pass the door of a woodcutter's hut in the forest of Lions, in front of which a black dog with a flame-colored beard was barking, without exclaiming to yourself: 'Breloque, we're not lost—there's Brisquet's house!'

"What shall I say about the localities? You have no need of a compass, or guides, or maps, or an itinerary, or statistics, or an almanac to direct yourself in the land, and if a good woman emerged from the aforementioned hut, still young, with a benevolent physiognomy, a slightly worried but very mild gaze, who says to you: 'Since Monsieur is going toward Mortener, he can take the short cut between the hill and the pond, but the route isn't safe,' you would reply, without reflection: 'A thousand thanks, Madame; my intention is, in fact, to take the high road to Puchay, passing by the Croix aux Anes.' Alas, if Homer had imprinted a character of verity as naïve to his beautiful topography, of which I am far from contesting the merit, we would know the country of Troy better than the Plaine Saint-Denis.

"As for style, I am obliged to confess that it is neither picturesque, nor romantic, nor poetic, nor oratory, but it is what it ought to be: clear, simple, expressive, appropriate to the persons and the objects, intelligible to all minds, and, in consequence, essentially suitable."

I bit my lips until they bled. *The Amours of Gervais and Eulalie* were already printed but I threw my China paper copy far away over the pickets of the pond of Goupillière.

After that fine speech, Breloque swelled up like an orator on the left bank of the Seine reading three immense columns in the *Moniteur*, printed in *petit nompareille* or *parisienne*, or *sédanoise*, by means of which he had proved the day before, to the great advantage of his commentants, that one can easily make a balloon into a lantern by putting a lighted candle inside.

I had, however, something to respond, for all my humility does not forbid me a fit of impatience . . .

But I posit, in fact, that there is not a single person somewhat honorably placed in society who cannot judge by experience of the immense and sudden diversion produced in the most preoccupied mind by a post chaise stopping outside your house, especially if you are, by chance, the only tenant in residence . . .

Pif, paf, piaf, patapan . . .

I believe, in truth, that that merits another chapter.

Invention

Pif paf piaf patapan.
 Ouhiyns ouhiyns. Ebrohé broha broha. Ouhiyns ouhiyns.
 Hoé hu. Dia hurau. Tza tza tza.
 Cla cla cla. Vli vlan. Flic flac. Flaflaflac.
 Tza tza tza, Psi psi psi. Ouistle.
 Zou lou lou. Rhurlurlu. Ouistle.
 Cla cla cla. Flaflaflac.
 Ta tat a. Ta tat a. Pouf.
 Ouhiyns. Enrohé broka, Ouhiyns ouhiyns.
 Ta ta—ta ta—ta ta—ta ta—hup.
 A u ho. Tza tza tza, O hem. O hup. O war!
 Trrrrrrrrrrrr. Hup. O hep. O hup. O hem. Hap!
 Trrrrrrrrrrrr. O hup. O he. O halt! O! Oooooh!
 Xi xi xi xi! Pic! Pan! Baoûnde.
 Hourra!!!!!!!!!!!

Interpretation

In the name of Heaven, Théodore, recover your senses! What language are you speaking?

Can you misunderstand it? Is it not the consecrated language, the imitative and descriptive language of decennial prizes, the patented loquacity of the imperial Muses?

Is it not the perfected interpretation of human thought for which the Iroquois journal demands insistently a patent of invention?

You do not remark, in addition, that the page in question, unique among all the written monuments of speech, hides, under the appearance of a simple *jeu d'esprit*, the most powerful effort of a creative imagination, the secret of the *Novum organum* and the *Caractéristique*;[1] the universal intelligibility for which the Kantians, the eclectists and the doctrinaires, so amorous of clarity, are still groping!

You do not know that if Nemrod (or Nembroth) had been apprised of that discovery on the day of the defection of the laborers of Babel, I could offer you today a very nice bachelor apartment a few thousand toises above the summits of Chimborazo, whereas, if God does not provide, we shall be at great risk of sleeping in the street this winter!

---

1 *Novum Organum* (1620) is by Francis Bacon; the second title is probably a reference to *La Caracteristique géométrique* (1677), the French translation of a treatise by Gottfried Leibniz.

In fact, read that chapter with a certain savor of inflection before a lexicographical committee formed in the name of the human race, and where the most barbaric peoples are represented, without excepting the Romantics and the Eskimos, and I shall submit to whatever punishment you want to inflict upon me—a musical soirée of amateurs, a session at the Atheneum, a benefit performance, the reading of a tragedy, an unexpected rendezvous with a woman one loves, a day when one has been subjected for too long to a rendezvous with a woman one no longer loves—if anyone among your innumerable auditors is mistaken in regard to the implicit meaning of that sublime composition, of which no dictionary has furnished the elements.

And if genius consists of rendering a natural depiction with an energetic and naïve simplicity, I tremble to say that perhaps no one . . . But I will leave that for my editor to say in the preface to the eighth edition, which will be the same as this one, save for two or three insets.

From the first line (it only depends on me to call it a line of verse, for it has six syllables, and would be held to be exactly metric in Timbuktu) . . . from the first line, you can hear the chargers whinnying impatiently; and afterwards, listen; they are still quivering and whinnying! Automedon (that is the figurative name of the coachman) has launched himself forward. He covers them with his gaze, he warns them with his voice; the whip is deployed, whistling thongs split the air. For a long time he only excites his team with benevolent cadences or interjections devoid of anger. The whip still resounds, and the sonorous lash still whines without wounding. They trot, they trot, they whinny, the flying horse gallops. It aspires to the nourishing grain that I dare not name, but which I designate very elegantly in saying that an emperor had it clad in golden leaves for the banquets of the only consul who had struck the ground with four dusty feet.[1] Can you hear the wheel turning, which makes the trembling planks and the heavy ironwork of the drawbridge rebound? Can you hear the wheezing horse slipping and the pavement groaning under his fall? You are in the castle, and all the inhabitants utter a cry of welcome and joy.[2]

---

1 The reference is to Incitatus, Caligula's favorite horse, according to legend, alleged by Suetonius to have been made a consul; Cassius Dio alleges that he was fed oats mixed with flakes of gold.

2 Author's note: "A just sentiment of modesty obliges the translator to declare that he has not the slightest intention of battling with the original, which is much more expressive." The retranslator can only agree, wholeheartedly and regretfully.

Solution

"What portcullis, what drawbridge, what castle!" cried Victorine.

"Oh, my God! My good friend, the portcullis and draw-bridge of the castle of Koenigsgratz . . .

"Or Konigingratz, or Konigingretz," added Don Pic, rubbing his eyes. "The city surrendered in 1423 to Jean Ziska."[1]

"Koenigsgratz? Is it possible? Are we already in the saddest of the seven castles of the King of Bohemia?"

"We are there, dear Victorine, since you wanted it . . ."

"Oh my friend, how tedious last season was at the waters of Toeplitz! Can you not regale us this year with some historiette more amusing that that long rhapsody of blind people, mummies, academicians, wigs, pantoufles, spaniels and lapdogs?"

"That's up to me," replied Breloque, sitting down with a composed expression at the reading table of the salon in Milan and finishing dissolving a refractory sugar-cube in his glass.

He was about to commence when a fateful finger . . .

I will not say that it was the one that minuted, in laconic argot, on the walls of the palace of Belshazzar, whom the

1 The Hussite military leader "Jean Ziska" (Jan Zizka, c1360-124), who played a prominent role in the civil wars in Bohemia, a pioneer in the use of field artillery; he remains a Czech national hero, and became familiar to the French Romantics as the eponymous hero of an 1848 novel by George Sand.

Greeks called Nabonadios, the definitive sentence of the monarchy of Babylon,

It was simply that of my publisher, who had only given me three hundred and eighty-seven pages of cavalier vellum to fill[1] and a twenty-centimeter inkwell to empty, in order to perfect the futile work of conceit and idleness that is vulgarly called a book.

Breloque was about to commence, as I said, when that positive and calculative finger traced, in large capitals, at the foot of my completed page, the syllables:

THE END

---

1 This sentence appears on page 387 of the original edition.

Recapitulation

Printer's Note:

We have carefully noted the page numbers of the chapters, their logical sequence being of great importance for the intelligence of the book.

Correction

I declare formally that, after having read this excellent story with all the attention of which I am capable, I have only found a single word therein to change, and that it has required long reflection and laborious research to assure myself of the necessity of that erratum; and I ought to warn the reader that the modification in question does not concern a fault of language nor a locution in bad taste, nor a repetition in bad grace, nor one of the pedantic neologisms of which timorous journalists accuse me, nor one of the unintelligible archaisms for which I am reproached in salons, but a finesse of synonymy that can only be grasped by the most delicate minds.

I beg the enlightened and sensible persons for whom the reading of *The Story of the King of Bohemia and his Seven Castles* has become a daily need, like the study of Monsieur Jacotot's *universal education* or Monsieur Marle's *ortografe perfeksioné*,[1] to substitute mentally the word *babouche* for the word *pantoufle* everywhere that there is a question of Popocambou's *pantoufle*, which must necessarily have been a *babouche*, which

---

1 Joseph Jacotot (1770-1840) created an eccentric method of education that he called "intellectual emancipation," which became briefly fashionable in his native Belgium and part of France; Nodier routinely made sarcastic references to it in his works. Charles-Louis Marle, the editor of the short-lived *Journal grammatical et didictique de la langue* (1826) was one of several educationalists who campaigned in France for phonetic spelling in the early nineteenth century.

will be abundantly demonstrated when a fossil *pantoufle* has been found.

Babouche participates in a certain sovereign majesty. *Pantoufle* suddenly gives birth in thought to the sentiment of an intellectual civilization more complete, in truth, but less primitive and less solemn.

It is sufficient to pronounce the two words to prove that the babouche is the veritable pantoufle of kings, and that the pantoufle is, at the most, the babouche of patricians.

One says an august babouche, but one says a pretty pantoufle. A pretty babouche would be inappropriate, an august pantoufle would be burlesque.

The intelligence of languages has pronounced on this question by virtue of certain indications; pantoufle has a diminutive, but babouche has not.

The idea of a pantoufle linked to all ideas of inconsideration and stupidity; the idea of a babouche has all the habitudes of sagacity and gravity. Young women have pantoufles and grandmothers have babouches.

Pantoufle is an object of pejorative comparison: the new member has reasoned like a pantoufle, the president has responded like a pantoufle. One has much more regard for babouches.

There can only be question of babouches in the biography of Popocambou the Broken-toothed, since it is written that babouche is appropriate to the sublime style and pantoufle to the tempered style.

Approbation

I, the undersigned, expert weigher of ideas, patented translator of equivocal words, sworn despumator of abstruse cogitations, executor of bass-works and great literary provost of Timbuktu, certify to whom it may concern that I have tried to read, by order, The Story of the King of Bohemia and his Seven Castles; *that the aforesaid work is neither impious, nor, obscene, nor seditious, nor satirical, and that it is, in consequence, very mediocrely pleasing; but that the* table of chapters *appears to me to be a very agreeable invention and a usage very convenient for the grave, religious and right thinking societies that exercise, on winter evenings, the edifying and instructive game of corbillon.*[1]

𝕽𝖆𝖒𝖎𝖓𝖆𝖌𝖗𝖔𝖇𝖎𝖘[2]

---

1 In the children's game of *corbillon* [literally, "little basket"] the players take turns to answer the question "What is in my little basket?" with a series of rhyming suggestions, thus teaching them to expand their vocabularies and to savor the charm of poetic phonetics.

2 Raminagrobis, a name attributed by Rabelais to a poet, is synthesized from roots signifying "ruminating tomcat," and was thus used as a familiar term for a tomcat or a fat man.

ON THE PHENOMENA
OF SLEEP

I am neither a physician, nor a physiologist, nor a philosopher, and all that I know of those noble sciences can be reduced to a few common impressions that are not worth the trouble of being subjugated to a method. I do not attach to these any more importance than the subject merits, and as it is a matter of dreams, I only offer them as dreams. If these dreams have any place in the logical series of our ideas, it is evidently the last.

What is frightening for human sagacity is that on the day when the most eccentric dreams of the imagination are weighed in a reliable balance with the most accepted solutions of reason, if it does not remain equal, only an incomprehensible and unknown power can make it tilt.

It might seem extraordinary, but it is certain that sleep is not only the most powerful but also the most lucid state of mind, if not in the temporary illusions that it envelops, at least in the perceptions that derive therefrom, which it enables to spring forth at its whim from the confused weave of dreams. The ancients, who had, I believe, few things to envy us in experimental philosophy, depicted that mystery wittily under the symbol of the transparent door that gives access to the dreams of the morning, and the unanimous wisdom of peoples has expressed it in an even more vivid manner in the significant locutions of all languages: *I'll dream about it; I need to sleep on it; the night brings counsel.*

It seems that the mind, obfuscated by the darkness of exterior life, is never liberated with more facility than under the mild empire of that intermittent death, in which it is permitted to repose in one's own essence, sheltered from all the influences of the conventional personality that society has made for us. The first perception that creates light through the inexplicable vagueness of dream is as limpid as the first ray of sunlight that dissipates a cloud, and intelligence, momentarily suspended between the two states that divine our life, is rapidly illuminated, like a dazzling flash of lightning running from the tempests of the sky to the tempests of the earth. It is then that the immortal conception of the artist and poet springs forth; it is then that Hesiod wakes, his lips perfumed by the honey of the Muses, Homer, with his eyes descaled by the nymphs of Meles, and Milton, his heart delighted by the last glance of a beauty that he never saw again.

Alas, where can one rediscover the amours and beauties of slumber? Take away from genius the visions of the marvelous world, and you take away its wings. The map of the imaginable universe is only traced in dreams. The sensible universe is infinitely small.

The nightmare, which the Dalmatians call Smarra, is one of the most common phenomena of sleep, and there are few people who have not experienced it. It becomes habitual because of the inoccupation of the positive life and the intensity of the imaginative life, particularly in children, passionate young people, idle people who are content with little, and in inert and stationary states that only require a vague and dreamy attention, like that of a shepherd. It is, in my opinion, from that physiological disposition, placed in the conditions that develop it, that the marvelous of all countries emerges.

It is imagined, inaccurately, that the nightmare is only exercised in lugubrious and repulsive fantasies. In a rich and animated imagination, nourished by the free circulation of pure blood and the robust vitality of a beautiful organization, there are visions that overwhelm the thought of the sleeper by means of their enchantments, as the others do by means of their fears. It sows suns in the sky; it builds in order to approach them cities higher than the celestial Jerusalem; it erects in order to attain them resplendent avenues with fiery steps, and it populates their borders with angels with divine harps, the inexpressible harmonies of which cannot be compared with anything that has been heard on earth. It lends an old man the flight of a bird in order to traverse seas and mountains, and compared with those mountains the Alps of the known world disappear like grains of sand; and in those seas, our oceans are drowned like drops of water. There is all the mythism of a religion, revealed from Jacob's ladder to Elijah's chariot, and the future miracles of the Apocalypse.

In order to oppose to that a more plausible theory, it would first be necessary to establish that the perception, extinguished by awakening, can neither be prolonged nor propagated in the pale and cold atmosphere of the real world. That is the veritable placement of the question. Well, it will be demonstrated in the narrow and positive state of rationalism to which the long disenchantment of social life has reduced us, that that argument is worthless against the utterly naïve impression of primitive societies, which have always regarded sleep as a privileged modification of intelligent life; and from where does the marvelous proceed, I ask you, if not from the credence of the first societies?

The Bible, which is the only book that is held to be true, only supports its most precious traditions on the revelations of sleep. Adam himself was dreaming "a slumber sent by God" when God gave him a woman.

Numa, Socrates and Brutus, who are the highest types of ancient virtues, especially the two who never had any need to deceive peoples because they were neither legislators nor kings, reported all their instinctive sagacity to the inspirations of sleep. Marcus Aurelius, who dates from yesterday in the philosophical history of society, testifies that he owed the salvation of his life to dreams three times, and the salvation of Marcus Aurelius was that of the human race.

If the perception of sleep is prolonged to that point in the most powerful intelligences of an intermediary age, what immense sympathy must have moved it in the cradle of the world, under the tent of the revered patriarch, who recounted on getting up from his mat the marvels of creation and the great works of God, as they had been shown to him in the mystery of sleep.

Even today, the perception of sleep still vibrates long enough in the faculties of the waking human being for us to be able to comprehend without effort how it must once have been prolonged in primitive humans, who were not enlightened by the torch of science and lived almost entirely by imagination. It is not long since one of the most ingenious and most profound philosophers of our epoch recounted to me on this subject, that having dreamed several nights in succession in his youth that he had acquired the marvelous property of sustaining himself and moving in the air, he could never disabuse himself of that impression without attempting a trial in passing over a stream or a ditch.

In place of the scholar who had studied the secrets of intelligence profoundly but who nevertheless submitted to that preoccupation with such abandon, place the pastor of the solitudes who only judged the reality of things by the equally striking sensations from which he has never departed, but who has remarked within himself two variant existences, one of which flows in material facts, without poetry and without grandeur, while the other is transported outside the positive world into sublime ecstasies. He will necessarily conclude that he contains two beings infinitely disproportionate to one another, whose attributions are separated by awakening. He will launch forth from that sole idea to the theory of the soul; he will penetrate, on the faith of the guide that sleep gives him, into the most remote realms of the spiritual world; and if he has enthusiasm and genius, you will have a prophet, and perhaps a god.

As there is nothing more difficult and more perilous than saying what has never been said before, I cannot affirm without trembling what I firmly believe, which is that all religions, with the exception of the one whose verity cannot be put in doubt, have been taught to us by sleep.

The narrators of unusual and marvelous things have conserved for posterity the names of certain men who have never dreamed. Is it not remarkable that those men were atheists, and that the list that ends with Lalande commences with Protagoras?

We can descend again from that principle to applications that are no less new; but here, all the elements of the discussion become sufficient tangible to bring them out of the category of true or plausible propositions, which do not have the good fortune of obtaining the approval of the schools or the safe-conduct of the academies. They are what are known in France as paradoxes.

Natural somnambulism and spontaneous somniloquism are phenomena of sleep as uncontested as the nightmare. No one has ever doubted that there are people who can voice their thoughts while asleep, who can execute them while asleep, and who can come to the end of them thanks to the state of potency that sleep can sometimes acquire in the most common organizations by means that have escaped the meditations of philosophers, with a facility that defies the subtlety of the clever and frightens the audacity of the bold. Human memory and books are full of such histories.

I do not believe that it can be argued that any of these phenomena—somnambulism, somniloquism and the nightmare—excludes the others; and as they are, on the contrary, essentially congenerate, there is nothing surprising in finding them united in the same individual. That accumulation of eccentric faculties will be encountered most frequently in the circumstances that I have supposed—which is to say, in a state of society in which humans only encounter the general forms of civilization at a small number of points, and in which the soul, which a commencement of education has revealed, has only developed in itself and only exercises upon itself:

The celibate individual isolated from the entire world, in whom all thought rises, descends and rises again incessantly from the flock of his ewes to the innumerable flock of the stars;

The futile and ejected old woman who only sustains her poor life by collecting insipid roots in the words to nourish herself, and dry branches to protect herself from the cold of winter;

The amorous and suffering young woman who has not found the soul of a man to comprehend a young woman's soul . . .

You will see that those people are more subject than others to the contemplative aberrations that sleep elaborates, transforms into hyperbolic realities and into the midst of which it throws its patient, like an actor with a thousand faces and a thousand voices, in order to perform for him alone, with his knowledge, an extraordinary drama that leaves far behind all the caprices of the imagination and genius.

There he is, that ignorant, credulous, impressionable and pensive person, walking and acting, because he is a somnambulist; talking, moaning and weeping, because he is a somniloquist; and who sees things unknown to the rest of his fellows, walking and talking, because he has the nightmare. There he is, waking up to the freshness of a penetrating dew, at the first rays of the sun that pierce the mist, two leagues from the place where he lay down to sleep; he is, if you wish, in a clearing in the wood, where three large trees are huddled that are often struck by lightning, from which the sonorous bones of a few malefactors are still hanging.

At the moment of opening his eyes, fleeting perception allows him to retain in his ear a little frightful laughter; a streak of flame or smoke, which is only effaced gradually, marks for his frightened sight the track of the demon's chariot; the trodden grass all around him conserves the imprint of nocturnal dances. Where do you expect him to have spent that night of terrors, if not at the Sabbat? He is found, his face distraught, his teeth chattering, his limbs numb with cold and molded by curvature; he is dragged before the judge and interrogated; he has come from the Sabbat; he has seen his neighbors, parents and friends there, if he has any; the Devil was present in person, in the form of a goat, but a giant goat with eyes for fire, whose horns spit lightning and who speaks a human language, because that is how the animals of the nightmare are made. The tribunal pronounces; the flames consume the unfortunate, who has confessed his crime without comprehending it, and his ashes are thrown to the wind. You have seen the phenomena of somnambulism open Heaven to you; now they have opened Hell.

If you agree that the history of sorcery is in that, you are not far from thinking, like me, that the history of religions is too. What man accustomed to the hideous visits of the nightmare cannot comprehend, at first sight, that all the idols of China and India have been dreamed?

Often, the pastor, preoccupied with the fear of wolves, will dream that he has become a wolf in his turn, and sleep will appropriate to him the bloody instinct so deadly to his flocks. He is hungry for palpitating flesh, he is thirsty for blood, he drags himself on all fours around the animal shed, uttering the species of savage howl that is proper to the nightmare and which recalls so terribly that of famished hyenas. And if some fatal hazard enables him to encounter a poor stray animal, still too young to flee, perhaps you will find him, his hands entangled in its fleece, already threatening with his teeth the dearest of his lambs.

Do not say that werewolves do not exist. Lycanthropy is one of the phenomena of sleep; and that horrible perception, more subject to prolongation than the greater number of the ordinary illusions of the nightmare, has passed into positive life under the name of a malady known to physicians. I do not know whether they have ever recognized its origin, for I have never read a book of modern medicine; but I regret it if it has not, because it seems to me that that theory, examined by a philosopher, would not be useless to the treatment and cure of the majority of monomaniacs, who probably only have the prolonged perception of a sensation acquired in the fantastic life of which half of ours is composed: the life of human sleep.

If, by chance, the monomaniac reenters, in going to sleep, the realties of his material life—as I am not far from believing, for all our functions tend perpetually to equilibrate—he would be, relative to the exercise of his thought, as reasonable as the physician who cares for him, if the latter dreams every night. What confirms me in that idea is that I have never seen a monomaniac suddenly woken up whose first impression was not perfectly lucid. His perception is obscured in being extended, as ours is clarified.

Great God, who will ever fathom these impenetrable mysteries of the soul, the depths of which give vertigo to the most assured reason?

Twenty-four years ago, I was traveling in Bavaria with a young Italian painter I had met in Munich. His society suited my character and my imagination at that time, because there

240

was a dolorous conformity between our sentiments and our misfortunes. He had lost some time before a woman whom he loved, and the circumstances of that event, which he had often recounted to me, were of a nature to leave an ineradicable impression. The young woman, who had followed him obstinately in the misery of a cruel proscription, and had disguised the deterioration of her strength from him, ended up by yielding, during one of their vagabond nights, to the excess of a fatigue that had reached the point that she only aspired to the repose of death.

Bread had been lacking them for two days when they discovered a rocky hole in which to hide. She threw herself upon his heart when they were sitting down, and it seemed that she said to him: "Eat me if you are hungry." But he had lost consciousness, and when he recovered enough strength to hug her in his arms, he found that she was dead. Then he got up, loaded her on to his shoulders, and carried her all the way to the cemetery of the first village, where he dug her a grave that he covered with earth and grass, and on which he planted a cross composed of his staff, which he has traversed with his sword. After that, he was not difficult to capture, for he no longer budged. A few commonplace events then set him free, but his happiness was ended.

My traveling companion, who only conserved twenty-two years in the lineaments of a handsome and noble face, was extremely thin, perhaps because he scarcely ate enough to sustain him. He was pale, and beneath his slightly bronzed epidermis, the pallor of an Italian is livid. The activity of his mental life seemed to have taken refuge entirely in two eyes of a bizarre transparent blue, which scintillated with an inexpressible power between two red eyelids, the lashes of which it appeared, had been devoured by tears, for his eyebrows were also quite beautiful.

As we had confessed to one another that we were subject to the nightmare, we had acquired the habit of sleeping in two adjacent rooms, in order to be able to wake one another up at the sound of those lamentable cries which, as I have said, have more of the wild beast than the human about them. But he had always demanded that I lock the door on my side, and I attributed that precaution to the anxious and suspicious habit of an unfortunate individual who had long been threatened in his liberty, and who had not long enjoyed the good fortune of confiding himself to the guard of a friend.

One evening, we only had one room and one bed for the two of us. The hostelry was full. He received that news with an expression more anxious than usual, and when we were in the attic that had been assigned to us, he divided the mattress in such a way as to make two beds, a delicacy that I would perhaps have appreciated, and which did not shock me. Then he threw himself on his and, throwing me a packet of ropes with which he was equipped he said to me, with an expression of bitter despair: "Come and tie my hands and feet, or blow my brains out."

I am recounting, I am not making up an episode of a fantastic story; I shall not report my response and the details of a conversation of that nature; they can be divined.

"The unfortunate woman who told me to eat in order to sustain my life . . ." he cried, falling back with horror and covering his eyes with his hands, "there is not a night when I do not disinter her and devour her in my dreams . . . not a night when the fits of my execrable somnambulism do not make me seek the place where I left her, when the demon that torments me does not deliver her cadaver to me! Judge now whether you can lie down next to me, next to a vampire!"

It would be even crueler for me than for the reader to arrest his attention on that story. What I can do is to attest on my honor that all that is essential in it is exactly true; that it does not even have the embroidery of a writer who increases the dimensions of an idea by covering it with words; and that, if I have modified anything in it, it is not that which contradicts a vain hypothesis, abandoned, as it merits, to amateurs of hypotheses, but that which, aggravates the frightful reality therein by means of details that the pen cannot write.

Five years later I visited the frontiers of the Morlachs[1] with an ardent desire to know that curious and special people, whom my destiny, always opposed, had not permitted me to see as I would have wished. I had never recounted my anecdote because I regarded it as a frightful, and perhaps unique, anomaly in the bizarre history of human intelligence. When I had passed the Croatian frontier I was astonished to learn that the supposed anomaly in question was, throughout a large province, an endemic malady.

There is scarcely a hamlet of Morlachs that does not count several *vukodlacks*, and there are some where the vukodlack is found in almost all the families, like the saint or the cretin of the Alpine valleys. Here, the malady is not complicated by a degrading infirmity, which alters the very principle of reason in its most vulgar faculties. The vukodlack suddenly awakes to all the horror of his perception; he fears and detests it, like my Italian painter; he struggles against it furiously; he resorts, in order to counter it, to the remedies of medicine, the prayers of religion, the section of a muscle, the amputation of a limb, and sometimes to suicide; he demands of his children that when he dies his heart should be traversed by a stake and nailed to the planks of the coffin, in order to free his

---

1 The Morlachs were an ethnically-distinct pastoral community living in the mountains of Croatia in the fifteenth century, who were stigmatized as barbarians during the subsequent conflicts on the borders of the Ottoman Empire, but Romanticized by some Western European writers as "noble savages" of a kind. Nodier would have encountered the prejudice against them during his time in Illyria, and would have been naturally inclined to react against it.

cadaver, in the slumber of death, from the criminal instinct of the slumber of the living man.

The vukodlack is otherwise a good man, often the example and counsel of his tribe, often its judge or its poet. Through the somber sadness imposed on him by the perception of memory and the presentiment of his nocturnal life, you divine a tender, hospitable, generous soul that only asks to love. It is necessary for the sun to set, it is necessary for the night to imprint a leaden seal on the eyelids of the poor vukodlack for him to go to scratch with his fingernails the grave of a dead man or to disturb the vigils of a nurse asleep beside the cradle of a newborn, for the vukodlack is a vampire, and the efforts of science and the ceremonies of the church can do nothing against his malady. Death does not cure it, so long as he conserves in the coffin some symptom of life; and as his conscience, tortured by the illusion of an involuntary crime, reposes then for the first time, it is not surprising that he is sometimes found fresh and cheerful in the tomb: the unfortunate has never slept without dreaming!

Almost always, that mental aberration is limited to the intuitive illusion of the unfortunate person who experiences it. It can also be accomplished in all its circumstances, because all that is necessary for that is the concurrence of the nightmare and somnambulism. There commences the domain of medical philosophy, which has not noticed two essential facts that I regard as certain. The first is that the perception of an extraordinary act, which is not familiar to our nature, is easily converted into dreams; the second is that the perception of an oft-repeated dream is easily converted into action, especially when it is acting upon a debilitated and irritable individual.

Thus, the monomanias that I have observed ordinarily affect women, and the women of whom they take possession are, for the most part, afflicted in advance by an extreme intellectual debility; it is not necessary, in justice, to ask them how they have lived, but how they have slept, for the secret of their crime is far less the secret of their positive life than that of their sleep. That is because the perception, I repeat, is especially prolonged in isolation, and that stupefaction is induced by a species of isolation in which the perception develops without obstacles, and ends up absorbing all the faculties of thought.

Do you want a singular proof without reply? Our judiciary annals have fortunately furnished only two examples of the incomprehensible crime of anthropophagy, that of Ferrage and that of Léger;[1] those two monsters were stupid and solitary. Scholars who know languages are not unaware that the ancients had only one word to designate the *solitary* and the *idiot*.

Supposing the indefinite prolongation of the perceptions of sleep that causes monomania to be established—I do not have the space here to elaborate that idea in a manner to bring it to the last degree of evidence—I shall arrive at another theory that appears to me to be no less demonstrated: that of the propagation of those perceptions of the nocturnal life between auditors and witnesses who have a disposition appropriate to them. That would explain the endemic nature of vampirism among the Hungarians and the Morlachs, and a few other aberrations of that nature, which are infallibly reproduced everywhere that they have burst forth, but with a

---

1 Blaise Ferrage was an eighteenth-century thief and murderer whose conviction caused something of a sensation because of the introduction of accusations of anthrophagy; the case was popularized by an account contained in the *Journal historique et littéraire* in April 1783, which was reprinted with various embroideries in Jean B. Chamagnac's *Chronique du crime et de l'innocence* (1833) and B. Saint-Edme's *Repertoire general des causes celebres* (1835). The case of Antoine Léger, tried at the Assize Court of Versailles in November 1824 for child rape and murder, became the lead item in Étienne Georget's *Examen médical des procès criminels nommés Leger, Feldtmann, Lecouffe, Jean-Pierre et Papavoine, dans lesquels l'aliénation mentale a été alléguée comme moyen de defense* (1825), which a pioneering legal study of pleas of insanity employed as a defense in court.

relative intensity, in accordance with the infinitely modifiable conditions of time, space and the age, sex and education of the subjects. Somnambulism, somniloquism, and the nightmare above all, are contagious. Children, women and invalids reproduce more readily the impressions of a dream that has been recounted to them than the most vivid impressions of real life, because there is a more energetic sympathy between the sensations of the sleeping human bring than between the sensations of the waking individual, and I have no need to state the reason for that to physiologists. In France, and in all the lands into which I have penetrated by means of voyages and by means of study, I have heard it said by people that the communication of *fasting* dreams—which is to say, when the perception of a dream has been able to be prolonged in a waking individual—becomes deadly to the dreamer or to others. The idea of the contagious extensibility of the perception of sleep is therefore not precisely new, since it is as old as the world. It is undoubtedly a superstition, and I am convinced of it, but dare I ask you what local verity is not a superstition, and what universal superstition is not a verity?

I do not have the pretention of teaching anyone anything; but it would be difficult to explain to me the propagation of a monomania that did not have sleep as an intermediary. All those who visited the lair of Trophonius came out melancholy or mad when they had slept therein.

I shall descend from these heights, to which the Royal Society of Medicine would not forgive me for having elevated myself, if the rumor of my existence ever reached as far as that, and return to my stories. Here is one that Fortis recounted in his *Voyage en Dalmatie* ten years after my birth,[1] and which I

1 Nodier's chronology is slightly mistaken; Abbé Alberto Fortis' *Voyage en Dalmatie* was published in French in 1778, two years before his birth, having originally been published in Italian as *Viaggio in Dalmazia* in Venice in 1774. Fortis' *Voyage* has a long section on "Morlacchi" [Morlachs] (pp 43-90 in the English translation of 1778), which appears to have played a

246

found forty years later, sufficiently different from his in a few matters of detail for me to be obliged to imagine that it as reproduced more than once:

The witches, or *ujèstize* of the land, more refined than the vukodlacks in their abominable feasts, seek to feed on the hearts of young men who commence to love them, and to eat them roasted over an ardent fire. A fiancé twenty years old whom they surrounded in their ambushes, and who often woke up just in time when they began to sound his breast with their eyes and hands, had the idea, in order to escape them, of assisting his sleep with the company of an old priest, who had never heard mention of those redoubtable mysteries, and who did not think that God permitted similar forfeits to the enemies of humankind.

The priest therefore went to sleep placidly, after a few exorcisms in the chamber of the sick man, whom he had the mission of defending against the demon; but sleep had scarcely descended on his eyelids when he believed that he saw the *ujèstize* hovering over his friend's pillow, frolicking and crouching down around him with ferocious laughter, rummaging in his torn bosom, snatching out their prey and devouring it avidly, after having disputed the fragments over blazing fires. As for him, bonds that were impossible to break rendered him immobile on his bed, and he strove in vain to utter cries of horror that expired on his lips, while the witches continued to fascinate him with frightful eyes, wiping their bloody mouths on his white hair. When he awoke, he no longer saw anyone but his companion, who got out of bed unsteadily, attempting a few ill-assured steps and fell dead at his feet, pale and cold, because he no longer had a heart.[1]

role in popularizing the notion of that supposedly-primitive culture with writers associated with the Romantic Movement, but it only contains one cursory paragraph relating their superstitious belief in vampires, which is far less melodramatic than Nodier's account.

1 In Fortis' version of this anecdote the friar gives the young man the

The two men had had the same dream, in consequence of a perception prolonged in their conversation, which had killed one of them, and which the other had seen. That is what can happen when our reason is abandoned to the ideas of sleep.

No one, after reading this, if anyone has read it, and after having verified it on pages 64 and 65 of the Italian edition of Fortis' *Voyage*, will fail to recall that the same story is the subject of the first book of Apuleius,[1] which was probably not known either to the poor Morlach or the old priest. That is not all; that story of Apuleius, which resembles certain stories of Homer, is reported in Pliny as particular to lower Mysia and the Esclavons of whom I speak; and Pliny supports himself, on that subject, on the testimony of Isigone. The famous voyager Pietro della Valle[2] rediscovered it on the oriental frontiers of Persia; it has made the tour of the globe and the centuries.

The impression of a man's life that sleep usurps from his positive life, as if to reveal another existence and other faculties to him, is thus essentially susceptible to prolonging itself and propagating in others; and as the life of sleep is much more solemn than the other, it is the one whose influence must initially have predominated over all the organizations of a certain order; it is the one that must have given birth to all the elevated thoughts of social creation, initiating peoples into

"well broiled" heart supposedly extracted by the witches; he eats it and is restored to health—Nodier presumably changed the denouement in order to make his thesis of a shared dream seem more plausible. Fortis merely suggests that the friar, who allegedly spread the story, had experienced a drunken hallucination.

1 *Metamorphoses*, more commonly known in English as *The Golden Ass*.
2 Pietro della Valle (1586-1652) made a pilgrimage from Venice to Jerusalem in 1615 after an amorous disappointment, and then went on to Baghdad, where he "discovered" the sites of ancient Babylon and Ninveh, making descriptions of them that are a trifle fanciful; he went on to Isfahan and Persepolis before sailing for India in 1623 and returning from there to Rome in 1625. His account of his travels influenced many early ethnographers, but more recent scholars tend to be skeptical about its reliability.

248

the only ideas that rendered them imposing before history. Without the omnipotent action of that imaginative force, of which sleep is the only hearth, amour is only a brutal instinct and liberty the frenzy of a savage. Without it, human civilization cannot sustain comparison with those that regulate the sage discipline of beavers and the prudent industry of ants, because it is devoid of the invariable instinct that maintains those sublime mechanisms.

Look at what reform has made of Christianity in bringing it closer to the positive principle. Look at what the philosophy of the eighteenth century has made of the science of Pythagoras and Plato. Look at what the poetry of pedants has made of the divine art of Orpheus, Homer and David. Look at what the economic egotism and practical statistics have made of the magnificent politics of the ancients. Look at what the morality and intelligence of the species have gained from the monstrous representative "perfection" that has calculated the individual value of the citizen in sous and deniers, which would make the vilest of barbaric peoples blush with shame and indignation.

I do not want to make any application of these ideas to politics, but I cannot refrain entirely from the inductions that emerge from them in spite of me.

As there are two powers in human beings; or, if one can put it thus, two souls that regulate, like individuals, the peoples of which they are the unitary expression, in accordance with the growth or the decay of the faculties that characterize the individual or the species, there are also two societies, one of which belongs to the imaginative principle and the other to the material principle of human life. The contest of those forces, almost equal in the beginning, but which overflow by turns, is the eternal secret of all revolutions, under whatever aspect they present themselves.

The frequent and convulsive alternation of those two estates is inevitable in the life of old peoples, and it is necessary to submit to it in every sense when the time has come.

The peasants in our villages who could read legends and tales of enchantment a hundred years ago, and who believed in them, now read gazettes and proclamations, and believe in them. They were insensate, they have become stupid; that is progress. Which is the better of the two conditions? Take your pick.

If I dared to state my opinion, as a human being cannot escape at an unknown tangent the obligation to accept and fulfill the conditions of his double nature, they are both impossible in exclusive application. The best is one that includes both, like the human being, and very nearly such as Christianity has given us. When the possibility of such a combination no longer exists, all will be said and done.

In a country where the imaginative principle became absolute, there would be no positive civilization, and civilization cannot do without its positive element. In a country where the positive element attempts to set itself exclusively above all opinions, and even above all errors—if there is an opinion in the world that is not an error—there only one thing left to do, and that is to abandon the title of humanity and retreat to the forest with a universal burst of laughter, for such a society does not merit any other adieu.

POLICHINELLE

Polichinelle is one of the great characters entirely outside private life, who can only be judged by their exterior and regarding whom more-or-less hazardous opinions are formed in consequence, for want of having penetrated the intimacy of their domestic habits. That is a fatality attached to the noble destiny of Polichinelle; there is no human grandeur that does not have its compensations.

Since I have known Polchinele, as everybody knows him, for having encountered him frequently on the public highway and in portable houses, I have not spent a day without desiring to know him better; but my natural timidity, and perhaps also some difficulty in finding a means, have prevented me from succeeding in that. My ambitions have been so limited that I do not recall that I have known anything but disappointments in that regard, and I know nothing comparable to the inconsolable dolor that would be left to me at the final moment if I had the misfortune to depart without having had a familiar conversation with Polichinelle in private audience. How many secrets of the soul, how many curious revelations of mysteries of genius and sensibility, and how many observations of a true and profound philosophy there would be to collect in Polichinelle's conversation, if Polichinelle wished!

But Polichinelle resembles all the great men of all eras; he is restive, eccentric, umbrageous and deeply melancholy. A bitter experience of the perversity of the species, which initially rendered him hostile to his peers, and which he has converted since into a disdainful and insulting irony, has dissuaded him from committing himself to trivial social relationships. He only consents to communicate with it from the height of his oblong box, and he toys with the vain curiosity of the crowd, which pursue him, without finding him, behind the curtain of old fabric with which he covers himself when he pleases.

Philosophers have seen many things, but I do not believe that there is a single philosopher who has seen through Polichinelle's curtain. In the midst of the multitude that flocks to the sound of his voice, Polichinelle has found the solitude of a sage and remains a stranger to the sympathies that he excites everywhere; his heart, extinct by virtue of experience and misfortune, no longer sympathizes with anyone, except perhaps his accomplice, about whom I shall speak at another time. I am too occupied now with Polichinelle to stop at accessories. A single ingenious episode can take its place in ordinary histories, but the episode would be vain, inconvenient and, I dare say, profane, in the history of Polichinelle.

People will appreciate, I hope, at its true value, my great work about Polchinelle, if I ever complete it, by virtue of a single fact that is fortunately well known and which I report without vain pride as without false modesty. Bayle adored Polichinelle.[1] Bayle spent the finest hours of his laborious life upright before the house of Polichinelle, his eyes fixed by pleasure on the eyes of Polichinelle, his lips parted by a soft smile at Polichinelle's gibes, his expression idle and his hands in his pockets, like the rest of Polichinelle's spectators. That was the Pierre Bayle that you know, Bayle the advocate general of philosophers and the prince of critics, Bayle who wrote

---

1 Pierre Bayle (1647-1706), author of the *Dictionnaire historique et critique* (1647-1706), which influenced the philosophers of the Enlightenment and was an important forerunner of the *Encyclopédie*.

the biography of everyone in four enormous folio volumes; but Bayle did not dare to write the biography of Polichinelle. Nevertheless, I am not seeking reasons to feel proud, like a writer in love with his own works. Civilization has marched on, but it has not arrived; that is the fault of civilization, it is not the fault of Bayle. Polichinelle required a century worthy of him; if this is not it, I renounce it.

The ignorance that we are in of the intimate facts of Polichinelle's life was one of the necessary conditions of his social supremacy. Polichinelle, who knows everything, has reflected for a long time on the instability of our political faith and that of our religions. It was doubtless him who suggested to Byron the idea that a system of belief ought not to last longer than two thousand years, and Polichinelle is not a man to accommodate himself to two thousand years of popularity, like a legislator or a sectarian. Polichinelle, who has for a motto *Odi profanum vulgus*,[1] has sensed that solemn positions demand a great reserve, and that they lose their authority progressively in lowering themselves to excessively vulgar relationships.

Polichinelle thought like Pascal—if it was not Pascal who thought like Polichinelle—that the weakness of the highest celebrities of history is that they touch the ground with their feet, and that is the origin of the immense vicissitudes that have led him to say to Mahomet: "My empire is destroyed if the man is recognized." Polichinelle, a logician as always, has never touched the ground with his feet. He does not show his feet. It is only on the faith of tradition and monuments that one can be sure that he has clogs.

You will never see Polichinelle, cafés and drawing rooms, like an ordinary great man, nor at the Opéra, like a domesticated sovereign who comes complaisantly once a week, in

---

1 The full quote from Horace is *Odi profanum vulgus et arceo*: "I have the masses [and avoid them]."

order that the multitude might observe his material human identity. Polichinelle has a better understanding of the decorum of a power that only exists by virtue of opinion, He maintains himself wisely in his entresol above the heads of the people, and no one would want to see him anywhere else, so much is that one suited to public comfort, and fortunately exposed to the line of sight of the spectator.

Polichilnelle does not aspire to occupy superbly the summit of a column; he is too well aware that one falls therefrom; but Polichinelle does not descend to ground level like Pierre de Provence, because he also knows that Polichinelle on the pavement would scarcely be more than human; he would only be a marionette. That lesson in philosophy of Polichinelle's is so grave that empires have been seen to crumble for having forgotten it, and the only well-established political systems known today are those that have passed into dogma: that of the Emperor of China, that of the Grand Lama and that of Polichinelle.

Thus there are sophists—there is no lack of them in these paradoxical times—who will tell you boldly that Polichinelle is perpetuated from century to century, in resemblance to the Grand Lama, in forms that are always similar in individuals that are always new, as if prodigal nature could furnish incessantly the reproduction of Polichinelle.

It is nearly half a century, to my great regret, since I have seen Polichinelle; throughout that time, I have scarcely seen anything but Polichinelle, and I declare in the sincerity of my conscience, not far from the moment when I shall have to account to God for my philosophical and other opinions, that I cannot conceive how the world could contain two of him.

The secret of Polichinelle, which has been sought for such a long time, consists of hiding appropriately under a curtain that which ought only to be lifted by his accomplice, like that of Isis, of covering herself with a veil that only opens before her priests; and there is a closer relationship than one might think between the accomplices of Isis and the high priest of Polichinelle. His power is in his mystery, like the power of talismans that lose all their virtue when the magic word is surrendered. Polichinelle, palpable to human senses like Apollonius of Tyana, Saint Simon and Debureau[1] would perhaps have been only a philosopher, a tightrope-walker or a prophet; Polichinelle, ideal and fantastic, occupies the culminating point of modern society. He shines there at the zenith of civilization, or, rather the present expression of perfected civilization is entirely in Polichinelle; and if it is not, I would like to know where it is.

To exercise to such a degree the incalculable influence that is attached to the name of Polichinelle, it is not sufficient to combine the near-creative genius of Hermes and Orpheus, the adventurous temerity of Alexander, the strength of will of Napoléon and the universality of Monsieur Jacotot. It is necessary to be *endowed*, in the sense that enchantment attaches to the word—which is to say, provided with a multitude of faculties of choice appropriate to compose one of those omnipotent individualities that only have to show themselves to subjugate nations. It is necessary to have received the nature of the fortunate and cheerful loquacity that captures all hearts, the tone that reaches the soul, the gesture that binds and the gaze that fascinates. I have no need to say that all that is found in Polichinelle; he would have been recognized without being named.

I have already said that Polichinelle is eternal, or rather, I have had the honor of reminding you of it in passing, the

---

1 Jean-François Deburau (1796-1846) was a famous mime who appeared at the Théâtre des Funambules as Pierrot, and in that guise became a favorite symbol of Romantic and Symbolist art, beloved by Théophile Gautier, Charles Baudelaire and many others. Nodier could not know when he wrote this essay that in 1836, when he killed a small boy who addressed him in the street as "Pierrot" by striking him with his cane, Deburau would be charged with murder—but the jury acquitted him.

eternity of Polichinelle being, thank God, the least contested of all dogmatic questions, to my knowledge. I have, at least, read all the books of religious polemic that have been written since people have taken the trouble to write, and in all my life I have not found a single word that could put in doubt the indubitable eternity of Polichinelle, which is attested by monumental tradition, by written tradition and by oral transition.

For a start, his mask has been discovered, striking in its resemblance, in the excavations in Egypt. Everyone knows whether it is possible to be mistaken regarding the resemblance of the mask of Polichinelle, and I am assured that the portrait in question is at least as well demonstrated as the autograph testament of Sesostris that has recently been found somewhere, to the great satisfaction of people of taste who could not do without the testament of Sesostris.

As for the written tradition, it does not go back as far, but we know that Polichinelle existed identically and nominatively in the epoch of the creation of the Académie, which shares with Polichinelle the privilege of immortality, by virtue of royal letters-patent. It is true that Polichinelle is not in the Académie, and that it even speaks of him in rather light terms in its *Dictionnaire*, but that is naturally explained by the sentiment of bitterness that competition for glory generated by two great notabilities.

Finaly, for the oral tradition, you will not encounter anywhere a man old enough to have seen Polichinelle younger than he is today, and who has heard his grandfather speak of any other Polichinelle. The cradle of Jupiter has been found on the island of Crete, but no one had ever found the cradle of Polichinelle. "The adult age is the age of the gods," says Hesiod, who must not have believed in the cradle of Jupiter. The adult age is also that of Polichinelle, and I do not intend to draw a rigorous consequence from that, which would risk being an impiety. I only conclude from it that it has been given to Polichinelle to fix the fugitive present that always escapes us. We grow old incessantly, all such as we are, around Polichinelle, who does not age. Dynasties pass, kingdoms fall, peerages, more vivacious than kingdoms, lapse; newspapers, which have destroyed all that, will go away for want of subscribers. What am I saying! Nations are effaced from the earth; religions descend and vanish into the abyss of the past after religions that have disappeared; the Opéra-Comique has already closed twice, but Polichinelle never closes. Polichinelle always fustigates the same child; Polichinelle always beats the same wife; Polchinele will knock out tomorrow evening the Barigel that he knocked out this morning—which does not justify in any manner the suspicion of cruelty that historians, ignorant or prejudiced want inappropriately to weigh upon Polichinelle. His innocent rigors are only deployed upon wooden actors, because all the actors in Polichinelle's theater are wooden. Only Polichinelle is alive.

Polchinelle is invulnerable; and the invulnerability of the heroes of Ariosto is less proven than that of Polichinelle. I do not know whether his heel remained hidden in his mothers hand when she plunged him in the Styx, but what does that matter to Polichinelle, whose heel is never seen? What is certain, and what the whole world can verify at this very moment in the Place du Châtelet, if these laudable studies still occupy a few good minds, is that Polichinelle, labored with blows by the police, assassinated by bravi, hanged by the executioner and borne away by the Devil, will infallibly reappear a quarter of an hour later in his dramatic cage, as frisky, as fresh and as gallant as ever, only dreaming of clandestine flirtations and licentious mischief. Polichinelle is dead, long live Polichinelle! It is that phenomenon that has given the idea of legitimacy. Montesquieu would have said so had he known; one cannot know everything.

I shall continue. Polichinelle, eternal and invulnerable, as one would like to be when one does not know what life is worth, has the gift of tongues, which has only been given three times: the first time to the apostles, the second time to the Societé Asiatique and the third time to Polichinelle. Travel the habited earth, if you have the time and the means; go as far from Paris as it is possible—and in truth, I wish you would, from the bottom of my heart—and seek Polichinelle, who will search for you. I challenge you to suspend your hammock in any corner of the globe where Polichinelle has not been before you.

Polichinelle is cosmopolitan. What you mistake at first for a savage's hut is the house of Polichinelle under its twill curtains—and you know whether it will be announced at a distance by the joyful circle that surrounds it; Polichinelle, still asleep, his head on his arm and his arm on the barricade of his open-air podium, like La Fontaine's Aurore, will only wake up at the abrupt appeal of his accomplice or the clink of coins, which ring harmoniously on the pavement, when you will see him shudder, start, bound, dance, and you will hear him express himself lightly, like a native, in the idiom of the country. Personally, a nomadic voyager through all the regions of the old world, I have not covered twenty leagues without finding Polichinelle again, without finding him naturalized by mores and speech, and if I had not found him again I would have come back, and I would have said like the companions of Regnard: *Sistimus hic tandem nobis ubi defuit orbis.*[1]

Polichinelle's box is the Pillars of Hercules of modern civilization.

That is not all; Polchinelle possesses the veritable philosopher's stone, or, what is even more convenient in its manipulation, the infallible denier of the Wandering Jew. Polichinelle

---

1 "We stopped when we ran out of earth": the last line (slightly misquoted in Nodier's text) of a quatrain by Jean-François Regnard (1655-1709), a comic poet who undertook an epic northward trek in 1681 with two companions, but could not continue after they had climbed the mountain of Metawara in Lapland. The line was quoted by several Romantics, including Victor Hugo in *Notre Dame de Paris.*

has no need to drag in his wake a long procession of financiers and to send his courtiers as messengers and his bankers as ambassadors, through kingdoms. Polichinelle exercises a power of attraction that acts on the meanest metals like the word of a minister on the vote of a public functionary, an avowed, reciprocal, solid, synallagmatic, amiable power disarmed of requisitions, summons, executions and coercive means, to which the contributors submit of their own accord and without demands; which has never been seen in any other budget since the representative system has been in vigor, and which will perhaps never be seen again, for the concord of payers and payees is even rarer than that of brothers.

There is no meager proletariat that has not taken pleasure in being inscribed, at least once in its life, among the spontaneous contributors of Polichinelle. The ex-capitalist ruined by a bankruptcy, the disappointed solicitor, the scholar devoid of a pension, the pauper who has neither a hearth not a home, a philosopher, artist or poet, all keep a luxury sou for the civil list of Polchinelle. See how they rain down, without being requested, on the humble parvis of his wooden palace. That is because the tributary nations have only ever been unanimous once regarding the legality of power, and that was in favor of Polichinelle; but Polichinelle was the expression of a noble thought, of a powerful social necessity, and every statesman who does not understand that mystery—I can prove it if you wish—is unworthy to shake the noble hand of Polichinelle's accomplice.

When the incomparable minister whose private secretary I had the honor of being in the time when ministers still responded to the letters that were written to them, complained one day of my regular inexactitudes, I tried to excuse myself like a schoolboy, by the pleasure I had obtained in stopping for a while before Polichinelle's box.

"Good," he said, smiling, "but how is it that I didn't see you there?"

A sublime remark, which reveals an immense range of study and political vision. Unfortunately, he only kept the portfolio for fifty-three hours and a half, but I did not feel sorry for him, because I knew the strength and stoicism of his intelligence.

By chance, Polichinelle had just stopped outside the minister's house: Polichinelle insouciant and free, in his quality as Polichinelle, of the caprice and ill humor of kings. The disgraced minister stopped, by virtue of one of those changes of method that signal a good education, in front of Polichinelle's box. Polichinelle was still singing; the minister resumed, listening with as much joy as if he had never been a minister, and perhaps you could still see him there, although you would see, alas, that no one went there to look for him.

Notabilities are not lacking in front of Polichinelle's box. Everyone passes there in his turn. Few are worthy of fixing themselves there. The bewildered idler leaves it in disdain; the stroller, impatient for new emotions, salutes it, at the most, with a glance of recognition; the pedant, petrified in his stupid science, blinks while blushing, with an ashamed glance. You do not dread there the brazen contact of the vulgar populace with blasé and brutalized tastes, the scum of the riot and the orgy, a filthy crowd that rolls around the monsters of the crossroads the gymnastic disputes of the cabarets and scaffolds of the Palais; it has seen children without heads and children with two heads; it has seen heads cut off; it no longer cares about Polichinelle.

Polichinelle's ordinary clientele is much more composed. It is the student, freshly molded by his province, who is still dreaming about the pleasures of his family and his mother's adieux. Hasten to savor on his face the fresh and cheerful expansion of his final joy; tomorrow he will be classic, romantic or Saint-Simonian; he will be doomed. It is the young député, a patriot by conviction, an honest man by instinct, who braves the call to vote in order to come to meditate momentarily with Polichinelle on the rational institutions of society. Praise God, who has put him on the right path! Polichinelle's podium will teach him more verities in a quarter of an hour than the other can un-teach him in a session. It is the disinherited peer who descends from his cabriolet, having become more modest, to educate himself with scorn for human grandeurs, in the example of Polichinelle. Fortunate man among all men! He has lost the peerage but he has gained wisdom. It is the erudite man exhausted by toil, whom Polichinelle relaxes and renews, or the philosopher worn out by futile speculations who comes, in despair of his cause, to humiliate his mistaken doctrines at the invisible feet of Polichinelle.

And there is even better than all of that!

Behold Polichinelle, the great, the true, the unique Polichinelle! He has not appeared yet, but you can see him already. You recognize him by his fantastic laughter, as inextinguishable as that of the gods. He has not appeared yet, but he is whispering, whistling, humming, babbling, crying out, speaking in the voice that is not a human voice, the accent that is not derived from human organs, and which announces something superior to human beings—Polichinelle, for example. He launches forth laughing; he falls, he gets up again, he walks, he gambols, he jumps, he argues, he gesticulates, he collapses, broken down, upon a platform that resonates with his fall. He is nothing; he is everything; he is Polichinelle. The deaf hear him and laugh; the blind laugh and see him; and all the thoughts of the intoxicated multitude are confounded in one cry: "It's him! It's him! It's Polichinelle!"

Then . . . oh, it's an enchanting spectacle, that one! Then, the little children who were holding still in a curious alarm in the arms of their nursemaids, their eyes fixed anxiously on the empty stage, suddenly move and agitate, further widening their lovely round eyes in order to see better, moving forward and disputing the best place. They will dispute many more when they are grown up! The wave of the forestage rolls over its surface of little bonnets, little caps, little shakos, toques, helmets and headscarves, pretty white arms contending, pretty white hands repelling, and all that, do you know why? To seize, to catch Polchinelle alive! I understand that marvelously, but I, poor children, going gray there behind your fathers, have been waiting for it for forty years!

In the second row, meanwhile, the nursemaids are huddled, and the wet-nurses, expansive, red-faced, as joyful as the other children, under pointed bonnets and round bonnets, wimples with floating bands and madras turbans; high society nursemaids especially, chambermaids of a sort, with pinched necks and disdainful shoulders, rounded gestures and sharp oblique gazes that dart violet irises between long lashes, which promise everything and refuse everything. I don't know whether that has changed, but I remember that they were charming.

It is here that the history of Polichinelle ought logically to have commenced, but these philosophical prefaces have drawn me into considerations so profound regarding the moral needs of our unhappy society that tenderness has overtaken me at the first chapter of the history of Polichinelle. The history of Polichinelle is, alas, the entire history of humankind, with all its blind beliefs, blind passions, bind follies and blind joys. The heart breaks over the history of Polichinelle: *sunt lacrymae rerum.*[1]

---

1 The full quote from the *Aeneid* is *sunt lacrimae rerum et mentem mortalia tangunt*: "There are tears for things, and mortal things are the most touching," but the first three words are often rendered in isolation, and sometimes misconstrued—but not by Nodier—as "the tears of things."

I promised, however, the story of Polichinelle. Oh, my God, I'll tell it one day, and I'll tell more than that; for it is decidedly the only book that remains to be written; and if I don't do it I advise you, as a friend, to ask two men who know it better than I do: Cruyshank and Charlet.[1]

---

1 "Cruyshank" is a skewed rendering of the name of the caricaturist George Cruikshank (1792-1878), whose *Punch and Judy*, illustrating Giovanni Piccini's version of the show, appeared in 1828, and rapidly went through several editions. The lithographer Nicolas-Toussaint Charlet (1792-1845) was best known for his military illustrations, including numerous archetypal images of Napoléon I, but two of his best-selling prints were "L'Enterrement de Polichinelle" and "Danse petit Polichinelle" (1828).

THE BIBLIOMANIAC[1]

---

1 The term bibliomania was popularized, if not actually coined, by the Reverend Thomas Frognall Dibdin, whose *Bibliomania, or Book Madness, A Bibliographical Romance in Six Parts* (1811) transformed into satirical fiction, in the manner of Thomas Love Peacock, an earlier (1809) account of the hypothetical disease, which he alleged mischievously to be rife in the English aristocracy; Nodier obviously identified with sufferers from the disease.

You all knew the good Théodore, on whose grave I have come to throw flowers, praying to Heaven that the earth will be light upon him.

Those two remarks, which are also familiar to you, will announce to you sufficiently that I propose to consecrate a few pages of a necrological notice or funeral oration to him.

It is twenty years since Théodore withdrew from society in order to work or to do nothing—which of the two was his great secret. He dreamed, and no one knew of what he dreamed. He spent his life in the midst of books, and only occupied himself with books, which had led some to think that he was composing a book that would make all the books unnecessary; but they were evidently mistaken. Théodore had obtained too much from his studies to be unaware that that book had been written three hundred years ago. It is the thirteenth chapter of the first book of Rabelais.[1]

Théodore no longer talked, no longer laughed, no longer played cards, no longer ate, no longer went to any ball or comedy. The women whom he had loved in his youth no longer attracted his gaze, or, at the most, he only looked at their feet, and when an elegant shoe of some bright color struck his

---

[1] The chapter in question is entitled "Come Grandgousier reconnut à l'invention d'un torche-cul la merveilleuse intelligence de Gargantua" (modernized editions render it slightly differently). A torche-cul is a device for setting farts alight.

gaze, it drew a profound groan from his breast. "Alas," he said, "what a waste of morocco!"

He had once sacrificed to fashion; the memoirs of the time tell us that he was the first to knot his cravat to the left, in spite of the authority of Garat,[1] who knotted his to the right, and in spite of the vulgar, who are still obstinate today in knotting it in the middle. Théodore no longer cared about fashion. He had only had one dispute with his tailor in twenty years. "Monsieur," he said to him one day, "this coat is the last I shall receive from you if you forget once more to make me pockets *in-quarto*."

Politics, whose ridiculous chances have created the fortune of so many fools, could never distract him from his meditations more than momentarily. It put him in a bad mood, since the foolish enterprises of Napoléon in the north, which had made Russian leather dearer. He approved, however, of the French intervention in the revolutions in Spain. "It is," he said "a fine opportunity to bring back romances of chivalry and *cancioneros* from the Peninsula." But the expeditionary army did not take the trouble do that, and he was piqued. When anyone said *Trocadero* to him he replied, ironically, *Romancero*, which caused him to pass for a liberal.

The memorable campaign of Monsieur de Bourmont on the African coast transported him with joy.[2] "Thank Heaven,"

---

1 Pierre-Jean Garat (1764-1823) was a singer renowned as a sartorial trend-setter.

2 The Comte de Ghaisnes de Boumont was an émigré who fought with the counter-revolutionary army and joined the insurrection in the Vendée in support of George Cadoudal, but took advantage of an 1807 amnesty to rejoin the French army and rose to the rank of general, although he was never trusted and betrayed Napoleon's plans to the Prussians during the Hundred Days. Favored under the Restoration, he was given command of the invasion of Algiers in 1830, to which the present comment refers, but after the July Revolution he refused to recognize Louis Philippe as King and fled to Portugal—hence the remark about Théodore's enthusiasm for him obtaining him a reputation as a Carlist.

he said, rubbing his hands. "We shall have Levantine Morocco cheap"—which made him pass for a Carlist.

He was walking last summer in a populous street with his nose in a book. Honest citizens, who were emerging from a tavern unsteadily, came to beg him, with a knife at his throat, in the name of freedom of speech, to cry: "Long live the Poles!"

"I'd like nothing better," said Théodore, whose thought was an eternal cry in favor of the human race, "but may I ask you in what regard?"

"Because we're declaring war on Holland, which is oppressing the Poles, under the pretext that they don't like Jesuits," replied the friend of enlightenment, who was a rude geographer and an intrepid logician.

"God forgive us," murmured our friend, crossing his hands piteously. "Shall we be reduced to Monsieur Montgolfier's pretended Holland paper?"[1]

The eminently civilized man broke his leg with a blow of a stick. Théodore spent three months in bed studying book catalogues. Always disposed to take his emotions to extremes, that reading inflamed his blood. In his convalescence, even his sleep was horribly agitated. His wife woke him up one night in the midst of the anguish of the nightmare. "You've arrived just in time to prevent me dying of fright and dolor," he said, embracing her. "I was surrounded by monsters which would have given me no quarter."

"What monster can you fear, my good friend, you who have never done anyone any harm?"

"It was, if I remember rightly, the shade of Purgold, whose deadly scissors were biting an inch and a half from the margins of my bound Aldes, while Heudier's plunged my most

1 When not pioneering the sport of ballooning, the Montgolfier brothers were paper manufacturers, whose business thrived by importing technical innovations made in the Netherlands. The wordplay is based on the fact that "Holland paper" was a prestigious kind employed in producing fine illustrated books.

beautiful first edition pitilessly into a corrosive acid, and I took it out entirely blank; but I have good reason to think that at least they are both in purgatory."[1]

His wife thought he was speaking Greek, for he knew a little Greek, to the extent that three shelves in his library were laden with Greek texts whose pages had not been cut. In consequence, he never opened them, and contented himself with showing the front and the back to connoisseurs of his acquaintance, indicating the place of impression, the name of the printer and the date. Simple folk concluded that he was a sorcerer. I do not believe it.

As he was visibly deteriorating, his physician was summoned, who chanced to be a man of intelligence and a philosopher. You can find one if you try. The doctor recognized that cerebral congestion was imminent, and he made a beautiful report on the malady in the *Journal des Sciences Médicales*, where he called it "morocco monomania" or "bibliomaniac typhus," but there was no discussion of it at the Académie des Science because of competition from Cholera Morbus.[2]

He was advised to exercise, and as that idea made him smile he set forth early the other day, I was too worried to quit him by a step. We headed for the quais, and I rejoiced because I imagined that the sight of the river would soothe him, but he did not take his eyes away from the level of the parapets. The parapets were as empty of displays as if they had been visited in the morning by the defenders of the press who had drowned the archbishop's library in February. We were more fortunate on the Quai aux Fleurs. There was a profusion of second-hand

---

1 Purgold is not easily identifiable from extant sources, although mention is made in some sources of a bookbinder of that name; Alde Manuce was a famous Venetian printer; a M. Heudier was given joint credit for devising a chemical method of restoring the print of old documents with the aid of acid.

2 The term Cholera Morbus was bandied about in the medical literature of the 1820s in connection with an epidemic of the disease in Calcutta observed by several European physicians.

books, but what books! All the works that the newspapers had reviewed well months ago, which had infallibly fallen there into the fifty-centime boxes from the editorial offices or the depths of the bookshop: philosophers, historians, poets, novelists, authors in all genres and all formats, for whom the most pompous announcements are only the insurmountable limbo of immortality, and who pass, disdained, from the shelves of shops to the rim of the Seine, a profound Lethe from which they contemplate, while going moldy, the assured terminus of their presumptuous flight. I deployed there the satined pages of my octavos, between five or six of my friends.

Théodore sighed, but it was only in seeing the works of my intelligence exposed to the rain, poorly protected by officious awnings of waxed cloth.

"What has become," he said, "of the Golden Age of open air booksellers? It is here, however, that my illustrious friend Barbier collected so many treasures that he succeeded in composing a special bibliography of several thousand articles. It was here that the sage Monmerqué, while going to the Palais, and the sage Labouderie, while emerging from the metropolis, made their learned and fruitful promenades for entire hours. It's here that the venerable Boulard picked up a meter of rarities every day, measured by his graduated cane, for which his six houses, plethoric with volumes, had no space left. Oh, how many times he desired, on such occasions, the modest *angulus* of Horace or the elastic capsule of the fays' cavern that would have sheltered, if necessary, the army of Xerxes, and accommodated as conveniently the sheath of the knives of Jeannot's grandfather![1]

1 The librarian and bibliographer Antoine Barbier (1765-1825) was charged with distributing to the libraries of Paris the books confiscated during the French Revolution, His dictionary of anonymous and pseudnymous works is still an important reference book. The magistrate Louis Monmerqué (1780-1860) wrote many biograhical articles and published numerous collections of old documents. Abbé Jean Labouderie

"Nowadays—what a pity!—you only see the inept cast-offs of that modern literature which will never be ancient literature, the life of which evaporates in twenty-four hours like that of the flies of the river Hypanis: a literature well worthy, in fact, of the charcoal ink and pulp paper to which a few shame-faced typographers, almost as stupid as their books, deliver it regretfully. And it is to profane the name of books to give it to those muddy rags, which have hardly changed destiny in quitting the rag-picker's basket. The quais are henceforth only the Morgue of contemporary celebrities!"

He sighed again, and I sighed too, but not for the same reason.

I was in haste to draw him away, for his excitement, increasing at every step, seemed to be threatening him with a mortal fit. It must have been an unlucky day, since everything was contributing to aggravating his melancholy.

"There!" he said, passing the pompous façade of Ladvocat, the Galiot du Pré of bastardized letters of the nineteenth century, an industrious and liberal bookshop that would have merited being born in a better age, but whose deplorable activity has cruelly multiplied new books to the eternal prejudice of old books; the unpardonable eternal promoter of cotton paper, ignorant orthography and the mannered vignette, the fatal guardian of academic prose and fashionable poetry— as if France had had poetry since Ronsard and prose since Montaigne![1] That Palace of Bibliopolis is the Trojan horse that

(1776-1849), a preacher at Notre-Dame, was an antiquarian with a particular expertise in the Auvergnat language. The administrator of the lycées of Paris Antoine-Marie-Henri Boulard (1754-1825) was a prolific translator who amassed a legendary book collection.

1 Pierre-François Ladvocat (1791-1854), also known as Camille Ladvocat, was the most celebrated Parisian bookseller of the early nineteenth century, the proprietor of a stall in the Palais-Royal before opening a shop on the Quai Voltaire. He was closely associated with the burgeoning of the Romantic Movement, his entrepreneurial endeavors obtaining initial publication for many of its younger authors; Nodier and Balzac were

has carried all the plunderers of the palladium, the Pandora's box that has given passage to all the evils of the world! I still like the cannibal, and I shall write a chapter for his book, and I shall never see it again!

"There," he continued, "is the shop with green walls of the worthy Crozet, the most amiable of our young booksellers, the Parisian most able to distinguish a binding by Derome the elder from a binding by Derome the younger, and the last hope of the last generation of book-lovers, if one can still arise in the middle of our barbarity; but I shall not enjoy his conversation today, in which I always learn something. He is in England, where he is disputing, with the just right of reprisal, with our avid invaders of Soho Square and Fleet Street the precious debris of the monuments of our beautiful language, forgotten for two centuries on the ingrate land that produced them! *Macte animo, generose puer.*"[1]

Retracing his steps, he said: "There is the Pont-des-Arts, whose useless balcony will never support, on its ridiculous guard-rail a few centimeters broad, the noble deposit of the three-hundred-year-old folio that flattered the eyes of ten generations with the sight of its pigskin cover and its bronze clasps; a profoundly emblematic passage, in truth, which leads to the château of the Institut by a road that is not that of science. I might be mistaken, but the invention of that bridge

---

among the writers who produced hackwork at his behest, the exact extent of which is now incalculable; the present story was published in his series *Paris: Le Livre des Cent-et-un*. The probably-pseudonymous Galliot du Pré was a sixteenth-century predecessor, one of the first entrepreneurs to pay printers to produce books for him and to obtain a royal privilege licensing their sale.

1 Joseph Crozet (1808-1841) took over his father's bookshop in the Rue du Lycée in 1829. Nodier wrote his obituary, in the *Bulletin du bibliophile*, in 1841, giving further details of the expedition to London mentioned here. The Derome family of bookbinders was active in the eighteenth century. The Latin quote from the *Aeneid*, the original of which continues *sic itur ad astra*, translates roughly as "Buck up, noble youth (this is the way to the stars)."

of sorts ought to be for the erudite a flagrant revelation of the decadence of fine letters.

"There," Théodore said again, passing into the Place de Louvre, "is the white sign of another active and ingenious bookshop; it made my heart palpitate for a long time, but I no longer perceive it without a painful emotion since Techener has taken it into his head to reprint with the characters of Tastu, on dazzling paper with an elegant binding, the Gothic marvels of Jeahan Bonifns of Paris, Jeahan Mareschal of Lyon and Jehan de Chancy of Abignon, undiscoverable bagatelles that he has multiplied in delectable counterfeits. Snowy white paper horrifies me, my friend, and there is nothing that I don't prefer, except what it becomes when it has received, under the thrust of an executioner of the press, the deplorable imprint of the dreams and stupidities of that century of iron."[1]

Théodore sighed more deeply; he was going from bad to worse.

We arrived thus in the Rue des Bons-Enfants, at Silvestre's rich bazaar of public sales, honored by scholars, where more inestimable curiosities have succeeded one another in a quarter of a century than the library of the Ptolemies ever contained, which might not have been burned by Omar, as our unreliable historians say. I had never seen so many splendid volumes on display.

"Those who are selling them are unfortunate!" I said to Théodore.

"They're dead," he replied, "or dying."

But the hall was empty. We only remarked the indefatigable Monsieur Thour, copying with a patient exactitude on

---

1 This reference is oddly uncomplimentary, although it was penned before Nodier entered into collaboration with the bookseller Jacques-Joseph Techener (1802-1873) to found the *Bulletin de bibliophile* in 1834. Nodier could not know that the shop in question would eventually be taken over by François-Noël Thibault, alias "Noël France," and thus become the cradle of Anatole France, who would take over the mantle of the nation's greatest writer after the death of Victor Hugo.

carefully prepared cards the titles of works that had escaped his quotidian investigation the day before. A man fortunate among them all, who possessed in his boxes, in order of subject, the faithful image of the frontispieces of all known titles! It would be in vain, for that one, that all the productions of printing might perish in the first and imminent revolution that the progress of perfectibility assures us. He would be able to bequeath to the future the complete catalogue of the universal library. There was certainly an admirable tact of prescience in foreseeing at such a distance the moment when the time would come to compile the inventory of civilization. A few more years, and no one would be talking about it any longer.

"God forgive me, worthy Théodore," said the honest Monsieur Silvestre, "You've mistaken the day. Yesterday was the last vacation. The books you can see are sold and awaiting collection."

Théodore shuddered and went pale. His forehead took on the color of slightly worn yellow morocco. The blow that struck him resonated in the depths of my heart.

"That's all right," he said, with a dejected air. "I recognize my customary bad luck in that frightful news. But in that case, to whom do these pearls, these diamonds, these fantastic riches belong, by which the libraries of Thou and the Groliers would have been made glorious?"[1]

"As usual, Monsieur" replied Monsieur Silvestre, "these excellent original editions of classics, these old and perfect examples autographed by celebrated scholars, these piquant philological rarities of which the Académie and the Université have not heard mention, revert by right to Sir Richard Heber.

---

1 The libraries of Christopher de Thou and Lyonnaise Grolier family are extensively featured in the latter chapters of T. F. Dibdin's "sequel" to *Bibliomania*, *The Bibliographic Decameron* (1817), where the obsessive bibliophile Sir Richard Heber (1773-1833)—the dedicatee of *Bibliomania*—is also mentioned extensively.

It to the English lion that we are yielding with a good grace the Greek and Latin that we no longer know.

"These beautiful collections of natural history, these masterpieces of method and iconography, are going to the Prince de ****, whose studious tastes further ennoble, by their employment, a noble and immense fortune.

"These mysteries of the Middle Ages, these phoenix moralities whose menechme does not exist anywhere, these curious dramatic essays of our ancestors, will augment the model library of Monsieur de Soleine.

"These ancient farces, so svelte, so elegant, so dainty and so well-conserved, compose the lot of your amiable and ingenious friend Monsieur Aimé-Martin.[1]

"I have no need to tell you to whom these fresh and bright moroccos with triple threads, broad dentellations and sumptuous compartments belong. It's the Shakespeare of petty propriety, the Corneille of melodrama, the skillful and often eloquent interpreter of the passions and virtues of the people,[2] who, after having undervalued them somewhat in the morning, purchased them in the evening for their weight in gold, not without muttering between his teeth like a mortally wounded boar and turning tragic eyes shadowed by black eyebrows upon his competitors."

Théodore was no longer listening. He had just put his

---

1 A detailed account of the library of the writer "Louis Aimé-Martin" (Louis-Aimé Martin, 1782-1847) was compiled when the latter died by the aforementioned bookseller Jacques-Joseph Techener. Martin had been a close friend of the proto-Romantic writer Bernardin de Saint-Pierre, whose widow he married and whose works he edited; most of his own works were published after the present story was penned, and he was a leading contributor to the *Bulletin du bibliophile*.

2 This unnamed character is undoubtedly René-Charles Guibert de Pixérécourt (1773-1844), a theater director and prolific writer of successful melodramas highly esteemed by Nodier, a notorious bibliomaniac who was later to catalogue Nodier's own library in collaboration with the longtime member of the *cénacle* Paul Lacroix, "le bibliophile Jacob."

hand on a volume of rather good appearance, to which he hastened to apply his elzevierometer—which is to say the six-inch ruler divided almost infinitely, by which he measured the price and, alas, the intrinsic value of his books. He approached it ten times to the accursed volume, verified the distressing calculation ten times over, murmured a few words that I did not hear, changed color again, and fainted in my arms. I had a great deal of difficulty getting him to the first fiacre that came along.

My insistence in trying to extract the secret of his sudden dolor was unsuccessful for a long time. He was not talking. My words were no longer reaching him. *It's the typhus*, I thought, *the paroxysm of the typhus.*

I hugged him in my arms. I continued to interrogate him. He appeared to yield to an impulse of expansion.

"You see in me," he said, "the most unfortunate of men. This volume is the Virgil of 1676, in large format, of which I thought I had the giant exemplar, and it is taller than mine by a third of a ligne.[1] Hostile or alerted minds might even have found half a ligne. A third of a ligne, great God!"

I was thunderstruck. I understood that he was being overtaken by delirium.

"A third of a ligne!" he repeated, menacing the heavens with a furious fist, like Ajax or Capaneus.

I trembled in all my limbs.

He fell gradually into the deepest depression. The poor fellow was only living to suffer. He only repeated periodically. "A third of a ligne!" while gnawing his hands, and I repeated silently: *The harvest of books and typhus!*

"Calm down, my friend," I whispered in his ear, tenderly, every time the crisis was renewed. "A third of a ligne isn't very much in the most delicate affairs of this world."

---

1 A ligne is a twelfth of a French inch, which was slightly larger than an English inch, and a third of a ligne is thus approximately 0.75 millimeters.

"Not very much!" he cried. "A third of a ligne in the Virgil of 1676! It's a third of a ligne that has augmented by a hundred louis the price of Nerli's Homer at Monsieur de Cotte's. A third of a ligne! Would you count for nothing the third of a ligne of an awl that punctures your heart?"

His face was utterly distraught, his arms stiff; his legs were seized by a cramp with iron fingernails. The typhus was visibly taking hold of his extremities. I would not have wanted to elongate by a third of a ligne the short route that separated us from his house.

We finally arrived. "A third of a ligne!" he said to the porter.

"A third of a ligne!" he said to the cook who came to open the door.

"A third of a ligne!" he said to his wife, moistening her with his tears.

"My parakeet has flown away!" said his little daughter, who was weeping like him.

"Why did you leave the cage open?" said Theodore. "A third of a ligne!"

"The people are up in arms in the Midi and the Rue du Cadran," said his aged aunt, who was reading the evening newspaper.

"What the devil do the people have to do with it?" replied Théodore. "A third of a ligne!"

"Your farm in Beauce has been burned," his domestic told him, while putting him to bed.

"It's necessary to rebuild it," replied Théodore, "if the domain is worth the trouble. A third of a ligne!"

"Do you think it's serious?" the nurse said to me.

"Haven't you read the *Journal des Sciences médicales*, my girl? What are you waiting for to go and fetch a priest?"

Fortunately, the curé came in at that moment for a chat, as was his custom, about a thousand trivial literary and bibliographical details, from which his breviary had never distracted him completely—but he was no longer thinking about that once he had taken Théodore's pulse.

"Alas, my son," he said to him, "the life of a man is only a passage, and the world itself is not firm on its eternal foundations. It must finish, like everything that begins."

"Have your read, on that subject," Théodore replied, "the treatise on *son origine et de son antiquité?*"[1]

"I have learned what I know from *Genesis*," the respectable pastor replied, "but I've heard it said that a sophist of the last century named Monsieur de Mirabeau[2] has written a book on the subject."

"*Sub judice lis est*," Théodore interrupted, abruptly. "I have proved in my *Stromates* that the first two parts of the *Monde* were by the sad pedant Mirabeau and the third by Abbé Le Mascrier."[3]

"My God," said the old aunt, lifting up her spectacles. "Who made America, then?"[4]

---

1 *Le Monde, son origine et son antiquité* (1751) by Jean-Frédéric Bernard, was revised and extended by Jean-Baptiste de Mirabaud and Jean-Baptiste Le Mascrier. The last-named had earlier edited Benoît de Maillet's proto-evolutionist text *Telliamed* (1750).

2 The abbé is probably confusing the economist of that name with his more famous son, the Revolutionary leader. Either Théodore's reply substitutes "Mirabeau" for "Mirabaud" or the witness reporting the conversation misheard the name.

3 *Stromata* [*Stromates* in French, meaning "patchwork"], sometimes reprinted as *Miscellanies*, is the third volume of a trilogy of works by the Chrstian apologist Clement of Alexandria written in the second century A.D., but Théodore might be referring obliquely to a volume of *Miscellanies* published by Charles Nodier. The Latin phrase Théodore employs is one habitually used by lawyers to indicate that one should not make statements about a matter that is still under adjudication. As an admirer of Georges Cuvier, Nodier is probably accommodating the phrase "parties du monde" to a hypothesis of recurrent creations, which the bibliomaniac Théodore thinks of as new editions.

4 The aunt's remark reflects the fact that "parties du *Monde*" is ambiguous even without Nodier's further gloss, translatable as "continents of the world."

"It's not a matter of that," continued the abbé. "Do you believe in the Trinity?"

"How can one not believe in the famous volume of Servet's *Trinitate*," said Théodore, raising himself up from his pillow, "since I've seen it ceded, *ipsissimus oculis*,[1] for the modest sum of two hundred and fifteen francs, from Monsieur MacCarthy,[2] a copy for which the latter paid seven hundred livres at the La Vallière sale?"

"We're talking at cross-purposes," exclaimed the apostle, slightly disconcerted. "I'm asking you, my son, what you think of the divinity of Jesus Christ."

"Good, good," said Théodore. "It's just a matter of understanding, I will sustain against anyone that the *Toldos-jeschu*,[3] from which that ignorant satirist Voltaire has taken so many stupid fables worthy of the *Mille-et-une Nuits* is nothing but a wicked rabbinical ineptitude, unworthy of figuring in the library of a scholar."

"Yes, indeed!" sighed the worthy ecclesiastic.

"Unless someone rediscovers one day," Théodore continued, "the exemplar *in carta maxima* of which there is mention, if I remember correctly, in the unpublished nonsense of David Clément."[4]

The curé groaned this time, quite intelligibly; he rose emotionally from his chair and leaned over Théodore in order to make him understood, without ambiguity or equivocation, that he had attained the final degree of the bibliomaniac typhus of which there is mention in the *Journal des Sciences*

---

1 "With my own eyes."

2 Justin MacCarthy Reagh (1744), ennobled in France as Comte MacCarthy.

3 The *Todelot Yeshu* is a Medieval Jewish document offering an alternative biography of Jesus to that given in the gospels.

4 There is mention of a nine-volume catalogue of hard-to-find texts, *Bibliothèque curieuse* (1750-60) by David Clement, which is itself very hard to find, in Dibdin's *Bibliomania*.

médicales, and that he ought not to occupy himself with anything other than his salvation.

Théodore had not retrenched his life under the impertinent negation of the incredulous, which is the science of fools, but the dear man had pushed too far in the vain study of letters to take the time to attach himself to the spirit. In a full state of health a doctrine would have given him a fever and a dogmatic tetanus. He would have lowered the flag in moral theology before a Saint-Simonian. He turned to face the wall.

The long time that passed without him speaking would have made us think that he was dead if, on drawing nearer to him, I had not heard him murmur dully: "A third of a ligne! God of justice and bounty! But where will you render me that third of a ligne, and up to what point can your omnipotence repair the irreparable blunder of that bookbinder?"

One of his bibliophile friends arrived a moment later. He was told that Théodore was dying, that he was delirious to the point of believing that Abbé Le Mascrier had made a third part of the world, and that he had lost the power of speech a quarter of an hour ago.

"I'll make sure," replied the book-lover. "By what fault of pagination can the true 1635 Elzévir edition of *Caesar* be recognized?" he asked Théodore.

"153 for 149."

"Very good. And the Terence of the same year?"

"108 for 104."

"Damn!" I said. "The Elzévirs were unlucky with numbers that year. They did well not to choose it for printing their logarithms!"

"Marvelous!" said Théodore's friend "If I'd listened to these people, I'd have believed you to be within an inch of death."

"A third of a ligne!" Théodore replied, his voice fading away by degrees.

"I know your story," but it's nothing compared with mine. Can you imagine that I missed, a week ago, in one of those bastard and anonymous sales that are only advertised by a poster on the door, a 1527 Boccaccio as magnificent as yours, bound in Venetian vellum, with pointed *a*s, uncut pages everywhere and not a single page renewed?"

All of Théodore's faculties were concentrated on a single thought. "Are you quite sure that the *a*s were pointed?"

"Like the iron tip of a lancer's halberd."

"It was, therefore, undoubtedly, the *vintisettine* itself!"

"Itself. We had a nice dinner that day, charming women, green oysters, witty men, Champagne wine. I arrived three minutes after the adjudication."

"Monsieur," cried Théodore, "When the *vintisettine* is for sale, one does not dine!"

That final effort exhausted the residue of life that still animated him, which the emotion of the conversation had sustained like a bellows playing on an expiring spark. His lips, however, babbled again: "A third of a ligne!"—but they were his last words.

Since we had renounced the hope of considering him, his bed had been wheeled next to the bookshelves, from which we took down one by one each volume that appeared to be summoned by his eyes, holding those we judged most likely to flatter him exposed to his sight for longer. He died at midnight, between a Deseuil and a Padeloup, his two hands pressed amorously to a Thouvenin.

The next day we escorted his hearse, at the head of a numerous gathering of weeping morocco-lovers, and we had his tomb sealed with a stone charged with the following inscription, in which he had parodied for himself the epitaph of Franklin:[1]

---

1 Benjamin Franklin, a printer by profession, composed his own epitaph, of which he made copies for his friends, which vary slightly. The standard version reads: "The Body of/B. Franklin,/Printer;/Like the Cover of an

HERE LIES,
BENEATH THIS WOODEN BINDING,
A FOLIO COPY
OF THE FINEST EDITION
OF A MAN,
WRITTEN IN THE LANGUAGE OF THE GOLDEN
AGE,
WHICH THE WORLD NO LONGER UNDERSTANDS.
HE IS TODAY
AN OLD BOOK
WORN,
STAINED,
TATTERED,
WITH AN IMPERFECT FRONTISPIECE,
WORM-EATEN,
AND GREATLY DAMAGED BY ROT.
ONE DARE NOT AFFIRM FOR HIM
THE BELATED AND FUTILE HONORS
OF A REPRINTING.

---

old book,/Its contents torn out,/And stript of its Lettering and Gilding,/ Lies here, Food for Worms./But the Work shall not be wholly lost;/For it will, as he believ'd, appear once more,/In a new and more perfect Edition,/ Corrected and amended/By the Author,/He was born Jan. 6, 1706. Died 17**."

A PARTIAL LIST OF SNUGGLY BOOKS

www.ingramcontent.com/pod-product-compliance
Lightning Source LLC
Chambersburg PA
CBHW020403110726
47899CB00006B/1837